Body Holiday

Derek E Pearson

First published 2014
Published by GB Publishing.org

A catalogue record of the printed book is available from the
British Library

Cover Design © Mary Pargeter Design

GBP ®

GB Publishing.org
www.gbpublishing.org

For Sue
for suffering this protracted birth with me

Acknowledgement

Grateful thanks to Christopher Ritchie for his faith and help,

George Boughton for his willingness to take the risk and

Brenda Marsh for her great enthusiasm and insight

3

Contents

Prelude

TWO men sit in an atmosphere of self-absorbed silence. The air in their windowless room is thick and rankly organic, like a changing room at a men's sports club. This is an intimate place, a private space, stuffy and redolent of long-term occupation. There is a strong sense of restrained violence. Blood will be spilt by hand or by proxy.

The men spend a lot of time here, seated on comfortable, ergonomic chairs and surrounded by large 3D monitors and crowded banks of black, high-capacity computers – computers equipped with the most advanced graphic and editing software. A great deal of money has been invested in providing the very best facilities, and they have always brought a healthy return.

If they want, or need to, they have more than enough core skills and talent to make a movie by utilising nothing more than their technical know-how and the potential contained in their equipment, but they'd rather not.

Their exclusive, wealthy clientele know exactly what they want and demand nothing less. To a man (and some women, though surprisingly few) they call for the freshness and surprise that only real pain can bring. Facile, virtual thrills and spills were all very well for the commercial marketplace, and it's true some scripted productions offer genuine genius, but for this audience nothing can replace the specific pleasure of watching real people strive to cope with the horrifically unexpected.

Their viewing experience improved immensely when people catastrophically failed to cope, and they could goggle from front row seats while unwitting performers desperately suffered for their entertainment, most often just before meeting grim death in front of the cameras. The trick to success was to ring the changes with these deaths and serve up something new and fresh whenever possible.

For their client base the possibilities inherent in the men's specialist work floated a whole flotilla of boats. Clients wanted to see nothing less than torture, fear, humiliation, pain and death combined with a liberal dose of tits-and-ass and up-close and personal hardcore porn. They howled for lip-smackingly rare entertainment designed to titillate the jaded palates of blood-thirsty, voyeuristic cognoscenti. Faire-snuff, as they say in the business.

The clients wouldn't recognise either man in the flesh. They were unsung heroes who brought talent and imagination to their projects without gaining any credit from their faceless audience. But that was fine. They were well paid and loved their jobs.

However, when between jobs and with little worthwhile to do, it was not a good psychological position for either to be in.

One is eating a sandwich, picking through the filling like a beachcomber and sniffing pieces of food, before gingerly placing the scraps in his mouth and chewing thoroughly. The other is playing a complex 3D video game that occupies three of his screens and involves knife play against voluptuous, naked vampire women. The women's teeth seem to be the least obvious attributes on show and certainly the least mobile in 3D.

The atmosphere in the room is one of occupants passing time while waiting for a main event. A sense of expectancy is palpable: like soldiers relaxing on their bunks reading a novel or letter from home when edgily aware of an imminent call to arms, or medics in an emergency room taking a break, always with an eye on the entrance doors; like a girlfriend spending time with her boy while aching to be his bride. The men play while they wait – at least most of the time. Sometimes even genius takes a holiday.

The game player farts loudly, rising slightly from his chair and rolling his backside to the left to allow lengthy emission while taking neither eyes nor hands from his game. The room's atmosphere thickens. His hands move swiftly and surely across his keyboard; like a virtuoso musician's, they dance and flicker with absolute precision. His movements indicate total comfort with what he is and what he does.

He isn't quite sane.

The sandwich-eater grimaces, his movements lost in the shadows. Looking regretfully at the remains of his sandwich, he dumps it in his bin.

He fans his hand in front of his face to waft away the worsening sulphur stink but says nothing. There's no point. His colleague would hear nothing through his headphones, and anyway, sandwich-eater has seen this level of concentration before. He would need to hit the man with a hammer to get any kind of response.

Sometimes the idea of inflicting stark violence on this game-playing, eruptive person with whom he is so creatively bonded brings a creamy smile to the sandwich-eater's face.

To use some heavy blunt instrument – anything, it needn't be a hammer – and smash it down into that dreadful, clever head would be therapeutic; to be pounding again and again until the skull is just pink pulp and the brain scatters and splashes across the black ceramic floor. The idea is very attractive: to still that aching strangeness, kill the alien other and bring order to the day. Sandwich-eater sighs with frustration.

He is Omega to the other's Alpha; he knows this. Once combined, their differing talents shine a unique light onto their projects and in this darkened room they create dark poetry. Now, this waiting for a job grates on sandwich man's nerves worse than a long sleepless night on an unfamiliar bed.

He needs the fresh dawn of another project. *Give me a fucking job to do*, he thinks, *or...* His colleague lifts up his buttocks and erupts another sticky fart. The sandwich man's hands clench, nails pressing into flesh. *A fresh job soon, or there'll be murder.*

The monitors flicker into life and sandwich-eater turns. Hello? Oh yes.

Across the room the player switches off his game and crouches over his keyboard. He's a toad, poised to leap. He belches with anticipation.

• • •

Part one: The Women

Chapter one: The Shutterbox

PRINZ felt like he ruled the Earth that day when he strutted out onto the Centre Court for the Wimbledon final. He could do anything. He was unbeatable. He was *only* ranked world number 12, but he planned to beat world number one seed Monos and he'd paid good money for the privilege.

His hired accomplice was out in the crowd. He won the toss and decided to serve second. The game went according to plan. His competitor was good but psychologically Prinz's performance was being telepathically boosted. Monos didn't stand a chance. Prinz's powerful telepath was sitting in the crowd helping to ensure Centre Court was his, a sunny place where he would win no matter what.

She was also filling his opponent with despair, sapping his will to win. The first set went down six-two, the second six-one. Prinz could taste victory. Every stroke was delivered with a powerful grunting howl, a winner's war cry.

Then something went wrong. The world altered for Prinz as if the colour and vibrancy drained out of his game; green grass became grey and the sun shone weakly through a watery veil.

On the other side of the net, Monos regained his focus as well as his cat-like agility and strength. It felt like someone pulled a curtain from his mind and set him free to play the game he loved so much. He reared back to deliver his trademark serve, and for the first time in the game Prinz had absolutely no idea where it would land.

Monos won that Wimbledon final in five sets – the world's audience focusing on the players' sharp variations in style for weeks afterwards: Prinz had seemed to lose control just as Monos got his second wind.

Conspiracy theorists posited a complex notion around kidnapped loved ones rescued in time to allow the Romanian to play like a true champion. Others thought the German shot his bolt too early and couldn't sustain that level of play.

After the second set it was a completely different match – the Eastern European took command of his game against an increasingly faltering German. Prinz was frantic, desperately trying to collect his scattered thoughts and to claw back the sense of power and authority that had simply leeched out of his body. He didn't notice the plain-clothed police officers who pressed through the crowd to a large panicked-looking woman dressed in layers of coloured cloth.

She was yellow as a canary from the turban on her head to the stained plastic sandals on her sweaty feet. Her skin had a jaundiced cast too.

When she removed those sandals for the body search back at the station, she practically cleared the room. The thick calloused skin that coated her soles was cracked and infected.

Her armpits and pubic hair were untended and unwashed. Her teeth were damaged and diseased. The officers in charge considered her completely revolting.

Frika was a transmitter, a telepath who could push words, ideas or sensations into another person's mind. In her home town in Lithuania she'd been employed by the local supermarket owner. Under her influence people purchased ageing cheese or elderly cake, slightly stale fish or wilting vegetables. They weren't really aware of what they'd done until they got home and unpacked their goods.

She was happy in her job. Executing minor mind crimes in retail suited her equally minor intellect. However, the honeymoon phase couldn't last; she had a potent talent and was quickly tracked down by powerful people using 'tied' TPs, for whom her mind chimed like a loud and lucrative bell.

Thereafter her talent was put to more profitable uses. For a number of years Frika had been earning a relative pittance for herself but good money for her bosses by pushing thoughts into other people's minds.

She wasn't very bright, however. In some of the events she rigged, she needed to concentrate very hard on the colour of the clothes contestants were wearing to correctly direct her thoughts. Sometimes she got it wrong and confused the outcome. Her bosses soon learned to provide her with a companion who could direct and keep her focused on her target.

The science behind people like Frika was not steadfast. The talent manifested itself in three basic types. *Transmitters*, like Frika, would usually demonstrate a poor IQ but could push thoughts into another's mind so strongly that they could affect the outcome of any sporting event or, more dangerously, tip the balance in politics or business. Some researchers saw contemporary transmitters, who invariably presented a low IQ and low self-esteem, as an evolutionary trait; otherwise they would end up ruling the planet through mental domination.

Others parried this theory by asking, 'And how do you know they don't already? Can you explain some of the stupid choices voters have taken in the past?'

Receivers specialised in gathering information: what is your opponent thinking? What is the other fellow planning? Putting a receiver on the job would guarantee a fully itemised dossier of everything a target was thinking – and all done without a dangerously traceable phone tap, hack or statscan.

Unlike a transmitter, the receiver wouldn't need to be in the same room or even on a clear sightline to 'read' their prey. Instead, working within a set parameter, he or she could sample all the minds around them one by one until they found the person they were looking for. After that their task would become as simple as picking up a ringing phone to listen in on a conversation, plucking thoughts from their victim's mind.

The *Shutterbox* was considered the most dangerous to Frika's family of TPs but mostly harmless to everyone else. The Shutterbox was usually female. She couldn't strongly influence anybody, or anything about her, but could – when the psychic wind was blowing in her direction – pick out others of her ilk, even when inactive. She could also register the emotions of all the people around her: anger, lust, sweet love, sour disdain, hearty jollity...

Unlike the receiver she could 'hear' people's moods and dip into the emotions of everyone around her. Once this was established she could tighten her focus and isolate the mood of a specific passing stranger.

She could predict an action, foresee danger and recognise something different in one person in a crowded room. She could cause people to ignore her; using her talent she could become a blank person, unseen in plain view.

One such was Milla Carter.

Milla worked freelance in security, and it was she who homed in on Frika. Her job was often busy and varied, one of the reasons she loved it. In one week she worked Wimbledon; next was the ancient but revered O2 Arena. The week after that she was at the NEC. Wherever one TP could be used to divert the thoughts of a person for gain, Milla could hopefully pick up the telepathic influences and alert her colleagues. And she always sensed when something was out of kilter, beyond normal, which made her a useful tool in finding criminals whose minds worked outside accepted parameters.

Frika was arrested, admitting her guilt without ever meeting her accuser. Her life for the next few years would become very predictable; it would certainly involve improved physical cleanliness and better dental care. Until she once again emerged from captivity, to find her sponsors waiting patiently to take her back into the fold. Frika was happy for a while. She even learned how to read. after a fashion.

Milla, however, walked off to a future that held two meetings she was never likely to forget.

• • •

Chapter two: Real Weather

PEARCE looked across at Ruth. She was exercising on the apartment's spacious balcony, drenched in cool rain and naked. He, as usual, was running his business from a handheld slaved to his implant while watching cooking programmes on his 3D.

He loved food and enjoyed cooking when the fancy took him, but because most meals were delivered pre-prepared by his automated kitchen, he was just getting ideas for the day's menu.

Ruth didn't watch TV much. She did her own thing – most of it physical.

At 62, she looked every day of 30. Even at a time when good nutrition and excellent medical care meant nearly the entire population of Europe lived longer and healthier lives, she was exceptional.

In her youth she'd been a top glamour model, actively and enthusiastically sought by senior producers wanting her to perform in 3D porn productions; a career move to which she almost succumbed, as the hysterical sums offered spiralled ever upwards.

She'd also been approached by legitimate studios asking her to appear in mainstream cinema, but she had no ambition to pursue an acting career.

Her startlingly beautiful elegance gathered a lucrative fan-base on the global glamour circuit. But she knew, or thought she knew, she lacked that special indefinable quality that transcends physical beauty and transforms loveliness into iconic acting talent. In any case, in her own way, she was too vain to be a second-rater.

But her long legs, taut butt, high full breasts and sensuously rounded yet slender belly so very nearly introduced her to a career as one of the royalty of the 3D porn circuit.

Meeting and marrying Pearce changed all of that.

She stood in the rain, looked up as she sensed a movement from Pearce, then watched as he paused his programme and shrugged himself out of his clothes. He was 86 but looked about 50, and had a penis so long, thick and heavy that she couldn't remember ever seeing it higher than half-mast at any point in over 30 years of marriage.

Ruth was never vain about her looks, despite her classic male-fantasy figure. Her breasts had been permanently augmented in her teen years using stem cell technology. She was very pretty, beautiful in fact, her face illuminated by keen intelligence and good humour. And the camera loved her – all of her.

From an early age her parents used the revenue she earned from the glamour work they pushed her into, despite her protests, to pay for a series of lucrative enhancements to make her even more bankable. But she suffered at school as a result.

On the day she finally – gratefully – escaped from academia, a small group of her classmates chose to pelt her with small, bean-shaped fruit chews they'd collected specially for the day. The 'Cherry Jellies' were delivered with envy, disdain and most likely frustrated lust. Despite her extra-curricular activities, Ruth was shy, uncomfortable with others and kept away from boys and girls alike.

As she protected her face from the falling shower of soft pink confectionery, and ran to the school gates where a car and safety were waiting, she heard her attackers crying, 'Whose tits are you wearing today, Hudson?'

The jellies were meant to reflect the full swell of Ruth's new breasts, in miniature, and mirror the thrust of her evidently engorged nipples; but, even though she was unhurt, nothing could mirror her fierce burn of anger that day. It was a consuming anger that never found an outlet in physical violence but which she channelled, instead, as a deep well of energy to help drive her career.

Truth to tell, the work carried out on Ruth's body had been more than a little over-enthusiastic from the word go, driven as it was by her parents' greed, for profit, rather than any thought for their daughter coping with what she'd been saddled with.

Once augmentation was complete she was forced to follow a strict, almost Olympian exercise regime – to develop and maintain the muscle to carry her extra poundage with anything like grace and dignity. Her newly enhanced figure was out of balance and threatened the curvature of her spine. Every moment she worked at it she cursed her parents, and that anger drove her further from them.

However, she worked hard and finally took possession of it, until her body was honed and sleek and true. Eventually she learned to accept and even enjoy her body. She appreciated Pearce's obsession with it, just as much as she enjoyed his respect for her mind. They made a good marriage. His business acumen and a hefty inheritance ensured they had enough money for just about anything they wanted, including a real window and a real balcony where she could enjoy real weather and relish the feeling of sunshine or cool, clean rain on her skin.

It helped make amends for Pearce's somewhat less than acceptable behaviour in so much of their relationship. She loved him for all that. The only man she'd ever loved.

Pearce joined her on the balcony, embracing her. As they slowly and gently began to make love in the warm rain, Ruth felt that nothing could ever spoil the precious life she and Pearce had made for each other.

She was wrong.

●●●

Chapter three: The Killer

MILLA blanketed herself in an isolation zone. Her ability to create such a place was a very useful gift and she was adept at it. Through careful training she was now able to maintain the zone while simultaneously sampling mental traits and signatures from the large group of people around her. She couldn't read thoughts and she wasn't a snoop, as she often assured herself. What she did was more like looking through people's mental windows to see how the décor of their minds was arranged but without needing to read through their personal diaries. She likened it to listening to many separate and highly individual strands of music without any resultant cacophony.

Here she was on a police swoop, and she was the talent out front.

She never liked being naked in a public place, not even in her dreams, but when the job demanded, she defrocked. The killer had to be here, and she was going to find him. A personality that vile would scream like a psychic banshee. Or so she hoped.

The NEC Skinfest was very popular. It happened twice a year and pulled huge ratings worldwide. It was a great employer and pulled in a tremendous return to cost ratio. Although few openly admitted watching, in a world of global TV and instant celebrity, Skinfests could earn the young, lovely or just plain lucky a great deal of fast money and fame. But only if they were prepared to put their flesh and sexual prowess out there on the screen in 3D, HD, full colour, up-close and very, very personal.

Tiny but very efficient cameras hovered almost invisibly above the contestants as they cruised the halls, chose their partners and began their 'performances'. The cameras would swoop down to more closely feature the straining faces of lovers or focus on details of penetration: oral, vaginal or anal.

This place, where Milla lay mentally blanketed and curled in her corner, was a hetero Skinfest hall. But there were also separate venues catering for gay and lesbian partners, dominance freaks, a little touch of S&M and even those who found animals a viable sexual option – literally enjoying it doggy fashion, though for these there was always a screened disclaimer: 'No animals were hurt in the making of this programme. In fact as far as we can tell, they enjoy it.' Such was not always the case with the humans involved; but they, unlike the animals, could sign away any legal rights to injury claims before engaging in cross-species couplings.

If there was cash to be made in the sexual pay-to-view market, there were 'Festas' willing to offer themselves up for it; though those with a taste for child abuse were not entertained, at least not in the legitimate 'theatre'.

Sick minds could always find an arena in which to share their tastes with like-minded perverts. They could even try to justify the ends they went to, to reap their miserable pleasures. But no matter how they approached their deviancy, they weren't welcome in polite society or at least not on prime-time television. Paedophiles were not the only predators stalking the sexual playground. There were others just as dangerous and just as vile. One of these, one of the worst, was why Milla lay at her station.

Milla would have made a fine Festa if she'd been that way inclined. She looked good and was an enthusiastic lover when the fancy took her; but she preferred a more private venue. And while she was at work today none of the roving, prurient cameras would be allowed to linger over her nakedness. That was a fixed part of the contract.

She was the girl in the corner who made no lasting impact on the paying viewers' 3D screens, even though the sight of her would have no doubt thrilled them. All the time her body lay still her mind was roving the hall, touching the thoughts and emotions of the people surrounding her.

She opened her talent to the crowd and felt the expected desire and lust, but also fear and nervousness alongside doubt and a touch of hope. Many of the Festas were alike in this, psychologically going through the same cascade of emotions: 'Am I worth it?' 'Will someone pick me?' 'What the fuck am I doing here?' 'I'm worth more than this.' 'Hello baby!' 'Fuck you then.' 'How much longer before you finish?' 'Are they catching my best side?' She let it wash over her like background noise.

Despite her abilities, Milla never saw herself as a mental voyeur. Instead she thought of what she was doing as enjoying the 'scent' of people's minds as if they were rare flowers. Not invading their privacy but skimming them, a light touch here and a more intense look there, then off to the next subject.

Then she felt him and her stomach clenched. She nearly pulled her knees up to her breasts in a defensive gesture. This was why she was here; this was the other part of her job. Here he was.

Milla was a consultant TP investigator for the Serious Crime Squad and this man was her target. By God and all his guardian angels she knew it with a profound certainty. He was here and he shone like a beacon.

He stalked the hall like a missile of flesh, his erection arching up out of the black tangle of hair at the base of his taut belly. He was lean and wide and ripped, good-looking in a sleek, dark way. But the smile on his face was predatory and the red mist in his mind teetered on a hot razor-sharp edge just barely contained on the social side of animal madness.

He wanted to fuck and rip and tear, hurt and kill, and the younger the flesh he could do it to the better. He knew how and when to release his demon and when to contain it, at least for now. Milla felt his terrible passion howl as he hunted his next victim, his penis tightened to his belly with concupiscence. She strengthened her isolation zone. She knew her coltish looks would act like a beacon for this sick, serial killer.

During the last four years, seven women between the ages of 18 and 23 had been found around the West Midlands, torn and bloody and discarded like so much meat. The injuries had been so severe that forensics experts needed to reconstruct the girls' faces using computer models, working from careful rebuilds of their slashed, distorted and battered skulls.

There seemed to be no connection between the girls other than youth, prettiness and the savage method of their murder.

The pattern of their deaths was one of the worst that a number of very experienced officers had ever seen. They were shocked by the slashed throats, genital mutilation and frenzied penile penetration of the victims' wounds. But they were most appalled by the uncontrolled assault on the girls' heads and upper bodies.

Facial features melted under the sustained battering. Bone was shattered and pummelled until the girls' skulls caved in and their brains squirted across the ground mixed with blood and bone. Teeth were shattered and scattered as well as eyes punctured and smeared across their sockets, before the sockets themselves were ground to paste and gore.

Once the girls had been identified, their parents were informed but the bodies were not released. How could anyone explain to a parent that their beautiful daughter's face was now just a bowl of unrecognisable pulp?

Just as disturbing was the fact that all this frenzy was controlled and cold; so much so that research found no DNA clues to their killer.

Then, one evening, a young police officer new to the case was gazing at the incident wall, studying the facial reconstructions pasted on the screens, while pondering what these lovely girls had done to end up as the pitiful subjects of a terrible murder case.

With a sudden jolt the officer realised she had seen each of the girls during episodes of *Skin TV*. She had that sort of memory and a mind attuned to pattern recognition. She saw beyond the grainy, eerily pale reconstructions on the incident wall to the warm, well-remembered originals.

She and her husband regularly watched *Skin TV* on recorded downloads as an inspirational prelude to their own bedtime activities. She hadn't just seen these girls during the twice-yearly TV scheduled NEC fuck-fest. She was also watching them in action as a regular part of her nightly pre-passion schedule. And she was absolutely sure of one fact: all these victims had been Festas.

Her revelation quickly mounted operation 'Cockroach Trap'. It resulted in a number of homicide officers being secreted within the buildings and grounds of the NEC, during the next Skinfest, with a TP surveillance team on hand to scan and isolate the performers.

On the presumption that the attacks followed a meeting at the hetero venue – where all the girls had last been seen, the operation was focused there. Milla was its point operator and it was time to snap the trap shut. She raised her hand to her ear, a set signal for her contact TP, a receiver, to tune in and look straight through her eyes.

She became acutely aware of another mind sitting behind her eyes, another person jostling to see what was happening.

Milla intensely disliked the sensation of being someone else's eyes, but this was a trained procedure and she was a professional.

One of the hovering cameras now became a dedicated follower of the hunter. He would be on camera right up to the time he made his move. If, or when, he made that move he would be taken, fast, before his victim was anything more than heartily scared. At least that was the game plan.

The hunter had now become the hunted and, though he didn't know it, his mind quickly became an open book to Milla's colleague. The police team moved smoothly into place.

Her job done, Milla quietly left the hall and gratefully went off to get dressed. She was thirsty and a little aroused by her triumph. Truth be told, she really badly wanted to pull on a pair of pants.

She had a smile playing on her lips born from the sense of a job well done, and a feeling of relief that responsibility for dealing with the guilty man had been passed on to others who knew best what to do with him.

She got changed in an otherwise empty women's locker room. Everyone else in the halls would probably be at the peak of their performances by now.

She washed briskly and collected together her stuff. It was late and all she wanted to do was get home to London and relax.

Her colleagues would let her know how things panned out once the case was resolved. She walked out into the atrium and headed towards the exit, thinking about her drive home, hoping the roads would be clear and the weather okay.

She jumped like a scalded cat when a man she hadn't sensed, with her now distracted Shutterbox talent, said, 'hello' so close to her ear that she felt his breath on her cheek.

●●●

Chapter four: A Gentle Shave

PEARCE was fastidious about depilating his wife, but he was so workmanlike about it she sometimes found it a strangely impersonal, unerotic event.

But not always.

From the time they first became intimate he made it plain he couldn't stand wisps of hair collected around her *mons veneris*. As soon as they became remotely noticeable, he would go after them with a tube of cream and a pouch of moisturiser.

The slightest shade to her groin was unacceptable. She had to be clean as an adolescent girl. But it wasn't her job to deal with it; it was his.

He whistled through his teeth as he worked between her legs and down her thighs. Sometimes the insistent smoothing and tickling of his busy fingers could be annoying. Other times, like now, she found it tickled in a soothing, tingling way. She found the process enjoyable if she relaxed and just passively accepted the strangeness of the act. It was part of the intimate culture of her marriage, as she had learned over the years. Most of the time she would rather be doing something else: reading a book, exercising, riding her horse or listening to music. Other times his cool, urgent fingers, slippery with cream, roused her and brought her to the brink of orgasm.

Sometimes they ended up making love. Other times they shared a cup of tea, and occasionally Pearce would say, 'Good job, Alice!' – his customary (and no longer humorous) reference to rabbit holes. Then he kissed her on her denuded cleft and went off to do something else.

She knew depilation was something he insisted on but she'd learned never to openly question why. She kept these

28

thoughts to herself. Pearce's quirk was part of the price she paid for her privileged and loving lifestyle. She reasoned other men would probably ask for worse.

Ruth once thought that perhaps it was those sought-after photographs of her – carefully lit, naked and smeared with lubricating oil, pinkly clean and lubriciously draped across whatever the photographer felt would look most arousing and thus most profitable – that brought Pearce to her in the beginning.

But he insisted he'd never seen her professional pics or vids. He maintained that he preferred sexual activity to be an honest, tactile reality between a man and his woman. He said he needed to 'keep it real' and claimed that if he wanted to pleasure himself he would rather use his imagination than rely on what he dismissively called 'fuck media'.

She believed him. What could he gain by lying?

And she realised that while he gently depilated her, completely absorbed in the reality of her and enjoying the particular pleasures he found in her, she didn't want to question anything he said, just love him back.

His eyes on her were possessive and his hands sure and tutored. Though, despite her arousal, she knew by his actions that this particular genital intervention would prove another bit of routine business, something to be dealt with and not an invitation to indulge in anything more passionate. Or would he?

Pearce finished what he was doing and blew an alarmingly warm breath across her groin. She reached down, pulled his head up until their lips were level, and kissed him firmly on the lips. Her tongue flickered around and against his mouth while she uttered a low, questioning moan. They were still naked from their activities on the balcony an hour before. His cock was still semi-hard, so she reached out and guided it between her legs. He just smiled and pulled away.

'No, Ruth,' he said as he walked over to his clothes and began pulling them on. 'The old man won't work again so soon. You know that. Anyway I need to see Ben about some business.'

He paused and let his eyes become wrapt in her smooth nakedness. Then he smiled, turned and left her alone in the room.

Ruth waited just a few moments after he'd gone before she frantically pleasured herself to a rapid, almost startled climax.

Her eyes closed tight and her mouth opened in a soundless, breathless howl. It was a performance that would once have left her many fans aching for more, literally aching, but she played the scene out now just for her own pleasure.

As the rain cleared and sunlight streamed through the open balcony window, her back arched, lifting her bottom up. Her straining legs opened wider as if to welcome the blue sky, throwing her furiously working fingers into sharp relief.

● ● ●

Chapter five: A Short Walk

MILLA felt the sick yearning wash from the man like a wave of feral slime. She wondered if she would ever wash his pungent stink from her mind. Her isolation zone must have slipped when she lost her concentration, before leaving the Skinfest, and he'd come after her like the vile predator he was. She suffered the equivalent of a mental gag reflex.

She could feel him now in every synapse of her talent. This man wanted to use her for his own purposes. With a dreadful, core-deep certainty, he knew from experience: that once isolated his victim could do nothing, not once he started his game. He had done this before. He was the Alpha male and she just a female plaything – a nothing, a pretty toy dog for the brutal entertainment of his inner wolf.

'So, why is the most beautiful girl in the room trying to make her escape?' He grinned through half-moon lips and big teeth – meat eater's teeth. *My, what a big smile you have*, thought Milla. Well I'm going to wipe it from your face.

'I didn't notice you until you started to move,' he continued, 'and then suddenly there you were on your way out.'

He put his hand on her arm, talking fast, chattering. 'I couldn't let you leave without saying hello and giving you the chance to see me again. I got straight out after you, dressed as fast as I could and waited for you here. Girls always take longer than men to get ready, don't they? They take more care, I suppose. In your case it's worth every second. Can I give you a lift someplace?'

'Thanks, no,' Milla answered. 'I've got my own car. Thanks.'

'Let me at least walk you to your car,' the man said. 'It's dark out there and you never know who might be lurking. Where are you parked?'

She told him. He nodded and steered her away from the well-lit atrium and out through the exit into the night. There was no sign of any buses, so he led her out onto the path to the eastern car parks.

At no point did he ask her why she'd decided to leave the Skinfest early. Why should he? What did it matter what decisions she made and why she made them? In his mind her life had just been drained of choices. Everything that happened to her in the next few minutes would be decided by him and him alone.

Her inescapable fate was to play the role of an orchestrated puppet, an extra in the movie he was running in his mind. No, more than an extra – she was important enough to make her appearance centre stage during the main event, essential in fact. But he was the star and his murderous desires would at last be free to run rampant once more. He would be steeped, washed clean in her torn flesh and spilled blood.

The path to her car ran away from the main atrium and up by the hedge bordering the glittering tower of the recently refurbished Hilton Hotel. She could hear his sharp anticipation build through his constant flow of chatter; feel his lust grow. They were alone now, completely alone.

Nobody in the area registered on her talent except the screaming lunatic beside her. She figured everyone around the NEC was either actively involved in the Skinfest or busy watching it. The grounds were deserted.

It was dark, a darkness clotted and marbled with scattered light from the hotel and painted with a mottled, rising mist. The walkers could barely be discerned as slight motions in the shifting, cloaking shadows even if there had been someone, anyone, to observe them.

However, they could be heard, his low incessant chatter rattling out like a child's. He said his name was Trapper without a trace of irony, and she had no doubt he was being honest. After all, he didn't expect her to survive long enough to tell anyone. She told him her name was Margaret, Mags for short, reasoning there was no point in sharing anything honest and personal with this creature.

They skirted the packed disabled car park (the NEC Skinfest catered for every legitimate taste) and then walked into the velvet dark of a pedestrian underpass leading to her car. His excitement began to crescendo. *It will happen here and now*, she realised. Trapper was too deeply immersed in the chain of events unfolding across his imagination's private movie screen to notice how Milla tensed beside him.

His hand tightened on her arm and she heard him swallow a flood of saliva. He stopped talking, just short of drooling with lust and anticipation.

You sad fuck, she thought as every move he made clearly telegraphed what was about to happen next.

She was ready. In a heightened state of awareness, reading him like the open book he was, she took a sharp breath. Steadying herself, she expertly blocked the knife-wielding hand Trapper was lancing towards her throat.

She raked the heel of her shoe down his shin, sensing his pain and confusion like a distant echo, and rammed her palm hard and straight up into his nose. She felt cartilage crack and the hot wetness of blood on her wrist.

'You cunt! You fucking cunt,' he sputtered, his words a high-pitched screech when she planted her knee fast and hard into his groin.

He was down. It had taken her mere seconds to change him from predator to prey and now she was going to make sure he never got up again.

She had his victims' ruined faces in her mind's eye as she lifted onto the balls of her feet and prepared to sweep a terminal roundhouse kick into the sobbing, gasping man's throat.

'It's okay, Milla. We've got the bastard,' said a calm voice by her side. 'We've got the whole thing recorded including his attack with the knife. He didn't know what a world of grief he was buying for himself when he tried that.'

The policewoman and her partner looped Elastomer ties around Trapper's wrists, pulled them tight, then dragged him stumbling and jerking to his feet – still doubled over his personal world of pain like an arthritic dog trying vainly to lick its balls.

'Come on, lover boy,' the policewoman said. 'We've rescued you from the nasty lady, but believe me – your nightmare is only just beginning.'

She led him hobbling away, bleeding and confused, trying yet failing to piece the last few minutes of his life together. What went wrong? How had he fallen so far and so fast?

Watching him go, Milla wondered if it added insult to injury that he was being arrested and marched away by a woman, a pretty and young one at that.

She hoped so. She really hoped so.

•••

Chapter six: Since New

RUTH rode her horse with elegant and fluid precision. If a renaissance Italian from one of the golden cities of 16th Century Umbria had walked into the vast, high-ceilinged room, he would have felt at home. Warm light flowed down in dusty, parallel streams from two rows of narrow, arched windows set high up on the long walls either side of her. Under her horse's clacking hooves a smooth, stone-flagged floor was strewn with sweet hay.

Pearce's major-domo Ben stood as he often did by one of the massive double doors set either side of the great opening in one of the end walls. He was watching her ride, intent and silent. She sometimes wondered what he was thinking while he watched.

She knew she looked good in traditional riding garb. The narrow-waisted jacket enhanced the flare of her hips, the tight pants and boots added even more appeal to her legs, and the high collar and lace cravat drew attention to her cantilevered bosom.

Back in the day her natural poise on a horse excited her producers to make a few equestrian films. They sold well, which was no big surprise. Seeing her with her golden thighs wrapped across a saddle (even, in a few cases, bare back) was as close as Ruth's admirers ever got to hardcore. The results were never anything short of beautiful. For the cognoscenti Ruth outshone Lady Godiva and needed no concealing cloak of hair. Dressed in nothing more than her own skin, she was fully clothed in beauty and freshness.

Back catalogue copies of video demonstrating what a cantering horse did to her naked figure still brought tears of pleasure to men's and some women's eyes. The sight of it could stop the breath in a viewer's throat. But all that was over now. These days she was happy to enjoy riding for its own, muscular sake.

The horse followed her instructions as if they shared a single mind. They were performing an intricate dressage: the horse now stepping in a jouncing, bouncing gait then almost skipping, prancing and dancing under her.

She knew it was stupid but something in Ruth's heart knew the horse got as much pleasure from the exercise as she did. Something was shared between mount and rider, something precious.

She rode around the great room tasting the relaxing air, bathed in the warm, antique light. She was acutely aware of the flow of muscle between her and the horse, the sense of oneness. Riding was one of the few things that always brought her heart into her mouth with joy and she revelled in it. Their movements together had a musical sense, poetical even. There was love in it.

Then from somewhere a noise began to impact on her sensibilities, a buzzing whine just on the inner edge of hearing, like an insect, audible but not too close.

She raised her eyes to look around and almost as if it sensed her lack of concentration her horse missed a beat, jittering awkwardly in mid-stride.

The grating, high-pitched sound began to annoy her. She knew it couldn't be an insect; that would be too phenomenal up here where her riding studio had been specially built. This room was high above the level where most insects flew.

Her horse jittered again and she brought her wandering focus back to the ride, keen to get back in the zone with her animal. Then she smelt an acrid stink of insulation burning and a fine haze of smoke caught at her throat. The horse began to lurch under her in an alarming fashion, its gait worsening until she pulled it up short and swung quickly out of the saddle.

A barely perceptible plume of whitish vapour was leeching out of the animal's flared nostrils and the insinuating whine became much more pronounced, needle-like. The animal offered a forlorn whickering, its head tossing in dismay.

'It looks like poor Neddy is in need of some TLC,' Ben observed as he strode towards her from his vantage point by the doorway. 'But then she is getting on a bit, poor old thing.'

Ruth put her ear against the beast's shoulder to listen more closely and identify the source of the noise. She jerked away smartly. 'It's hot!' she gasped. 'What's going on in there?'

Ben placed his hand on the animal's side. 'Feels pretty terminal. It could be some sort of meltdown, which can happen with these old, non-nano pre-solid-state systems,' he muttered. 'Something's fusing in the servos I reckon. That's why there's smoke, but I think we're a bit beyond the manufacturer's warranty on this one.'

He turned calm eyes on Ruth, cool grey under straight brows. 'She's a classic model though. I can look to see if I can get her repaired if you like. There's sure to be specialists for this kind of work. Or I can get quotes for a new one. Which would you prefer?'

'Do both please, Ben. Thank you.'

Ruth stepped back from her horse, gazing at it with alarm through welling eyes, as she and Ben had to jump away as the creature shuddered and performed what seemed to be an ugly, twitching caricature of the elegant dressage she shared with it so recently.

It juddered as if trying to walk to Ruth's side then emitted a metallic, grinding shriek before crashing stiffly to the floor. The metal in its skeleton clanged with an unexpectedly bright, clear sound against the stone flags, one of which cracked clean across.

Ruth choked back a rasping, shuddering breath, her belly visibly clenching and releasing in her tight riding garb. 'Forget the repair, Ben,' she gasped. 'Get me a new one, a young one. I couldn't ride that thing ever again without seeing how it fell, hearing it. Please, just have it taken away.'

She turned and walked slowly towards the oversized exit doors. Her head and shoulders slumped when she paused to gaze back at the ticking, twitching robotic ruin. Her cheeks were wet and her mouth quivered, snatching at words.

'I've had her from new, Ben,' she breathed. 'Now she's just a broken, wretched old has-been. And so am I. Why don't you get me a new body while you're at it?'

She hunched her shoulders and strode away without looking back.

She didn't see the expressions playing across Ben's face.

● ● ●

Chapter seven: Needy Yet Sly

MILLA reached the apartment she shared with her partner just after midnight. It had been a long day so she was relieved when her car finally parked itself in the Autorack and was lifted up to her floor before letting her out and tucking itself away for the night.

She took the opportunity for a brief doze during the journey home, though she'd never really been someone who could let the car's auto pilot do all the work. She took the controls on manual for part of the way, knowing she was probably foolish in doing this. After all, she reasoned, the car was a better driver than she and had a greater sensory awareness of what was happening around it. But she had her own mind and preferences and didn't beat herself up over it.

She and Franklyn had been together for several months now and were still in the first flush of something that could either prove permanent or just become another exciting interlude, good while it lasted. Either way she was enjoying it.

The apartment was hers and Franklyn was only there by invitation. Even so he maintained his room in a shared flat in another part of London just in case she ever wanted her privacy back.

Milla preferred her own company and always had, even when she was a child. She believed that some of her loner instinct was in part due to her telepathy.

She discussed her theory with TP colleagues and they agreed it's difficult to be alone if other people's minds are always there whispering on the edge of your sensory horizon. Milla had always chosen to avoid the company of strangers. She was even reserved with those she loved.

It had been awkward at home. She was raised in a small apartment shared with her parents, her brother and her grandfather. Then, as now, space was at a premium and families rubbed along sharing space as best they could. Inter-generational housing was very far from uncommon.

It was Granddad's place and as she got older she became increasingly stifled by her closeness to the old man. There was something needy and yet sly about him when he was around her. When she was very young her awareness of the old man's yearning looks, enhanced by her as yet untrained talent, confused her.

However, as she slowly entered puberty and took on the early mantle of her burgeoning beauty she became increasingly aware of his grasping attentions, something that seemed to escape her parents. He would touch her on every occasion he could, ask her to do little jobs for him so he could kiss her with thanks, perhaps grab a little cuddle.

Something in her, some alarm in her unfledged talent, predicted that the old man's unhealthy regard would boil over one day. When it finally did the result was both shocking and spectacular.

The psychic bellow she unleashed – when her grandfather tried to kiss her on her mouth while he wrestled with the belt of her jeans and tried to tug them down to her knees – was what first brought her to the notice of the authorities.

It was a TP team knocking at the door that brought the old man to his senses and sent him reeling, sobbing and apologising, away from her recumbent, half-naked form. It was some time before she could get the words through her chattering teeth and overcome her gulping sobs long enough to explain what he had done. One or two of the TP team eyed her miserable grandfather with patent expressions of disgust.

Incipient dementia was accepted by her family as the probable reason for the attack. The old man claimed his mind had slipped far enough away from reality that he became convinced Milla was his lovely young wife back from the dead. He also claimed he was deluded enough to believe he was once more her young and lusty suitor.

It was harmless perhaps and no charges were pressed. But everyone agreed it would be for the best if Milla accepted a boarder's room in the specialist training school to which she had been invited.

She never saw her grandfather again after the incident, and as her TP tutoring progressed she saw less and less of her family. These days they exchanged birthday cards and remembered family occasions but little else.

She wondered if the yawning chasm widening between her and her parents would have happened without her emerging talent. Were they afraid of what their daughter had become? Or were they embarrassed by what had happened to their girl in her own home, what they had allowed to happen? She wondered about it less and less as she became ever more deeply immersed in her life as a TP.

Over the years she honed her talent to the point where she was able to use it in the same way she used her eyes and ears. As the strength of her talent grew she began to depend on it to unconsciously read intentions of people and groups, which helped her stay out of harm's way.

It could predict danger early enough to warn. On one occasion she knew to step off a travelator moments before a crowd of 'steamers' rammed through the flow of commuters. The thugs violently muscled their way through the crowd, pushing and scattering people right and left. They cast some over the safety rails and down to the distant floor. Many were injured and too many died.

Milla was a key witness and her expert testimony helped with a number of arrests. It also introduced her to the right people and began her lucrative work in security plus a number of consultant jobs with the police. She earned enough to afford her own home and a limited number of comforts.

This was the home she dreamt of, her own space where she could at last enjoy peace away from the chattering minds of others. At first she was reluctant to share. However, she and Franklyn were enjoying a fun, kittenish relationship just now and he was good to come home to.

She opened her door gratefully and stepped into her quiet hallway. Then closing the door behind her, she took a deep breath. Peace at last, for now.

•••

Chapter eight: I Need a Holiday

MILLA's apartment was on the central core of the London sky tower, not far from the immensely strong yet slender cable that had once been part of a space lift but was now the central support of her home.

Space lifts had been predicted centuries before by Arthur C. Clarke, one of the patron saints of modern science. Using monomolecular technology immensely strong, almost indestructible cables had been woven for the specific purpose of creating lifts capable of carrying payloads up to a point beyond Earth's gravitational pull where it became economically viable to take them by rocket to destinations throughout the solar system.

Some brave pioneers were keen to colonise planets and moons viable for Terraforming, or at least those where structures could be safe and stable enough to support human life. Thousands took to the skies over the years, but it wasn't enough.

Writers and dreamers once predicted a great Diaspora out into the solar system but the draw of the home planet was too ingrained. Despite what might have been said before, outer space was not to prove the final frontier.

Living rooms set the boundaries and established the frontiers of human experience because on Earth space was becoming a rare and expensive premium.

The planet's population continued to spiral out of control. And without a regular war to clear the air every once in a while, somewhere had to be found to house people or catastrophe would be sure to follow.

Sky towers for mass housing became the most logical solution once cheap, reliable fusion reaction was cracked and cargo no longer needed to be carried beyond Earth's punishing gravity by space lift.

Pre-fabricated housing modules were manufactured in dedicated factories then mounted around the space lift cables. These were then raised up so that the next module could be placed below them, and so the towers began to grow. It was a great idea, but this process proved too slow and the pressing need for housing too urgent.

New factories were built into the geostationary lifting units that kept the cables taut and ran the space lifts when they were needed. The factories used materials mined from the asteroid belt and beyond to quickly manufacture more housing modules. These could be dropped down to meet the levels rising up to join them. In this way the build happened incredibly fast.

Beyond a certain height, living quarters needed to be sealed to contain the atmosphere. The very highest modules went beyond Earth's atmosphere to the edge of space, linking with geostationary space stations crafted from the now redundant factories.

Sky towers established a whole new class system. Below a certain level, wealthier residents could enjoy a window to the sky and *real* weather on their balconies. Some even established small gardens on their balconies, though most were reluctant to share their homes with soil considering it filthy stuff.

Milla's home was part of the housing module's inner core but was not so very far up. She had air-conditioning and could gaze out at a real sky in the communal, recreational and shopping areas, though in her living room and bedroom she had 'Virtuo' windows, considered by many to be the next best thing to real. In fact Franklyn was a real fan because the view from any Virtuo window could be changed at the touch of a button.

The window unit was slaved to real time, meaning the Virtuo sun rose when the real sun rose and set when it set. What many found most charming was that it could be made to look out on any scene the viewer chose, and Franklyn's choice was a specific street in Paris.

Milla knew that part of his choice was inspired by the tall buxom blonde who was brazenly, and nakedly, exercising in plain view in her living room just over the way and down the street a short distance.

She had no way of knowing who the woman was, but she did know that Paris no longer looked like it did in her Virtuo view. The blonde woman and even the building she was exercising in were quite likely things of the past.

She was more than confident in her ability to keep Franklyn's interest in her, over some vid of an old girl who was likely now to be in her sixties. Anyway she didn't look real, she was all out of proportion, and Milla maintained she was CGI.

Franklyn left a note on the kitchen work surface apologising for not waiting. He had an early start the next morning and so had gone to bed. He signed it, 'Kisses on the bottom the next time I see you.' Such a typical touch; so much about him made her laugh. And he knew she would head first to the kitchen. He really understood her.

Milla emptied what was left of a bottle of Namibian Shiraz into a large glass and sat in her kitchen sipping while crunching through a small bag of almonds coated in wasabi paste.

It was then she began involuntary shaking, not just with exhaustion but also with delayed reaction over how the operation had panned out at the NEC. She'd allowed herself to get so involved with her revulsion for the evil perp that she'd been willing, even eager, to take him out altogether. If the police hadn't turned up she would have likely killed him, and that wasn't part of her job.

She drained her glass, put it in the washer and went to get ready for bed. In the bathroom she looked directly at herself in the mirror and saw strain tightening her eyes and thinning her lips.

'Fuck,' she said quietly. 'I really need a holiday.'

For the second time in 24 hours she jumped out of her skin when an unexpected voice came from behind her. 'Funny you should say that.'

•••

Chapter nine: New Tastes

RUTH looked around the hall and sampled air redolent with rich aromas. Food, every aspect of food: its enjoyment its preparation and its digestion were deeply interesting to Pearce and Ruth always took part in culinary explorations.

Pearce understood why she wouldn't eat huge quantities of anything. Too much lard on top of her enhancements would prove a physiological nightmare. But she allowed him to tempt her with taste sensations. She nearly always joined him on his forays into foodie heaven, like today.

They were in Paris walking down an arcade of 'food booths' sipping and tasting their way through the variety of goods on offer.

Pearce was a very active, though often quite fierce, informed food critic. He had been invited by the event's organisers as an 'essential connoisseur' because his opinion was often reported in the global press and sought out on social media. They hoped his visit would prove positive.

There were few animals outside zoos in the modern world due to the population's changing needs and attitudes. The presumed effect of domestic kine's alimentary methane on the planet's climate had finally been frowned on where it mattered most, in the financial sector. The small contribution to power provision from animals, through harnessing that same methane for use as fuel, had been cancelled by nuclear fusion.

Now miners could stalk between planets to capture the mineral riches of the solar system and every home had light and heat without using an iota of organic fuel. As a result millions of tonnes of biomaterials became steadily redundant while hard technology filled the gap. Where once animals had been vital for man's welfare there was no longer the

47

space for grazing and feed production. That meant a culture historically evolved from an agronomic society was no more.

But people still had a taste for meat and ingenious minds made a living in feeding those tastes.

'This is the very latest range from the *Interesting MeatBeast* portfolio,' said the man with the carnivore smile. 'I have personally tasted every development in our portfolio and found it good.'

His smile widened further, showing pointed and polished teeth, which might have looked unnerving if so much of his attention hadn't been spent wandering with lingering gaze across the contour map of Ruth for her to take him seriously.

'So what am I looking at here?' asked Pearce. 'All this meat looks the same.'

'Ah,' said the sharply smiling man, 'try this.' He proffered some hot meat on a skewer, which Ruth and Pearce nibbled.

'Rabbit?' asked Pearce.

'No, that was zebra,' answered the smiling man. 'Now try this.'

Pearce and Ruth tried another slice of warm meat. 'Lamb?' asked Ruth.

'I think I need to direct you to more mundane flavours,' said the smiley man, though the edges of his smile began to look a little frayed. 'That was koala bear.'

'Try this,' he said. 'Now what,' he paused for effect, 'is *this*?'

Pearce and Ruth were losing interest in the game but were egged on for one last try.

'It's pork,' said Pearce with some conviction.

'I think so too,' quavered Ruth.

The pointy-toothed smile widened and the eyes narrowed in the smiley man's face. 'So many people say that. In fact when some of the ancient people who relished this meat were asked for a description they named it Long Pork. It isn't actually porcine, but I must admit the crackling is very much the same if you roast it right.'

'So, come on, what is it?' urged Ruth.

'Does the word cannibalism spring any surprises or ring any bells for you folks?' asked the smiley man and, receiving two blank stares, he nodded.

'Okay, some roan DNA got into the mix,' he spoke quickly, 'and human proteins were involved. Just one specific *MeatBeast* vat was infected, if that's the word. I suppose infected is the word, but in a good way, a really successful way, a delicious way. So the manufacturers worked hard to develop it, and here it is for your delectation.'

He almost slurped the words out as if saliva was washing around his wet mouth. 'This slice of meat is human flesh but entirely vat-grown. Please understand that no people were hurt in the production of this skewer. But God, it tastes good.'

Pearce took another bite then finished his skewer. He reached for a second. Ruth put hers down and took a decided step backwards.

'Hey Hun,' Pearce said. 'What's the rush?'

'I don't eat people,' she replied.

'This ain't people,' said Pearce. 'It's crackling, it's tasty, but it ain't people.' Ruth looked back at him with a glare that could probably cut stone and pierce ice.

'I don't eat any part of a man,' she said, 'even if he's worth the effort. You know that. But I'm not putting something in my mouth that hasn't even had a chance to sweat in a pair of pants.'

She turned to the polished-tooth smiley rep. 'G'night, you ghoul!' Then, spat to her reddening husband: 'See you back in the car.'

Pearce turned to the rep as Ruth stalked away to the exit. 'Thanks for lunch,' he said.

The rep grinned a rueful response. 'My pleasure sir, though perhaps it would be more accurate to say lunch was on him or her.' He indicated the vat-grown slices. 'So it was also their pleasure, Mr Pearce. I do hope your lady will be alright – it is never our policy to offend.'

Pearce smiled, picked up a last skewer of dripping man meat and chewed on it as he followed his wife out of the hall.

• • •

Chapter ten: Just As Any Woman

FRANKLYN opened another bottle of wine and poured them both a glass. Milla didn't argue. Neither of them were big drinkers, but sometimes they loosened the reins. They sat in companionable silence for a while, sipping and relaxing, gazing out over the desert scene she had chosen for the living room window.

'Thought you had an early morning,' Milla said, wondering if they had any more almonds in the kitchen.

'Just got a heads up,' he answered. 'Production's been put back till next week. Re-writes or something.'

'Ah,' she nodded, 're-writes. So what happens now?'

'I get to spend some quality time with you, if you want me.'

'Is that what you meant by a holiday?'

She looked at him; he was spare yet sensuous, almost pretty yet very male. His dark mop of hair was full and wavy with just a hint of curl, and his fine dark brows and long eyelashes set off his deep set, blue eyes. He was a striking figure, but more than that he was someone almost as genetically rare as she was. He was opaque to TP, meaning she couldn't read him at all. No emotions, no predictions – nothing came through.

With Franklyn she was just the same as any other woman with her man; she had only to read him using the usual number of senses and that suited her just fine.

For years Milla sampled men when the fancy took her. She had a type she liked but her attraction was often more about characteristics than specific physical attributes. However, once she got close enough her Shutterbox talent would lay the man's personality bare and she could see to the heart of their superficial words and actions.

She didn't need to hear the actual words in his head to read the mind of a man who was more interested in what they could do with her body than what they could learn about her as a person. True, most women had an instinct for what a man was after they smiled at her, but few enjoyed her cast-iron surety.

There was such a tedious similitude in so many of her dates that she began to doubt any man could offer a relationship beyond whatever it took to satisfy his physical urges.

And then she met Franklyn.

She didn't know what the future would bring from this armoured personality sitting in her flat sharing glasses of wine so late in the day (or was it early in the morning?), but she liked the intrigue and she enjoyed the mystery of wondering, just for once, how another human was feeling and where the relationship would take her.

And the relationship was not heading for sex tonight, at least she hoped not, because she was on the verge of sleep or tears and didn't know which. She wanted this companionable peace to last just a little while longer and give her time to sort her feelings out.

Would she really have killed that scumbag at the NEC if the police hadn't intervened? Where did her anger come from? Was it time for a little TP therapy from her peers? Or would she get more benefit from a bit of sunshine next to a pool somewhere with this man, who seemed to know when he needed to leave her alone with her thoughts?

'Penny for them?' she asked, before almost choking on the irony of what she'd just said. Of all the men she'd met...

'I haven't got a lot of money,' he replied. 'You know that.'

Milla said nothing but thought, *Well, this is a departure.*

Franklyn was in the arguably lucrative film business but also what was arguably the quality end of the UK market, so he was relatively cash-strapped.

To date, success in the UK movie stable meant producing affable rom-coms, period drama, gangster films (or both – these days gangster films *were* period drama) and porn. But instead of chasing the easy money Franklyn was into small, tight indie films with some kind of redemption message, an art slant, or at least a lot of rain on misty hillsides.

Milla liked the films she'd seen; there was one where an old girl and her son continuously bickered and raged against each other, steeped in apparent hatred, until one day the son was killed in an accident at work. The old girl didn't cry or rage anymore. She did nothing anymore.

Slowly, over the last part of the film, she turned to moss-spotted stone. The last word from her crusting lips was her son's name. Then she wheezed just once, smiled gently and was still.

Of the sculpture she morphed into, Milla liked the sad smile with something poetical and right about it. The figure was placed over her son's ashes and the local people took it in turns to place flowers there.

The penultimate scene was a long shot, showing the calcified woman seated amongst grey trees in the crematorium. It was spring. The sun came out and sticky buds were shown in close-up.

From one branch above her a drop of water fell onto the woman's stone face like a tear and travelled, rolling down her body to soak into the ground at her feet. The petals from the newest posy of flowers blew away on a quick breeze.

There was rain on the hillside before the credits, and Milla shouted a silent hurrah!

'But we need a holiday,' continued Franklyn, 'and we can make a bit of money while we do it.'

He stood and walked over to the bureau, which had become his putative possession in their relationship. Then he returned, holding out a tablet, which he had already keyed to the relevant page. Milla read: 'Body Holiday.'

•••

Chapter eleven: Where Do We Go From Here?

BEN took the car back to the apartment's parking slot. He said not a word to break the frosty quiet that unexpectedly enveloped his boss and his boss's wife when they returned from the food event.

He had his own feelings to deal with about Ruth, because his loyalty to Pearce was total. However, Ruth had become everything he valued in a woman, ever since his space pilot mother died hard by the rings of Saturn in a freak water-ice harvesting accident more than 20 years previously.

Ruth was a role model for dignity, caring and thoughtfulness, and God she had a body that kept a boy up at night. He worshipped her, not the ground she walked on, just her. And when she walked away from her ruined robot horse, when it collapsed onto the stone slabs of her riding stable, he wanted to either expunge everything that had just happened from her memory or give her another steed to ride. He would love to offer himself.

But then there was Pearce, his boss, someone who made his money from the colonies by doing the business right – while making sure people were properly cared for in the most dangerous places in the Solar System. Pearce was a good, though very original man. His head could churn figures faster than Ben could give them out. And he had some very lucrative brainwaves sometimes, more than Ben could keep track of. But he didn't have the powerful pheromonal magnetism his wife gave off. Ben took a deep draft of the air in the car, only savouring one of the scents available to him: a mix of flowers and citrus and something more primal.

But Pearce had become a friend as well as a boss, the fucker, so Ben just swallowed his feelings and hoped that he could control how he felt about the whole thing. He looked in the mirror at the couple he was employed to serve and protect, and thought, 'You, my friend, are perhaps not worthy of her consideration, but you are worthy of mine.' He keyed in the landing code and the car settled into its bay.

From the car landing in the garage to the pair entering their apartment took just a few minutes. Nevertheless Ruth forgave her man for his dietary transgressions before they'd closed the door and were finally alone. As was usual in the evenings, Pearce began to strip as soon as he was home and walking along behind him she saw his 'Old Fellow' unleashed to slap against his thighs and knew she wanted it sheathed before bedtime, but not in her.

Pearce paused in the living room and said, 'I've had an idea.'

Saying nothing, Ruth opened the big glass window doors that led onto the balcony, then took some drinks out of the chiller cabinet and handed one to Pearce. She sat and waited for him to elucidate.

They sipped in silence for a moment, Pearce unconsciously pulling at his penis with his free hand as was his wont. He leaned forward and gazed into Ruth's eyes.

'We need a holiday,' he said. 'You and me – away from everything we've been doing all these years, somewhere where we can do something completely new.'

The irony of his statement reignited her recent anger and she let fly with a vehemence that surprised them both. 'New?' she asked. 'What could possibly be new? You own half the fucking planet. Are we talking about going off-world again? Or are you still thinking about booking a window suite in that hotel under Antarctica? Or…are we thinking about that safari deal in Africa, the one with real animals?'

She looked back at him with the eyes of an injured child: too old for the perfection of her face, too deeply hurt to be those of an adult. Her mouth began to work like she didn't know whether to swear at him or howl with frustrated tears, her emotions stuttering from one state to another.

Swallowing the rest of her drink, she fetched herself and Pearce another. She wasn't a heavy drinker, neither was he, but sometimes she appreciated the intimations of unthinking languor that just a touch too much brought to her senses.

'What could be new, Pearce?' Ruth continued. 'After all we've done and all the things we've seen, where would we possibly go for something new?'

She started pinching and pulling at her body, then almost snarled, 'It doesn't matter where we go. We'll still be dragging these old bones around with us. And I've had enough of it.'

She took a sip from her glass before stalking round the centre of the room. 'My horse packed up because it was just too old to go on anymore, and I feel exactly the same way. You want to buy me a holiday? Then you just buy me a holiday away from myself. You give me a break away from Ruth Pearce because quite frankly I've had enough of her. And will you please leave your cock alone just for once while we're talking?'

Pearce jerked his hand away from his groin and spread his hands apart as if he wanted to prove the point. His eyes took on a familiar calculating glaze as they often did when he was dealing with a problem, thinking with speed and immense clarity. It was as if he was temporarily blind and deaf to everything except his machine-fast thoughts.

'Leaving my cock aside for the moment,' he began, placing a cushion over the offending member, 'Ben has been looking into something that will enable us, you and me, to do exactly what you are asking. We can take a holiday from ourselves, from these too familiar bodies of ours, and enjoy a month as other people.

'There is a facility, which is only open to the few among us who can afford it. By which we, you and I, can take what is called a Body Holiday – quite literally a holiday in someone else's body. What do you think?'

Ruth realised that Pearce's hand was back again, moving rhythmically underneath the cushion, but said nothing. One of the dues she knew she had to pay for the gift of Pearce's financial genius was his touch of Asperger's Syndrome demonstrated by jarring and inappropriate behaviour at certain times, as if he was coming at the world from a slightly different angle.

If he didn't see the point of accepted social mores he ignored them, which made him a difficult man to deal with for many of those he encountered in business. That's also why he often eschewed face-to-face meetings in favour of the more anonymous social media.

Though he could appear cold and off-hand, abrupt, rude and heartless in his dealings, he would be confused and upset if anyone told him so – because he always thought of himself as considerate and thoughtful of others. He just saw a problem or opportunity, worked out the best or fastest route to the desired end result and took it. Ruth gathered she was once again mired in one of Pearce's classic 'straight to the desired end result' gambits, and for a moment she was lost for words.

He continued, 'I've got the chap from the Body Holiday Foundation coming over tomorrow and we can look through samples from the catalogue before he arrives. The only limit to who we can be is that as a couple we have to be hosted – that's what they call it, 'hosted' – by another couple, because of the sex thing.

'They don't think it right for singles to go shagging wherever or whoever they want while being hosted. Can't see what's wrong with it myself, but there you are. But we can and will be young again for the duration of our stay. And that's it. What do you say?'

Ruth silently walked back to the chiller for fresh drinks, handed one to Pearce, and took a sip from hers before sitting down. The action gave her a chance to think, time to compose her thoughts. 'What if we don't like it?'

'We can opt out at any time, though we will forfeit the full fee of course.'

Ruth gazed at him for several heartbeats, took another sip from her glass, and then asked pensively, 'But what if we like it too much? What if we don't want to come back to our old bodies?'

Pearce folded both his hands around his drink, focusing for a moment on the coolness of the glass and its contents. 'We'll just have to deal with that if it happens.'

● ● ●

Part two: Body Holiday

Chapter one: Interviews

MILLA noted how the office in which the Body Holiday Foundation conducted its interviews had a real window but, due to its position up the sky tower, it was sealed. *Money on show*, she thought, *but not too much in your face. Cool.*

She sat back in a comfortable recliner with Franklyn next to her. The man addressing them was perched on a saddle seat, working with a state-of-the-art crystal clear tablet on the high table beside him.

Milla read the man when they'd entered his office, and found a harmless wage earner who saw them as little more than vehicles towards his next bonus payment – though his bantering flirtatiousness reinforced the sense she'd received that he saw them as a very likely pair indeed. He evidently saw them as the perfect route to hard cash in his pocket, so he was being nice.

'For the duration of the contract you will both become employees of the Foundation,' explained the man, who had asked them to 'call me Blake' over the initial handshakes.

Something about his grip was a little unsettling, which Milla put down to him being shy and awkward. It's funny, she mused, how many socially inept people gravitate towards sales. She reasoned it must be some sort of compensation activity.

'You will be under very firm constraints about just what you do with our clients' bodies,' continued Blake, 'but there's no reason not to enjoy yourselves.' He smiled and nodded keenly.

'The clients are all very wealthy, successful people, and you may recognise yourselves when you wake up in your clients' bodies. As a result you will sign a non-disclosure agreement beforehand and social media of all kinds is strictly prohibited during the contract. What happens in Body Holiday stays in Body Holiday, you understand?'

Blake waited while they nodded their affirmation then continued his lecture, his voice taking on a practiced, polished lilt. 'You will not be allowed to put our clients into embarrassing positions or put their bodies at risk. You will not be allowed to alter the bodies in any way, no piercings or tattoos for example.'

He smiled. 'One of our hosts spent the whole month swimming, reading and sunbathing. She ate only the healthiest food and looked after her client's body with great care and attention, planning to give it back looking better and fitter than when she got it.'

He shook his head and raised a warning finger. 'It all backfired because the client had a deep phobia about excessive exposure to sunlight. She had a silly fear of skin cancer or something. When she saw her deeply tanned face she went nuts and we had to refund her money plus take out lifetime insurance against melanoma, which is quite cheap these days of course. But it should never have happened.'

Blake looked intently at Milla and Franklyn. *Pause for effect* thought Milla, and he continued.

'The host didn't get her full payment, because we didn't get any of our payment. It's in the small print that in the event of an unhappy client who refuses our fee the host's payment reverts to scale, which is about a tenth of the original agreed amount. Sorry about that, but you have been warned. It's the client's holiday that counts, not yours.'

He stood up and began to count off stipulations on his fingers. 'You cannot take part in extreme sports, which includes skiing and skateboarding, fencing, most martial arts, cloud jumping and hill swooping, in fact any kind of unpowered flight or freefall activity. You are not allowed deep diving, speed racing or aerobics. Tombstoning and Spider-Man building climbs are both out.'

Pausing for breath, he continued: 'I won't waste your time or test your intelligence too much. You're bright or you wouldn't have got this far. For legal reasons there's a full list of dos and don'ts in your contract downloads if you want to read them all, but most of them are common sense.

'Put simply, if something you fancy doing might hurt or injure your client's body in any way, no matter how minor, don't do it.'

Blake stopped to ask if they had any questions so far. 'I suppose our clients...' Franklyn chewed the word as if he wasn't used to it yet. 'Our clients are likely to be old or disabled. What protection do we get from potentially dangerous medical situations?'

Blake nodded. 'Good question, Franklyn, and I'm coming to that. All those involved in the hosting, clients and hosts alike, are asked to wear a Mediband on their wrists. These are based on the old military model that's been in use for years. Our pilots wear them in space, of course.

'They can be taken off if the wearer so chooses, for an hour or two. But then the Mediband will send out a signal and the wearer will be asked, through the usual implanted communication systems, to put it back on.'

He stood up and walked over to the window, gazed out for a moment, then turned to the young couple. 'No doubt you know about the Mediband. It is discreet, comfortable, and monitors the wearer's health. Any problems and a medical team can be on hand within minutes. Be sure about it, I can promise you, there are no risks in taking a Body Holiday.'

By the time they left Blake's office, Milla and Franklyn had signed up as potential hosts. Though Milla, for one, wasn't sure about it. The money was great. Their willingness to let some old codgers rampage about for a month in their younger bodies would net them each a cool three-quarters of a million in credit, once the Holiday was safely completed.

However, Blake's parting comment gave the pair pause for thought. 'When you wake up in your clients' bodies, take it easy until you get used to things. You are in an alien environment: muscles won't work the way they should, weight distribution will be different, perhaps even your eyesight will be altered.

'You will also be fitted with painkilling implants and you may feel a little woozy until you get used to it. So take a little time to adjust. What I'm saying is, don't try to rush things and you should be fine.'

Milla asked, 'Why painkillers?'

Blake concluded his presentation as he led the pair to the door. 'These people, our clients, have been in their bodies all their lives while gravity and time have taken their toll. They've become used to all the stiffness and pains that slowly accrue over the years. They bear them because they have to, they have no alternative, and their bodies have learned how to accept the discomfort over the course of a lifetime.

'But you'll be taking them all on, in one fell swoop. Think about that. We've found painkillers have always been a great help in the early days. Trust me,' he laughed as he opened his door and saw them out into reception.

'You will be surprised by just how great it feels to get back into your own bodies when it's all over. I know, I've been there. It's like taking a Body Holiday all over again.'

With his promise to 'be in touch soon' still ringing in their ears, Milla and Franklyn joined the downwards East travelator and headed back across the tower to their flat. The mundane normalcy of the journey added extra strangeness to their recent interview. Without saying anything, they

stretched out hands to each other and didn't release their grip
until they got home.

●●●

Chapter two: The Joys of Youth

BLAKE stood at Pearce's balcony doors and breathed cool, fresh air flowing into the room. 'When I can, if I can,' he said, 'I'm going to get myself a home with windows that open like this.'

'The amount you're charging us for this holiday should go a long way towards paying for it,' riposted Pearce, joining him at the window and topping up Blake's drink.

'Oh, I'm on commission,' said Blake, 'and I love my job. But I won't get near this any time soon.' He drank in another deep breath and turned away from the view across golden-hued and pastel buildings stretching away to the perceptible curve at the horizon, all under a blue sky deepening to black.

'That view will haunt my dreams for some time,' he said, 'so thank you for the invitation to your home.' He turned to take a final lingering look, before swinging to face his potential client.

'Now to business.'

'At last,' said Pearce archly. 'I was beginning to wonder whether you came here for your pleasure or ours?'

'Yours!' came the answer, a shade too quickly.

Blake took a moment to gather his wits. 'Of course, I am here to provide you with the best holiday you have ever enjoyed. Have you found the time to look through our catalogue?'

'Yes,' said Pearce, 'and to be honest with you we're more than a little disappointed. Where did you find that bunch of has-beens and wannabees, a core house?'

Blake was again nonplussed. Core houses were where the most vulnerable, least able and poorest people once lived, at the centre of sky towers. They were crowded together with the sole purpose of creating renewable heat for the wealthier residents around them, and suffered in a fierce and sweltering environment as a result.

The violence, privation and sexual incontinence of those doomed to core house dwelling was infamous and frequently turned up in cheaper TV dramas and movies. Inbreeding resulted in some unusual looking offspring – the accusation of being a core house dweller was deemed a pretty fierce insult.

'Mr Pearce, I can assure you...'

'Pearce. Nobody calls me Mr unless I invite them to. Then I pay them for the privilege. Can I get you another drink?'

Blake took the proffered glass and sat down. He stood again as one of the most beautiful women he ever met entered the room and walked over with her hand extended. He was aware that his hand was sweating as he shook, but if she noticed she gave no reaction.

'Is my husband giving you a hard time, Mr...?'

'Blake. Just Blake, Mrs Pearce.'

'Ruth, please. And please sit down. Now, have you any more of those enchanting young people for us to see? Some of them are so lovely it will prove really hard to choose which ones we want to try on for size, so to speak.'

Blake brought out his tablet and after asking permission keyed it to the room's 3D screen. 'These are the very latest hosts to join us. I think you will be pleased with the choices on offer.'

'Shut up and scroll,' growled Pearce. 'We're not here to listen to your yap!' Thinking only of his commission, Blake bit his tongue and put the latest entries in his catalogue on slide show.

Images of couples appeared in various flattering poses, falling away to be replaced by others. All were attractive and young, but none elicited any response from Pearce until he suddenly said, 'Stop! Scroll back. There. Ruth, what do you think?'

His wife joined him and stood quietly examining the people who stood life-sized and still in the centre of the room. Pearce circled the image, his lips pouting in concentration, and barked at Blake, 'Has anyone used these two before?'

'No,' came the answer, 'they joined us this week.'

'Virgins, eh,' said Pearce, 'I like that. Untouched goods. They must not be used by anyone before us, guaranteed?'

'I can't...'

'I'll double your fee and theirs. Those are the hosts we want. Can you have them ready two weeks from Saturday?'

'I think...'

'Don't think, find out. Do it from here. Can I get you another drink?'

'Please...'

'Ruth, please get Blake what he wants. You, son, have just earned the right to call me Mr. Cheers!'

Blake keyed a number into his phone. A few moments later, Milla picked up at the other end. 'Hello?'

'Hello, Ms Carter. It's Blake.'

'Oh, hello Blake.'

'Ms Carter, you remember I told you I'd be in touch soon? Well, I've got some great news...' He looked over the Pearces' shoulders glancing from Ruth's classic profile to the startling fresh loveliness of Milla and the lean, good looks of Franklyn. *Gold dust*, he thought. *Pure gold dust.*

● ● ●

Chapter three: In the Male

BLAKE accompanied the Pearces in preparation for *Transition.* His colleague, Freedman, took Milla and Franklyn through their final checklists.

They were in a simple room with no windows, discreet lighting and plain though pleasant décor. There were two divan-style beds, side-by-side, above which a flat screen mounted on the ceiling displayed a hypnotically shifting light show.

'The beds are gel pools,' said Freedman, 'so they are about as comfortable as floating in warm salty water or breezing around in zero G. I've got one of these at home and man, I love my bed.'

He was a small man, very neat, with narrow wrists shooting from bright white shirt cuffs. His mass of tight, curly hair seemed to spring in a perfect halo from his coffee-coloured head, itself balanced on a narrow column of neck almost as if it were some alien plant recently bloomed from the tightly pinched collar of his jacket.

Milla just knew everything about Freedman was exactly the way he wanted it to be. Even his speech had a clipped, practiced precision and a slight bite to the consonants. He delivered each word like a polished gift. The overall effect would have been very annoying if it hadn't been for the genuine warmth of his smile and his idiosyncratic use of English.

'You hosts are in for a shock when you first sample a day in the clients' bodies, but I can promise you they will be as clean as an eagle's fart on a mountainside when you try them on for size. We'll make sure of that.'

'Are some clients a bit dirty?' asked Milla. 'I thought they were some of the wealthiest and most famous people in town.'

'Money don't buy manners,' laughed Freedman, 'and it don't teach people to wash much neither. You wouldn't believe the state of some creatures I've had through my hands. I wish everyone was as particular as you two.'

He leaned in, conspiratorially. 'The joke of it is that we have to dirty them up again afterwards before they wake up, because they get offended if they think we've fiddled with them while they've been away. So I have spray bottles of stale sweat, grime and all kinds of shit that I need to use.' He laughed uproariously when he realised what he'd just said. 'And I mean literally,' he giggled. 'Just imagine trying to put dirt back under fingernails, and don't even ask me about foreskins!'

Freedman sobered slightly. 'The first few days are going to hurt. I think Blake told you about that side of things but the Foundation looks after its hosts so don't worry. We want you to think about coming back while you're still young and fit enough to be a viable destination for holidaymakers. And may I say that a couple like you two will be a dream team for some years to come.'

He adjusted the temperature in the room while Milla read his deeply felt sense of duty, also his care and concern for his people. He wanted them to be comfortable and he wanted them to be safe.

Almost as if he was reading her mind, Freedman said, 'Now, for your comfort during Transition, I need you both undressed and tucked into your beds. You will fall into a gentle sleep. Then when you wake up, which will be tomorrow morning, you will be sharing space with your clients tighter than a duck's ass in a rainstorm.'

He walked to the door and turned the light down in the room, which had the effect of making the display on the ceiling brighten and cast shifting light patterns across the walls and the beds. 'Nice,' said Freedman. 'Now you good people get ready. Kiss each other. Do whatever it is you've got to do. Then get into bed and watch the birdie.' He indicated the ceiling.

'As for you, sweet lady,' he smiled at Milla, 'if you wonder where your man's gone when you wake up, don't you worry, he's in the male.' He chuckled, and his large eyes glowed in the half-lit room. 'Sorry folks, I just can't ever resist that one. See you soon.'

Once they were alone in the room, Milla and Franklyn looked at each other for long moments, the light from the display chasing itself across their faces. They moved together, held each other for a long moment, and then kissed deeply yet chastely. The thought of what they had committed to tugged at Milla's mind. She wondered whether it was too late to abort.

Too late. Franklyn started to strip and she automatically followed suit. When she folded down into her gel bed she found herself breathing shallowly, like a swimmer about to enter a cold pool of water. She shut her eyes tight rather than look up at the display and chased fearful thoughts around her mind. She was shocked to hear Franklyn suddenly burst out in uncontrolled laughter.

'What?' she asked.

'I just got it! I'll be in the male, you see. Clever. See you soon.'

She smiled. She looked up, and was lost.

●●●

Chapter four: She's so Bouncy

RUTH woke up feeling like she'd had the best night's sleep ever. She luxuriated under her light covers, stretching like a cat without popping her joints or straining uncomfortable muscles. She must get Pearce to order gel beds for the apartment.

Still a little drugged with sleep, she was confused to find she was completely naked. Since she got her augmentations, she always slept with a bra on, even after she married Pearce, because without nocturnal help gravity would have taken even more of a toll on her figure. Must have had a touch too much wine last night. Still, she had a bladder that needed emptying so she threw her covers to one side and swung herself into a sitting position. She bounced clean out of the bed and onto the floor, more shocked than hurt, rolling quickly to her knees.

When she stood up she nearly fell over backwards. Her weight was all wrong and she was closer to the ground than normal, or so it seemed.

Cool light washed in from glazed doors and she could hear what sounded like the susurration of waves on a sandy beach. She took a few steps towards the light and caught sight of a strange young girl gazing at her from a doorway. She too was naked. Ruth made as if to cover herself and the girl did the same, mimicking her exactly. Ruth was about to let fly verbally when the reality of her situation sunk home. She was the girl and the girl was her. The doorway was a recessed mirror and she had been on the brink of giving her new reflection some pithy abuse.

She laughed, enjoying the way her reflection's taut stomach tightened further when she did so, and ran her hands through her chestnut bob while admiring the small yet well rounded breasts as they lifted to her view. She took a close look at her host's well tended body and was pleased. Taking some time to admire both her front and back, she began to feel oddly voyeuristic about what she was doing.

She donned a short silken dressing gown and found her way to the bathroom. A full bladder must be dealt with no matter whose body it resides in.

As she sat and passed water she realised that the urine was nothing to do with her. Whatever this girl drank, it was imbibed before Ruth opened her eyes on this first day of her holiday. *She is none of me*, thought Ruth. *I am her custodian is all.* Then she fell prey to a cascade of emotions and confusion. Tears started from her eyes (*not my eyes*, she realised, *her eyes*) and she twisted the pretty mouth in something like fear.

Ruth always had a strong attitude to looking after other people's possessions. She had to give things back in the same condition as when she received them or better, from a book to a hire car, and here she was in somebody else's *body.* Another part of the problem was that the girl seemed so young and fresh. Ruth feared her well-seasoned mind might somehow sully her, age her prematurely. Part of her conscious mind understood: this girl had a life outside the Body Holiday Foundation. She hadn't been taken clean and fresh from a box for Ruth to inhabit for a spell then get put back until the next client turned up. This was a real breathing woman with bowel movements and sweat glands and a now empty bladder. But there was no escaping the fact she was brand new to Ruth, untouched and barely weaned.

Ruth flushed the toilet. She noticed it was a Medisan Premium model, which meant if she asked it could give her a fairly accurate health assessment based on her urine or stool samples. But there was no need. This body radiated health. It glowed with it, shone with it.

She washed her hands and took some time to study the girl's face, turning slightly left and right while she did so. Her ears were slightly too large for classical beauty, making her more striking as a result, and her rounded, deeply dimpled cheeks were hazed with a light dusting of freckles. The lips, full and up-tilted, looked as if she smiled more than she frowned. Or perhaps it was just that usage had yet to gouge its scars into her portrait.

The eyes appraised her with intense frankness and curiosity, hazel with flecks of gold lending depth and lustre. Was that intelligence she saw, inherent to this face? Or was any personality she gleaned simply borrowed from her own soul, now the temporary resident of this tender flesh, with muscles bending to her will? Ruth knew she would be unlikely to ever meet this girl socially once the month was over, but that wasn't the point. She had a duty of care as long as the month lasted.

While she looked at her reflection in the mirror she also saw echoes of her own face there, clues and hints that told her the old Ruth had not gone away but was still in the background looking after things. Clinging to old Ruth for a moment she looked deep into the girl's eyes and something maternal opened within her, something warm and protective. And she made a silent promise to the beautiful stranger that all would be well; she would make sure of it.

She brushed her teeth before enjoying her shower, a little surprised at the neat bush of pubic hair sprouting between her legs while also feeling a touch chastened by her strong temptation to linger and experiment there – a temptation she surrendered to for perhaps a moment longer than she thought proper.

Hair and body dried, deodorised and perfumed from a bottle she found in the bathroom cabinet (she was pleased to see it was the brand she preferred), she wrapped herself in her robe and walked barefoot, still a little unsteadily, to take in the view from the glazed doors.

She's so bouncy and fluid, Ruth realised. *It's like she's on firm springs.* She smiled as she remembered the sequence from one of her favourite childhood films, *Bambi*, in which the young fawn took its first wobbly steps. *Well maybe not quite that bad*, she chuckled, *but we'll have to take time to get used to each other my girl.*

Ruth stood in the doorway looking out across dazzling white sands, clean blue sky, turquoise sea and leaning palm trees scenting the fresh breeze – a picture post card.

She was just thinking that she'd have to check this place was equipped with the necessary bits she'd need when this girl's time of the month came round, which was sure to happen over the next four weeks, when the bedroom door burst open and a young man in a dressing gown erupted into the room. He gripped the front of his gown in both hands and grinned fiercely at her with something like a proprietary stare.

'You show me hers,' he said, 'and I'll show you his.'

•••

75

Chapter five: Nothing Prepares You

FRANKLYN was off somewhere and Milla was certain he was suffering, suffering badly. This woman she now inhabited was honed and tooled like an athlete. She also had an impossibly ethereal beauty, both somehow cool and deeply sexual at the same time, but she hurt in all sorts of places.

Her joints popped and ratcheted like cracked knuckles and her neck was an object lesson in keen agony. She spent 15 minutes practicing her most complex kata, out on the bedroom balcony, naked apart from the bra she'd put on in self defence against the swing and heft of the *Manga*-sized breasts she now had to cope with. The woman was slender and otherwise well-proportioned with good long legs and shapely hips. These chest ornaments were surely the result of design over nature. Why did she do this to herself?

Milla originally stepped out onto the balcony, completely naked, in order to enjoy the rare pleasure of a cool breeze with natural air flowing over her; while she practiced her kicks and turns, moving faster and faster. But because of the way these breasts seemed to start after she'd finished, and still be on their way up when she was on her way down, she'd reluctantly donned a support bra she eventually found in a drawer full of expensive underwear.

I feel like I've been in a car crash. I'm a recovering invalid, thought Milla as she tried to push her new body into a performance it was unsuited for. It surprised her that, during her initial close examination of her client's skin, she found no blatant bruises. She felt punched, bruised, kicked and violated in every part of her spine and across her shoulders.

'Where are those fucking painkillers we were promised,' she asked out loud and then realised that her mind was a little slower than usual, even wandering a bit. The painkillers were in and active. It was just that her young mind had never experienced what it felt like to be in a body four decades its senior.

I will never look at old people the same way again, she promised. *Nothing prepares you for this*. Then in a moment of insight she understood that only one thing can steel the body's nervous system to the point where it learns how to cope with this kind of constant pain, and that was time.

It takes decades of living through constant usage to season one's response to the damage inflicted on it over the years. And here she was, trying to come to terms with it on the first day of the 28 she had still to endure.

'Milla, you pussy,' she said out loud. 'Suck it up, like a soldier. Come on, chest out, shoulders back. Let's get you into some kind of shape.' From the balcony she was able to see herself in the large mirrored wall in their bedroom and her pose was such a classical fantasy one, even with the bra on. For the first time since she climbed aching from her gel bed that morning, she was surprised by laughter. But the pain to her neck caused by her heavily jouncing breasts soon quelled that.

A balcony with a view, it was a dream come true. She had the sky all to herself, so she couldn't be accused of putting her client into an 'embarrassing position' by exercising out here in her state of dishabille. She loved the air on her skin. She loved this balcony with its view out towards a curving horizon. She also loved the sense of privacy she was getting here. But could somebody please take away her cloak of nagging, grinding pain?

There was movement in the room and the old man Franklyn, slightly stooped and with pain tugging at his eyes and mouth, stepped into the light from the window. *He was a good-looking man for his age,* thought Milla, *but my lady is out of his league. It must be the money that keeps her home.*

No, she thought – *that's not it, not this girl. She could have anybody when she was younger and she could still turn most heads in the room today if she wanted to. Must be something else.*

'This guy is hung like a fucking bear,' whined the old man, 'but he might as well be a eunuch. It just hangs there like a piece of meat.'

'You in pain?' asked Milla.

'Sure I'm in pain. This guy was rolled in a barrel full of rocks before the Transition. I'm sure of it. He wanted to make sure that while he's off having the ball of his life in my skin, I'm going to rue every second I spend in his. The selfish fuck. There's so much pain that even the bits that don't hurt have come out in support of all the bits that do.'

From somewhere Franklyn raised an unsteady smile. 'Hey, I should write that down. That should be in a script, don't you think? But just now I need to lie down for a moment.' He groaned over to the bed and gasped himself painfully prone. He looked across at Milla, doing a double take. 'You know who you are?' he asked.

'Tall blonde with big tits. Dime a dozen.'

'No, seriously, do you know who you are? Look at yourself. Take that bra off for a minute and look at yourself.' A touch self-consciously she did as he asked, and he was right – she looked somehow familiar. 'Paris,' he said. 'From the window at home. You're the exercising woman from Paris. Fuck it!'

He slapped a mournful hand to his forehead and kneaded his temples. He whimpered in a way Milla found almost comical. 'Fuck it,' he repeated. 'I'm only sharing a bed with the woman from Paris and I'm in pain and saddled with a foot-long dick that won't perform. There's no justice, I tell you!' He looked at her, his eyes squeezed in pain. 'Now I ask you,' he groaned, 'what kind of sick fuck would write that into the script?'

•••

Interlude

TWO men sit in a darkened room surrounded by screens. One is watching Milla and Franklyn, the other Pearce and Ruth. They are recording everything taking place in the rooms: even Franklyn in the bathroom tugging vainly at Pearce's lengthy manhood and Ruth in the shower with her hands lingering between Milla's legs.

'Look at this,' said the first. 'See who she is?'

His colleague turned and squinted at the blonde woman in the room. 'Ruth Pearce. Or rather, the donor in Ruth Pearce's body. Rings bells though,' he answered. 'Nice tits. Want to swap?'

'No way, dude, this is a dream come true. That fine lady is Ruth Pearce, nee the extremely well known Horny Hudson, every thinking man's wet dream. At one time she was in everything except the hard stuff. I'm sure I've still got some downloads of her riding a horse naked. And here she is just for me, man 'o man, and I can't tell anyone about it but you.'

'Just concentrate on getting the best shots you can for the boss when he comes back,' came the retort. 'He'll cane your hide if you even think of talking about clients and donors outside this room. And compensate for the lighting a bit. You're overexposing Ms Hudson's pretty features. Her nipples look too pale.'

There was quiet in the room for a while, then the sound of slightly muted panting. 'You fucking obscene piece of shit,' warned the second voice. 'Don't you be doin' that in the same room as me. You set the cameras to auto and get yourself to the can.'

There was an urgent squeak. 'Damn,' came the first voice, breathlessly. 'It's all over the keyboard.'

'You incontinent prick,' growled the second. 'Clean it up before the boss sees it. Unplug the keyboard first. And sort yourself out. You smell like a dirty swimming pool.'

'Oh, man, I'm dripping down the leg of my pants.'

'Your system's slaved to mine now, so go clean yourself up. Clean your keyboard up, and try not to drip on the floor. And don't come back till you're decent for company!'

There was a scurrying sound and the darkness of the room was briefly swept by light from an opening then closing door. In the light the anger was plain on Blake's face – as he watched his hunched-over colleague hustle out of the room, open pants clenched in one hand, keyboard in the other.

Once the door was shut and he was alone in the renewed darkness, he chuckled. 'She's already taken out a seasoned professional in just a few hours,' he breathed, trying to keep an eye on all the screens at once. 'These four are a fucking gold mine. And it's just going to get better.'

●●●

Chapter six: Nettles in the Rose Garden

PEARCE stood before Ruth, his young frame almost vibrating with excitement. 'This body is fantastic,' he grinned. 'He's all slim muscle and jism. I feel I could run a mile, jump over a house and swim an ocean. I almost feel I could fly.' He bounced lightly on his feet. 'How's your girl?'

'I like her a lot,' Ruth smiled. 'She's looked after herself. I think I'd like her if I met her in the flesh too. I can't get over how she feels and I know what you mean about feeling like you could fly.'

Something eager passed between them. Without another word Pearce came to her, embraced her, and with some alarm she could feel his mounting need, his urgent penis hot against her belly. *Give me some time to get used to this at least*, she thought, and almost shrank back from this strange young man and his insistent hands.

Then she seemed to catch something of his fever and began to return his embrace. He quickly dropped his robe and then unpeeled hers, sliding it off her shoulders to fall in a silken puddle at her feet. He stood gazing at her with frank admiration, obviously enjoying what he saw until his inspecting eyes faltered and his expression changed.

'I see a patch of nettles in the rose garden,' he said archly. 'Stay there.'

He disappeared into the bathroom and quickly returned with his familiar depilation kit in his hands. She noticed with a curious glance that Pearce's host body had a smaller but quite elegantly curved cock. Its head was quite thick though mounted on a shorter, more slender stem.

It shrank away and curved downwards at first, while Pearce applied himself to her offending pubic bush. But as he worked it began to rise until its straining head was bobbing, nodding at her. His breath seemed to be catching in his throat and he swallowed back a surplus of saliva.

His gentle ministrations began to have their effect on her too. She felt every touch with increased sensitivity when he smoothed the cream onto her and massaged it in. Waiting for it to take effect, while breathing warmly onto her, he wiped away the scant fuzz before spreading cooling moisturiser around the girl's most private area.

Ruth was astonished at how deeply this girl reacted to physical touch and almost winced as her nipples peaked like small, rigid, rose-blushed fingertips. She gasped and felt it difficult to breath. She panted, 'Pearce, are you sure we should be doing this? We were told not to change anything in these people's bodies.'

'Don't worry,' he whispered. 'We have them for a month. You can grow back a whole field of nettles before we need to return them to their previous owners.'

He looked up at her with his host's urgent, flushed face, and she realised something of what she'd missed by not knowing Pearce as a young man.

'Let's enjoy them while we have them, girl,' he pleaded. 'Let's make this a holiday we'll never forget.' With that he blew gently across her denuded groin and applied a tentative tongue to her rising clitoris. Ruth nearly groaned. Pearce could wait no longer.

'Good job, Alice,' he said, then rose and placed his urgent cock into her moist cleft with a gently penetrating, practiced stroke. He lifted her up and easily turned onto his back, keeping their sexes joined so Ruth ended up riding him, pinioned on his cock. She felt its heat as it curved deeper into her, creating wells of pleasure even beyond its length.

'I daren't do too much,' grunted Pearce. 'It would be over too soon and I want us to enjoy this as long as we can.' He sat up and took her stiffly proud nipples into his mouth one after the other, rolling his tongue across them, sucking and chewing. He held her buttocks tight and guided her movements in his lap.

She had never before felt so much a part of another person. She was sharing everything with Pearce. They were moving as one. She could feel how his orgasm was mounting in tune with hers, a sweet crescendo. Then, as a small voice within her plaintively thought, 'Must it be so soon?' warmth and release flooded her body just as Pearce began spasmodically jerking and thrusting even harder into her, before he reached his own wordless, breathless conclusion.

She felt him come as if she touched his mind and shared his melting, spurting rush of release through her own nerve endings. She felt every sinew in his body squeeze then relax even as he sighed onto her shoulder and his mouth hungrily sought hers.

With him still hard inside her they kissed deeply and firmly, like the young people they were, the young people they had never before been as a couple. Slowly their breathing became more controlled. They regained their senses and became more aware of leaking, cooling fluids rolling down their skin onto the bed.

With a final touch of lips to lips, Ruth eased herself out of Pearce's lap and up off his penis. Clasping her hand to her wet crotch she scampered into the bathroom and turned on the shower, climbing in under the rigorous spray. Holding his still hard cock, Pearce joined her and they started to soap each other. This time he took her from behind while she braced herself against the tiled shower wall. It took longer but their mutual orgasm was even deeper and more satisfying as a result, surprising both of them with its juddering, out of control climax. They slipped and ended up on the floor of the shower, soaked with water, semen and foam, laughing and quivering.

They stood and rinsed off, cupping water from each other's bodies while enjoying the smooth litheness of each other, the hard, springy yielding of young flesh.

Then the mood in the shower changed. Something darkened in Pearce's face and an unlooked for, unwanted sense of doubt crept into Ruth's heart.

What Ruth couldn't know was that along with Milla's body she had also taken on her Shutterbox talent. For the period of the holiday she would be closer to her husband's mind than she had ever been in over 30 years of marriage. She was quite literally feeling what he was feeling, sharing his senses and moods.

Their lovemaking was so shattering because she was sensing and echoing Pearce's mounting sexual urgency in a fashion beyond the merely physical, in a fashion deeper and more affecting than anything she had ever previously known. And because she had been able to reflect Pearce's needs and meet them so exactly, their mutual enjoyment was heightened and more overwhelming at its conclusion.

Pearce turned off the shower and stood, somehow less buoyant, with water dripping from him like raindrops, like baffled tears. 'Ruth,' he said, 'would you leave me for a younger man?' He sounded confused, even hurt, and his proud cock had shrunk to a thumb-sized nubbin.

'No,' she answered firmly. 'I was just wishing I'd known you when you were younger. You've always been my mature, thoughtful man ever since I first met you. This is my first chance to see you like this, so young and passionate.'

She reached out and touched his cheek. 'But what about you with a younger woman?' she asked. 'Would you want to swap me for her?' She brought his face down until his eyes looked directly into hers. His was a face so strange, so unknown and yet so quickly intimate because she saw Pearce in there. He looked at her for a long moment without speaking.

'No, never, Hun,' he answered. 'I'm only and always for you. And that means I am for this girl too while you're at her rudder guiding her.

'They should have prepared us for this, you know, the bastards. This fear and doubt. But never mind, this is our time and these are our joys we're sharing, not theirs. We'll still have them as memories when we climb back into our crusty old shells.'

He cupped her chin and smiled at her. 'It's more than likely we will never know these kids outside of these rooms,' he said ruefully. 'But we can make the most of them while we're here.'

Once again he stepped to her and kissed her, pressed against her, held her close. Once again she felt hot stiffness grow against her skin.

'When do we stop to eat?' she wondered.

●●●

Chapter seven: See me with strange eyes

MILLA was disconcerted by Franklyn's attitude to her client's body, even while she was feeling genuine pity for the pain he was going through. Perhaps she was getting more inured to the aches and pains she was experiencing, or maybe the painkillers were finally kicking in, but she was already finding it easier to breathe and move around.

The muscles she was using were longer than her own – more tempered, somehow firmer. These legs were longer, as were the fingers tapering from the slender hands and elegant wrists. Yet she found herself growing accustomed to the Paris woman's marginally greater height and longer leverage.

It was going to take more time to become accustomed to The Breasts (she felt they deserved capitalisation). She even wondered if, as they were such an intrusive part of her anatomy, the Paris woman had pet names for them.

She was sure the old man would have a pet name for his ludicrous penis. What a couple they make, she reasoned, the beautiful but over-enhanced Paris woman living with an old man hung like the world's luckiest donkey. *What sort of a life do you have?* she wondered.

Of course the clients were rich. They'd paid to swap bodies for a month, and just part of that payment would help her and Franklyn afford luxuries that had never been within their reach before. There's big money changing hands here, she realised. Milla wondered what the Paris woman was doing just now, within her rented skin: how she felt about the girl she'd borrowed, what she was seeing through her eyes...

And what was going on with Franklyn?

She left the old man in bed, groaning, and went to rouse some breakfast. She found some cold roasted meats and cheese in the well stocked fridge, sorted herself a mug of coffee and took a tray laden with her selection to a table near the balcony in the living room. *A richness of windows*, she thought. *We are spoilt.* She would miss this when she got home.

She chewed and sipped with some initial appetite, but soon found her hunger was quickly assuaged. This surprised her. She had always been a person of real appetites, even feeling faint and sick if she couldn't get to food immediately she felt pangs in her belly. Maybe this woman is part solar-powered, she reasoned, or maybe you just need less food when you get older?

While she finished her coffee she scrolled through the early paragraphs of the advice leaflet – provided on the apartment's information tablet – noting where she could go and what she could do in her client's body. Within reason she was a free agent and the door locks were keyed to her client's ID implant. She would take a walk.

She cleared away the breakfast things and looked in on Franklyn, who appeared to be fast asleep. She once again walked out on the balcony and took a deep breath of air before going into the bathroom to make her toilet.

After showering, brushing her teeth and flossing, she dried her hair to a tousled blonde mound and used a deodorant. She was pleased to find a new bottle of her favourite scent on a shelf in the cabinet but was not sure if she liked the way it smelled when she sprayed it on her neck, wrists and inside her elbows. She was tempted to wash it off but instead decided to leave it, to see how it was once it calmed down.

She chose a simple sheath of a dress. It was cut in a way she would never have considered while in her own skin. It would have made her feel like she was playing at dressing-up but it was obviously hand-made for Paris woman. She looked good in it.

She had some credit loaded on her implant by the Body Holiday Foundation as part of the swap deal. So she decided to go shopping. She left the apartment and the silently sleeping old man (*Franklyn*, she reminded herself, *it's Franklyn in there no matter how weird he's acting*) and took her bearings in the corridor.

It was only the second time she'd had to find her way from the outer ring of a sky tower; the last had been when they left Blake's office. However, she was surprised at how quickly she was able to find her way to the nearest mall. Although this mall was nowhere she had ever been before, she soon got her bearings.

Sky tower malls were a homogeneous collection of places, despite their size, and all were based on the same model – much as has been said about all shopping malls over the centuries. If you know one you know them all, from the names of the coffee houses to the names of the shoe shops and the electrical goods retailers.

Milla found a branch of her favoured patisserie and sat in the corner to plan her day. She gave her order and was soon sipping a rich Americano and nibbling a sharply flavourful lemon tart. She enjoyed shopping and started eagerly making a list of where she would go and what she would buy. Then she became distracted, her mind drifting off the subject. What was it – what was the problem?

She keenly felt that something was wrong with the way people were looking at her, and so many of them were. She began feeling nervous, teetering on the brink of real fear until she realised what the problem was.

For the first time in many years she was out in a public place, without her talent, and she wasn't feeling anything from anyone around her. Thanks to the body swap, her

Shutterbox talent had deserted her. She couldn't even 'read' the furtive male (and female) glances continuously flickering over her, or even interpret the blatant stares of those greedily drinking of her beauty.

What were these people thinking? She didn't know. What were they going to do? She didn't know. *They see me with strange eyes*, she thought, and something at her very core gave way.

The Paris woman must have attracted this kind of attention all the time and probably developed a thickened skin about it. But for Milla, it felt like an intrusion and she tried to switch on her ability to fade from sight. That was gone with the rest of her talent. One man seemed on the point of coming over to speak with her, so she pushed her cup and plate away and made a hasty exit.

She hoped that a touch of retail therapy would settle her nerves. But once again, she couldn't be sure.

The man she thought was going to talk with her followed her from the café. She hastened her step until he'd disappeared from view. Then she slowed and caught her breath while admiring some shoes in a window display. *Maybe when all this is over I will be able to afford a pair of those*, she thought.

In the glass of the shop window, she saw the face at her shoulder smiling at her reflection. The man from the patisserie. 'Hello, Ruth...' he began.

This time she ran for it.

●●●

Chapter eight: The Sea, the Sea

RUTH finally admitted that she was beginning to feel sore, telling Pearce she didn't want to give her body back with painful friction burns. And anyway she was hungry, starving in fact, actually feeling sick with hunger.

The pair breakfasted like hungry wolves, ordering chorizo sausage and bacon and eggs with ciabatta toast followed by cereal, juice and coffee.

Sated, they sat for a few minutes just gazing raptly out of the French windows towards the sea. And for the first time Pearce seemed absorbed by something other than lust and his erectile ability.

'What's that noise?' he asked, leaping to his feet.

Ruth stood up as he hurried into the bathroom they'd recently vacated and from which she heard an irregular tapping sound. She felt a thrill of fear but also confidence that her man could cope with whatever he found. Pearce had trained in a number of martial arts but finally settled firmly on the Brazilian style known as capoeira – an almost balletic, fluid defensive art that was also quite lethal. He was also, he admitted in a conversation on the subject, happy to hit an assailant with a brick if there was one handy.

It was his training that helped keep him trim and flexible in his own body. What he would do to an adversary in this young one was something she hoped never to find out.

He came back from the bathroom, with the nearest thing to a goofy grin she supposed he could manage. 'Cleaner droid,' he said, 'tidying up after our exercises this morning. We made a bit of a mess in there I suppose.' He shrugged. 'Fancy a look around?'

They both donned shorts and flip-flops. Ruth sported a cropped top that left her midriff bare and Pearce put on a light, short-sleeved shirt he left unbuttoned. The sun pouring through the windows already promised a hot day and they were grateful for the cool breeze coming in off the sea when they walked out onto the sand. They reasoned they were in some isolated part of an island. The Body Holiday Foundation had promised a 'Dream Holiday, Paradise on Earth' without being specific. There was no activity out on the brilliantly turquoise waves and only the rustling of trees broached the silence. The horizon, far across the water, met the sky at a kind of blurred edge as the sun continued its slow journey – travelling from east to west, from a point just behind them. Their shadows were quite short. *It must be around 11 o'clock*, reasoned Pearce.

'If it gets too hot we should swim,' he said. 'We're on our own here so we don't need costumes or any of that nonsense. Imagine playing 360 Globe swimming here, in this place, under this light?'

One of the craziest sports Earth had never seen had to wait until resorts were put in space beyond the restricting gravity of the home planet. There, in carefully constructed spherical arenas, a body of water would be released into zero gravity. Eventually this water settled into a rippling globular mass at the centre of the arena and athletes could swim through it with the aid of specially designed breathing equipment. The aim: to pass through as many as possible of a network of hoops, at the centre of the mass of water, and do it faster than one's competitors.

It was the nearest a human could come to the sensation of flying without wings and it was something both Ruth and Pearce had done during their supra-planetary holidays. Both had enjoyed it thoroughly.

The beach stretched for a few miles one way. Then, when they returned and passed their discreet beach chalet set back in the palms, they found it also stretched just as far the other way. It was fenced off at either end by clear panels that seemed just as useful for keeping the couple in as they would be for keeping intruders out. But, at least, they didn't interfere with the view.

Behind the chalet they found a narrow path leading to a gate in a stout fence, which opened easily to Pearce's palm pressure. Beyond the gate was a finger-post sign, pointing down a palm-tree lined sandy path to their left, with the legend 'Town 3 kilometres'.

They closed the gate behind them and headed back to the chalet. A brief search turned up snorkels and masks, flippers, a chill bag, wine and some beach towels. Fully loaded, they walked back out onto their sandy beach.

On the towels they stripped out of their clothes, adjusted their masks to fit and threaded the snorkels through the straps. A quick blow through the mouthpieces made sure they were clear. Carrying their flippers they entered the warm water, sat side by side on the sand, and then felt the gentle waves well over them like the Earth's blessing.

'The sea, the sea, was a mother to me,' said Pearce, 'but now as a gift, I give her to thee.'

'I like that,' smiled Ruth. 'Where's it from?'

'Here, now,' he answered. 'I just made it up.'

She kissed him, tasting salt on his lips.

They rinsed their masks in salt water, spitting onto the clear acrylic, smearing the sputum all around then washing it out. They donned the masks and fitted the flippers, tested the snorkels again and then began a leisurely kick out into deeper water.

They swam until the sea below them was deep and purplish, the water a touch cooler than it had been closer to the shore. Cool currents found discreet pleasure points on Ruth's body and she revelled in her nakedness and the sheer joy of life.

Pearce took her hand and turned her to float upright, facing him in the water. Looking down she saw his cock engorged and pale in the water, pointing at her with obvious intent.

She took him into her there in the sea while fish swam below them, her legs looking for purchase, ratcheting up and down while his taut belly pumped up and up and up against her. Through their masks they watched themselves making love against the alien background of the rippling sea bed, upright in the sea with faces down in the water and arms out for buoyancy. Ruth felt as though she was dreaming; everything was so removed from everyday life. But there was one familiar fact to cling to, which was that she loved this man of hers with a hard passion.

Her climax surprised her with its uncontrollable convulsion. Her legs jerked down and threw her away from him, plucking him out from between her legs. Even while she watched he shot his seed into the crystal water as a jet of stringy white fluid, sinking down towards the purple belly of the sea.

Before it had gone more than a few metres, drifting and falling as a coherent thread, a fish swam up to it and snapped it down like a gourmet morsel before looking around, hungry for more.

Ruth learned two lessons that day: never say you've had enough of love in any of its aspects no matter how sore you feel. And never shout with laughter when you're wearing a snorkel.

●●●

Chapter nine: Not the Old Man

MILLA got back to the apartment in a state of almost complete nervous collapse. What on Earth had she been thinking? What could she even go shopping for? This body wasn't hers, so she couldn't buy underwear or shoes. She couldn't even buy her client a gift. The dresses the Paris woman already had hanging in her wardrobe were way beyond Milla's current budget.

Even the handbags and clothes she looked at, those she would have jumped at in her own skin, seemed cheap and shabby when she saw them in the mirror, held by this classic blonde with her hand-made dresses and expensive heels.

And everywhere she felt the eyes on her, the looks from passers-by, and the flagrant examination by strangers. What's more, she thought, all too often there was some sense of recognition evinced by a double-take and a slow smile. The Paris woman was evidently some kind of magnet for the steady gaze of all those about her, but was she also some sort of celebrity?

Milla had grown up learning how to disregard desirous looks from those who wanted to simply admire her fresh-faced charm, as anyone good-looking enough to garner such attention has learned to do. But this woman was attracting attention in a fashion leagues beyond anything Milla was used to.

She poured herself a cold chardonnay in a large glass, took a sip then shucked off her shoes and the dress. She'd worked herself into a flop sweat since leaving the patisserie and she felt dirty and unpleasant. She wondered if Paris woman ever felt this rotten then upbraided herself for being foolish. She was in danger of thinking of her client as some sort of superhuman being and that would be silly. She was just a woman after all. Like all of us she had sweat glands, bowels and a bladder.

Milla put the dress and underwear in the laundry unit, left the shoes where they fell, put the mostly full glass of wine on the kitchen table then walked into the bathroom where she gave herself a refreshing cool shower. She turned the heat up to wash her hair, then down again for her body.

Most of her physical awkwardness had gone now and the pain, twisting her body in knots that morning, had settled down to little more than a constant background ache. She mulled over her time in public that day and gained great admiration for her client, appreciating what it meant to look the way she did, to be constantly the centre of attention. *After all*, she thought with the return of her smile, *I have just walked at least a mile in her shoes.*

Milla realised how Paris woman became inured to other people's constant rapt attention. In the same way she had become used to the pain, it was simply a matter of time. Paris woman could comfortably walk under the attentive gaze of those around her because she had always experienced it. She would probably miss it if it stopped, as Milla now missed her talent.

Milla wrapped herself in a short robe and wound a towel around the long blonde hair, then walked back into the kitchen for her wine. Franklyn was sitting at the table, also in a short robe, and he had all but finished her drink.

'You look nice,' he said, raising the glass to her. He looked less strained; his sleep had obviously done something to lessen his discomfort.

'You're looking a touch more human,' she responded. 'How're you feeling?'

By way of an answer he stretched, spreading his arms and straightening his legs away from the table. The short robe did little to preserve his modesty and she was surprised to feel a profound touch of revulsion at the sight of him.

It's Franklyn, she reminded herself, *not the old man. It's the man I share my home with, not some old stranger.* However, no matter how hard she worked to see beyond this aged physical shell to the handsome young man inhabiting it, she was instead held in a trance by the slight wattle quivering at his neck and the liver spots on the back of his hands.

What she saw of the rest of this body was also way past its use-by date and the length of penis slung between the pale thighs looked like something major had prolapsed.

With something of a shock she realised Franklyn had been speaking for several minutes and she hadn't a clue what he was saying. '...I reckon we'll have earned that money by the time we get to the end of the month,' she heard when she managed to tune back in.

'I've spent most of today either asleep or in the bath.' He coughed a small laugh. 'If this old guy wasn't wrinkly before, he sure is now!'

Franklyn stood up and to Milla's horror opened his robe. Thankfully, instead of reaching for his groin as she'd feared he would, he took the two small mounds of man breast on his chest into his palms and jiggled them. 'Look at these,' he said, then somewhat unfairly: 'I've had girlfriends with boobs smaller than these.'

He went to the fridge and drew out the bottle of wine then found another glass in a nearby wall cabinet. He poured a full glass for Milla and topped up his own. Once more he raised his glass, waiting until she touched hers to his. He sipped the wine appreciatively. 'It's going to be a big ask, Milla, but we've got to make the best we can of this. And the only people we can depend on are each other.

'The place is grand, the facilities top class and the food matches the best I've ever eaten and then some. We just need to treat it like a top-class hotel and take advantage of what we have. What do you say?'

She nodded. Part of her mind was in complete agreement and the rest, in fact a good percentage of it, just wished he'd shut the fuck up and retie his robe.

Then the nightmare came true. Franklyn reached down to the length of flaccid meat between his legs and drew it out and up towards her, shaking the tip. He was talking again. 'Like most ladies I'm sure you would like to sample the delights of a ride on this sturdy old crossbar.'

No, she thought. *No, I really truly don't.*

He continued, 'But the fact is I need a bit more time to get used to this body before I can even think of doing anything more physical than take a piss with it.' He shook the cock again and snorted his little laugh. 'And with this thing here, I have to be careful where I aim because it's liable to go anywhere.'

To Milla's relief he finally tied his robe. But then, with the same hand he'd used to waggle his cock, he picked up his glass and took a good mouthful. 'Fancy something to eat?' he asked.

'I'll get it,' she said. 'You'll want to freshen up first.' *Or at least wash your fucking hands.*

She checked out the menu from the kitchen, made her order then looked through the wine list. There was enough in store to keep them both floating in booze for a year. *Good,* she thought. *I'm going to need something to stop me from running out of here screaming and going into hiding for the next month.*

She heard Franklyn come back into the kitchen and walk up behind her. His arms came round her waist and pulled her back against his bony chest. She felt a stirring length press

98

against her thigh. 'Perhaps we won't have to wait too long,' Franklyn breathed.

'Let's eat,' she replied, pulling away.

•••

Chapter ten: A touch too much sun

PEARCE had calmed down. He poured wine from the cooler and slathered sun lotion over her body, allowing her to do the same for him. They talked about some things that were important to them and others that were frivolous. They laughed a lot, drank the wine and ate their picnic.

By the middle of the afternoon they were asleep.

The cooling breeze playing over her reddened skin was what woke Ruth first. She quickly roused Pearce. They had been lying naked for some hours under a tropical sun, and she feared sun stroke.

The damage didn't seem too bad but they both re-entered the sea and took balm from the salt water. He licked the salt from her nipples, watching them harden and crinkle at his touch.

'She is just as responsive as you,' he observed.

Ruth put her hand down and held his aroused cock. 'Him too,' she answered. She led Pearce back to his towel and bade him lie down. She straddling his legs, then bending over until she brought his cock to her mouth, she began to work on it with hand and tongue.

Crouching low to her work, her mouth bobbed in a regular rhythm. Her breasts lightly grazed his tender flesh and her bottom was high and pert above her head. She had never done this for him before. He never asked for it but moved quickly from surprise to mounting appreciation.

The combination of what she was doing and the way she looked while doing it, glowing and lithe in the last golden light of the sun, stripped him of any reserve. He gave himself up fully to her ministrations.

His climax left him breathless and quivering after the unexpected strength of his release. Though he bucked and jerked against her, Ruth held him in her mouth until the last pulse drained him and left him prone on the sand.

He winced when she licked the last dribble of exudate from his wilting head, too tender and sensitive now for her touch. She kissed him and he tasted the chlorine saltiness of semen on her tongue.

Her eyes seemed to glow in her darkened face. Mischief ruled there.

'Why?' he asked. 'Why here and now? Is it this boy's body that excites you?'

Ruth chuckled. 'Silly. No, of course not.' She paused and shrugged. 'I just wondered what a fish knew that I didn't.' She smiled ruefully, her dimples very much in evidence. 'Frankly I think it's a fish thing.' Their laughter rang out across the sea and echoed in the palm tops. It was only silenced by a lingering kiss.

Finally, they collected together their stuff and carefully made their way back to the chalet. Behind them the sky slowly changed to resemble a navy velvet coverlet studded with insane stars, and the air musical with waves lyrically stroking the shore. It was all wasted; they saw nothing but each other.

Their shower was almost chaste, as they bathed under subdued lights. Freshened and clean they selected more wine and found bowls for olives and scraps of meat, a kind of impromptu tapas. Surprised by their hunger, they fed each other titbits while taking it in turns to revisit the fridge and replenish their supplies.

They even found how to call up hot treats of skewered meat with dips of savoury sesame and chilli. Pearce reminded Ruth of her reaction towards man-flavoured MeatBeast at the Paris festival and she laughed again.

When insects found their lamps they closed the chalet doors and the air conditioning automatically kicked in. It chilled them somewhat. Ruth felt fine hairs rise along her arms and her nipples stood out against the fabric of her robe.

Once they'd taken the dishes into the kitchen and loaded the washer, they took the last of their wine into the bedroom, where they lay in each other's arms murmuring drowsy thoughts to each other.

Neither was fully aware of the exact moment their day eventually succumbed to dream. Ruth was awake when Pearce pulled his arm out from under her shoulders because it had gone to sleep, but only just.

Amongst the last of her coherent thoughts, at the conclusion of that first day, was the realisation that she loved Pearce like an ache to her soul. Tears of happiness spilled onto her pillow.

She also wondered if it was proper for somebody to be so happy. *Today I have lived a poem to life*, she thought. *It has been perfect and at some point there will be a price.*

She was right. Too soon, indeed all too soon, the dream would become a nightmare far worse than anything she could imagine.

•••

Interlude

THE boss had been in and out of the editing suite for most of the day. He chatted with Blake and admitted he was pleased with some of the early material they already had on file. The clients in the young bodies had provided enough footage for a mini-series all of their own, although he insisted the prime shot would be Ruth Hudson getting royally fucked. The footage would be classic and completely unique. The fact that it was someone else in the skin would have no effect on its value.

Horny Hudson rising to the occasion on camera was something that could be auctioned to their exclusive clientele and would pay for an awful lot of luxury goods. The maths were simple: the harder the action and the deeper the penetration, the bigger the market.

'Ruth Hudson was a phenomenon in her day,' he said. 'She was so popular that she managed to avoid most of the nasty things big bad producers like me wanted her to do, asked her to do, even ordered her to do. She was that rare thing, a true star. The camera loved her and just as important, the cameramen loved her.

'She was lit better, posed better and looked better than any other woman in the business. And she learned her craft, my God she was good. She could put a stiffy in a red-blooded man's pants with little more than a smile and a twitch of that superb ass of hers. Yet, even though her vids never went all the way, her fans still felt privileged. Here she was all naked just for them.'

The boss leaned closer to the monitor and studied the sleeping face before him. There was the trace of a frown, her lips parted slightly. He raised his hand as if he would touch her cheek.

'She was the girl-child, the woman and the Goddess all rolled into one – vulnerable, aloof and available. Every man fell in love with her a little, every man wanted to fuck her until she was delirious with it, and every man also wanted to protect and keep her safe from harm.'

He turned and, even in the darkened room, Blake could see the wolf smile spread across his face. 'Then one day she was gone without a goodbye. She became the exclusive toy of Mister Sam, fucking rich bollocks Pearce. Well not anymore, because there she is and we've got every sweet inch in focus. And you know what?'

'What?'

'She's going to do more for us than she has ever done before. They all are. This is the big time, Blake. We're going to see it all in glorious 3D right here for our exclusive viewing pleasure. Then we polish it and cut it to perfection, before beaming it out to our sweet paying customers. They are going to lap it up like cats with a big bowl of cream.'

Blake grinned with pleasure. 'What's a cat?'

●●●

Part three: Cooling to Room Temperature

Chapter one: Avoid Confrontation

FRANKLYN eventually drank himself into a troubled sleep. Milla lay awake, listening to his light snores, very aware of the way he was fumbling and tugging at his increasingly engorged cock.

In the darkened room she could just make out the way the old man's features sank back against the bones of his skull: eyes sunk back into their sockets, cheekbones prominent and sharp. He had a good shock of platinum white hair and, despite everything Franklyn said about his body, the old man was in good shape for his age.

His belly was flat and the small mounds Franklyn had grabbed at earlier were in fact fairly well-defined pectorals. Perhaps at a later date in her life Milla could be attracted to a man like this.

She wondered how her appreciation of this man would be altered, if his body was still inhabited by its original owner. Franklyn's complaints about pain made the man pitiful. His patently greedy appreciation of her client's looks reminded her of the sly appraisal she'd experienced from her grandfather.

Perhaps that was part of the problem, she thought. Was she seeing her granddad here, gazing at her nakedness and now sharing her bed?

With a shiver of distaste running through her body, she slid from the bed and crept away from the snoring man. Behind her she heard him mumbling and smacking his lips, before he turned over onto his side and was silent.

She pulled the robe tighter around her and went to sit on the balcony. The heat of the day had leeched away into the night and she felt goose bumps erupt all over her body at the freshness of the air.

She breathed coolness into her lungs like a draught of fine wine, experiencing the thrill of it, enjoying the way this body seized every pleasure available to it. The wall of the balcony was high enough for security and safety but above knee-height it was completely transparent. She could gaze out across hundreds of kilometres of light-sprinkled landscape and even see the vertical glowing strip of another sky tower, curiously angled towards the sky thanks to the Earth's curvature. Perhaps that was Paris, Berlin or even Madrid.

The beauty of the scene numbed her to the cold. She had no idea how high she was or how far she was seeing but she just knew she would sit here for a while drinking in the subtle play of colours.

There was a constant movement playing across land and sky, like glowing arteries in a body of light. Mankind on the move, she thought, the unceasing traffic of civilisation. The bloodstream of humanity. Franklyn could make a film about this, she thought, though how he would move from this numinous scene to rain on a hillside escaped her.

She smiled, thinking of her man and his high-brow film career with its niche audience. For the first time since she woke that morning she began to feel some sympathy for the young man trapped in a body completely armoured in time-inflicted agony.

She wrapped her arms around herself and popped back into the apartment, moving to the kitchen without turning on the lights. She ordered a mug of Americano with milk and took it back to the balcony.

She warmed her hands round the warm ceramic and sipped at the flavoursome brew, tucking her feet up under her bottom.

She was on the point of tears. She felt too young for this Body Holiday arrangement and she didn't know how she felt about sharing her bed with Franklyn in an old man's hide.

With a shock she suddenly realised there was no way she could work out whether the sky tower on the horizon was Berlin or Madrid, because she didn't know where she was. She might *be* in Paris or Madrid and that distant strip of light could be London. She could be gazing at her own home, its majestic column reduced to little more than a firework sparkling in the night sky.

The tightness that had increasingly bound her chest all day broke and Milla wept into her coffee, tasting salt tears mingle with the rich roast espresso and water blended with milk. The scene before her blurred and the moving lines of light pulsed with her sobs.

The tears finally washed away the self-pity that had been toxically building up in her and stiffened her resolve. She finished her coffee dry-eyed, blew her nose on a tissue she kept in her sleeve and sat curled up in her chair looking out at the alien land of night time city and sky. She watched until the pale hint of dawn touched the curved horizon.

Never in her life had she seen anything so beautiful. The world resolved itself gently to her retina, clarifying details that changed from light-drenched abstract sculpture to architectural landscape pinkly glowing in the golden dawn.

The first warmth of the sun stroked her face like a hesitant lover and brought with it new understanding. She knew now that she was going to treat this Body Holiday for what it was: a step away from reality.

It wasn't her sitting here now but some strange woman she'd never met. She'd borrowed these hands and looked through these eyes but what she was experiencing was no more real than full immersion in a 3D computer game.

If Franklyn wanted to experience sex with Paris woman, it was no more than a husband's body choosing to make love with his wife's. Nothing out of the ordinary.

Milla preferred to avoid confrontation whenever she could and her new resolution brought calm to her mind. At some point soon sex was going to happen, so she might as well embrace it.

When Franklyn woke, some hours later, he walked out onto the balcony and stood for a while looking down onto the blonde woman's sleeping form. She was smiling. The expressions crowding across his face were complex: yearning and desirous yet protective with a touch of something else, something cold.

He gazed down at her like a tourist examining a relic, because it's on his itinerary and he's paid for the privilege to view it. Or perhaps like a collector, he was seeing something he'd always wanted in someone else's display cabinet and was reaching out with a criminal hand.

●●●

Chapter two: We Are Here For You

PEARCE made breakfast: ciabatta toast with chopped tomatoes and roast peppers, grilled chorizo sausage, rashers of unsmoked bacon and poached eggs. They washed it down with mugs of tea. They couldn't help but smile at each other all the way through the meal. Sunlight danced through the open windows and birds were making noise like musical chalk on a blackboard. Crickets sawed away creating a high-pitched drilling note, which soon faded unnoticed into the background.

They ate with appetite and appreciation, mopping the paprika-orange juices and egg yolk clean from their plates. They ate silently, catching each other's eyes with knowing glances, sometimes grinning around their food. They were like children with a mutual secret only they could share. Both were a little stiff after the previous day's exertions and their first tsunami of passion had quieted instead to lustful warmth. They were thrilled with joy.

They showered together and there was a lot of playful touching and kissing but no penetration. Ruth brushed her teeth and teased her hair into a look she liked. Pearce shaved scrupulously, stroking his chin afterwards to ensure he'd missed no bristles, then laid it next to his wife's smooth cheek. They kissed long and thoroughly.

It was going to be another warm day but, as they wanted to extend their adventure by going into town, they dressed a little more conservatively than they had the previous day. Still in shorts and thin shirts, Ruth also donned a bikini top and Pearce buttoned his shirt most of the way up. Ruth found a broad-brimmed straw hat that prettily shaded her sun-blushed face. After sleeping on the beach they both required liberal coats of after-sun and their complexions were more

111

pink than brown. The burn was most noticeable on Ruth's pubic triangle, which, shaved and exposed to the sun for the first time, had suffered and was uncomfortable.

Pearce tended to the area with after-sun and moisturiser, patently becoming aroused while he did so. Ruth begged off, asking for forbearance until things were a little less sore. Because of the burn she found baggy shorts more comfortable without underwear, something Pearce took advantage of with frequent touches of his cupped palm to her firm buttocks. That made her wriggle until she winced when the fabric of her shorts rubbed too firmly against her. After that, he left her pretty much alone.

In walking sandals, fitting perfectly, they strolled from their chalet towards town, gazing around them in companionable silence. They held hands until the heat made their palms sweat and they reluctantly let go.

It was approaching 11am when they saw a collection of buildings shimmering in heat haze at the end of the path. The buildings were blindingly white against the turquoise sea, modelled forms with blue-grey shadows. They were capped with orange-red tiled roofs and their doors and windows stood open revealing nothing of their blue-black, sun dark interiors. Some of the buildings had tables and chairs in front of them, baking in the sun, and awnings pressed shut above doors and windows.

Palm trees stood around them offering little in the way of shade. Fine, clean, smooth white sand reflected sprays of silvered sunlight into the shadows. 'If I was a painter I could make a fortune here,' said Pearce in a voice hushed by admiration.

It was not so much a town as a collection of dwellings, shops and cafés. On the beach narrow, sleek, brightly coloured boats with high prows painted with Egyptian eyes sported a single diagonal spar from their single masts. They had pontoons rigged to one side for stability in the water, a design dating back thousands of years to the very first oceangoing dugout canoes.

But these craft boasted more than primitive wind power. Outboard engines leaned down into the stern of the boats, from their hinged mountings at the centre of the transoms, with propellers angled high away from clogging sand. Small silver engine housings gave evidence that the props were powered by the very latest fusion technology – ancient and modern in a single snapshot.

'I've seen boats like these before,' murmured Pearce. 'In a painting by van Gogh. It's always been one of my favourites and now here I am in the middle of it.'

There were buildings and boats but little sign of any people. A single wire-haired terrier drowsed in the shadow of a palm tree and regarded them with a single weary eye as they passed. Its head came up and it looked round to its right.

The big door at the end of the largest building in the complex opened and a motley of town inhabitants streamed out, chattering, laughing and mopping their faces with bright handkerchiefs. There was no single type here but skins of every colour, a real mixture of races.

All were quite young apart from a few older, wiser looking characters who spoke with smiling authority. Last out of the door was a big, beaming woman in clerical robes who was shaking hands with her parishioners.

Her smile was huge and matched easily by her loud musical voice, which seemed to teeter ever on the point of laughter. She saw the couple standing on the path and strode through her flock towards them, whilst opening her arms in welcome.

'Mr and Mrs Pearce,' she sang, 'aren't you a beautiful sight on this delightful day. Welcome to the island. Sorry we weren't out to greet you when you arrived. We didn't expect

113

you so soon. Most people take a while to get their bearings before they venture out around here. You folk must be that bit more adventurous.

'We've just had our weekly debriefing with the Bossman,' she pointed upwards and rolled her eyes to the sky. 'It refreshes the soul and leads us by calm waters, so to speak.'

She shook their hands and spoke in a continuous stream, halting any questions Pearce and Ruth might have had. 'This is the Town and we're here when you need us. The food is fresh. I can recommend the fish, and the booze is top class. We have a nice chilled Sauvignon that's so good the grapes squeezed themselves, just to get in the vat. Or a Médoc from Pauillac that makes the nose want to die from happiness.'

She paused for breath so Pearce got his question in quickly before the woman could start again. 'Thank you indeed,' he said, 'but could you tell us where we are?'

If anything the smile got wider and Ruth almost found herself laughing out loud from the joy in it. 'Surely, Mr Pearce. This is the Town on the Island and we are here for you during your holiday. Whatever you need, any service or information' – at this she extended her arms as if to embrace all the townspeople who crowded round to see the two Body Holidaymakers, 'we are here for you.'

The day started so well for the couple, happily shaking hands with smiling people and hearing names they forgot almost as soon as they were spoken.

There was no way they could see the cloud coming to darken their horizon, nor realise the ruin it would bring.

● ● ●

Chapter three: Let me help

MILLA joined Franklyn in the kitchen, drawn by the aromas of toast and coffee. She was less sleepy than she thought she should be after her night-long vigil and eventual doze curled up on her chair, though her mind was clear and her body free from aches and stiffness.

She felt refreshed and talked with Franklyn about her night on the balcony. She didn't share her doubts about the Body Holiday arrangements or mention her tears. Instead she told him about the Earth's body of light and its bloodstream of vehicles, on land and in the air.

He nodded attentively while they breakfasted on granary toast, cheese and small slices of smoked sausage. Large bowls of cappuccino without cinnamon, something agreed on from the very first breakfast they shared together, completed the repast.

They took their frothy coffees into the living room and continued their conversation while developing foam moustaches, pointing these out to each other, wiping them away and laughing easily.

Franklyn told Milla he'd been reading the apartment's information folder and found they had exclusive use of an outdoor swimming pool they could access from the corridor just outside their door.

'I thought it might help ease these old joints,' he explained. 'And it's all completely private, so we needn't bother with costumes.'

Milla didn't hesitate in agreeing to the idea. Though she enjoyed swimming, it was an expensive pastime often pursued in crowded public pools that cramped her style and pleasure in equal measure.

Having performed their toilet and showered cleanly, they wrapped themselves in terry towelling robes before palming the outer door open. They turned left and walked barefoot to a pearlescent panel set at the end of the corridor.

Franklyn reached out and the panel swept sideways, onto a large white balcony which was fenced, as were those leading from the apartment, with high transparent walls. It was open to the sky, reflected blue in the clear waters of its full-sized kidney-shaped pool.

Two wooden and canvas sun loungers were placed either side of a round wooden table, from which sprouted a large closed parasol. There was a white chill cabinet set against the wall. A brief examination of its interior turned up a selection of ready-mixed alcoholic drinks, prepared for consumption by just peeling a protective seal from the salted rims of the glass.

They chose two drinks at random and carried them to the table. At this time of the morning there was no need for shade. They left the parasol down, peeled their drinks and toasted each other.

Milla's drink featured gin, lemon, lime and bitters. It was sharp and delicious. She let Franklyn try hers while she sipped his. It was salty and fresh with a real alcoholic kick. They passed glasses back and she agreed they should take it easy on the hooch before swimming.

'After all,' said Franklyn, 'we don't want to drown the old buggers while we're in them, do we?'

He shrugged out of his robe and dived cleanly into the water. His figure made a lean shape against the bottom of the pool. Between his legs she could see the cock performing a frenetic wagging motion as if it was urging her to join in the fun.

None of this is real, she reminded herself. *There's no way I'm standing by a full sized pool, on a sun-lit balcony, set halfway up a sky tower.* She disrobed, bending to place her robe carefully on her sun lounger.

The sun no longer stroked her with the hesitant touch it used at dawn. Proud against a flawless blue canopy its rays flooded down, sculpted her with bright clarity, and embraced her like a golden figurine. Worshipped her.

Franklyn was treading water. He was looking at her with steady eyes, nodding. She dived and the water streamed around her in a champagne flow of bubbles. She opened her legs and, on kicking out, felt the power in these long limbs as well as more drag across her breasts than she was used to. Nevertheless she flowed into a powerful freestyle and stroked quickly across the pool.

When she reached the far side she curled into a ball, poising the perfect orbs of her bottom briefly in the air, then turned and pushed away with her long legs. She swam some laps like that, knocking out some kinks she hadn't felt until now, then dived down to the bottom of the pool.

The cool water possessed her. She loved to swim and felt at home in the water. She wanted to breathe it like a fish, feel it flood into every part of her until she was cleansed inside and out. She floated for a moment, with her hair streaming around her head like a fine cloud and her arms out in a cruciform pose working the water.

The buoyancy of the water lifted and held her breasts, its cool touch hardening her nipples to jutting points. She made a striking figure. Franklyn was before her and his cock was jutting out at right-angles to his belly. The look of need was palpable on his face. He looked marbled and younger under water, firmer somehow, but still old.

She reached out for him and spread her legs to accept the pressure of his entry. He pushed. At first her body rejected his penetration. She was just too small for him and couldn't take the width or length of it. But then, like a dam giving

117

way, she felt it thrust into her. The thing felt enormous. It made her want to evacuate her bowels and empty her bladder at the same time.

Oh God I can't do this, she thought, almost panicking, before suddenly realising that Franklyn was beginning to struggle against her. His face was contorted. He needs to breathe, she realised, and they bobbed to the surface together still firmly conjoined at the loins.

Franklyn gasped air into his lungs in movements that did strange things to his cock, creating powerfully interesting sensations inside her. His distressed flailing caused it to begin sliding deeply in and out of her in long, smooth strokes.

He gasped, 'I don't think I can do this in the water. He's not quite strong enough.' He pulled out and Milla experienced a surprised moment of regret. Looking down she could see through the water that his cock had lost its tumescent pride and was curving away from the horizontal as if gravity had taken a firmer grip.

She put her hand out to cup his testicles, enjoying his moment of shocked surprise and pleasure. 'Come with me,' she said. 'Let me help you.'

● ● ●

Chapter four: Life's a Beach

RUTH and Pearce invited Pearly, the unelected but clearly popular Town spokesperson, to join them for lunch. She accepted a glass of wine, complimenting them both on their choice from the menu. The fish was fresh caught from the sea, she said, and a lure to the greedy and frugal alike. She called the restaurateur to the table, placed their order and raised her sweating glass to the couple.

Her personality enfolded them in its natural warmth, the three chatting easily and openly across a wide range of topics. But she declined the offer of a meal, explaining that she'd already accepted an invitation from a parishioner and couldn't disappoint them at such short notice. Perhaps another day.

'Anyway,' she observed, 'anyone getting between two such obvious lovebirds is a gooseberry. And I'm fruity enough already to not need that.' She walked away with a swaying yet light-footed gait, her large frame shaking with laughter, the sound of which set birds to calling and complaining.

Pearce looked across at Ruth and his eyes were brilliant with mirth, shining in his sun-browned face. *I shall remember every moment of this month,* she thought. *This impossible, wonderful month, this dream. When we're home again I shall love him as much as ever. But I shall miss this freshness between us. This all too brief and borrowed youth.*

Under the awning they were protected from the direct heat of the sun, enjoying a breeze sweeping in from the sea. The smell of charcoal-grilled fish brought saliva to their tongues and, while nibbling pitted black Kalamata olives marinated in a piquant sauce, their hunger rose to an exquisite peak.

119

Reverend Pearly was right about the fish. And the wine. With nothing more than a lemon, parsley and olive oil dressing, their crisply grilled sea bass were delicious. A leafy green salad, with crusty bread on the side, and glasses of crisp, cold white wine complemented the flavours. They revelled in the fresh tastes and textures. They feasted, cleaning the flesh from the bones down to the smallest morsel and wiping up the lemony juices with their bread.

Afterwards they walked along the beach, hair ruffled by the wind. Ruth left her hat back at the restaurant because it seemed a crime to hide away from this delicious weather. The salt tang from the sea breeze added a last touch of pleasure to the lingering flavours of their lunch.

Pearce turned to her suddenly in the sand and kissed her full on the lips. His tongue found hers and they explored each other's mouths until Ruth pulled away, coughing with laughter. 'Sorry,' she choked. 'I suddenly thought *the blighter's trying to nick my fish* and it was so silly it made me giggle.'

He joined her merriment and then stilled – gazing at her for a long moment while smiling, eyes dancing. He said, 'I want to remember you like this for the rest of our lives.'

She agreed, 'And I you. This is the happiest day of my life.'

He kissed her again, warmly yet gently. 'Don't be daft. The month just got started. Who knows what joys tomorrow will bring? And we still have the rest of today. Come on, let's walk off some of that fish.'

They held hands as they strolled barefoot along the margins of the sea. The beach was so white and clean it almost took on some aspects of hallucination, sand shimmering against the turquoise liquidity of the water under an endless depth of blue sky. The scene shifted Ruth's senses, tilting them from true. For a moment they seemed to be walking along a beach floating unsupported in an infinite space.

Ruth experienced a strangely profound sensation of minuteness. She felt like she was a microscopic creature walking across a narrow beach trapped in the heart of an immense translucent ball. A tiny thing poised beneath infinity of sky. Looking back she saw the Town was lost in the heat haze. They were alone in crystal blue, eternal space.

She stopped breathing for a moment. She was so light and irrelevant in all this space, so poised on the very edges of existence, she felt she would be snuffed out like a pale flame, burned away to nothing on the face of the sun.

Pearce picked up on some change in her demeanour and hesitated mid-stride, looking at her with a questioning glance. In that moment she was back with him. She felt her weight once more pressing the soles of her feet down into the sand and breath shuddered through her.

This man is my gravity, she realised, *my centre. I have no shadow without him, no dimension. I am defined by him.* She embraced Pearce with a fierce urgency, without seeing him for the tears that stung her eyes. He pulled away slightly and gazed at her with mounting concern. 'What's wrong, Ruth?'

'I...'

'What is it?'

She buried her face in his shoulder, her freely running tears dampening the fabric of his shirt. He held her for a long while until she calmed in his arms, until she stopped crying.

They embraced with all the strength of youth, pressed body to body, toe to toe. It was a timeless moment, a pregnant pause. There was no burning need for them to move, nowhere else they needed to be and no one else they wanted to be with. This was their particular time and place.

Ruth couldn't find a voice to explain the choking awe and love overwhelming her. It was a sensation too sacred, primeval even, to be sketched by crude words. Instead, her body impressed her discovery, her aching need, into Pearce.

Eventually they resumed their walk, starting first with arms around each other's waists before unlinking and clasping hands for greater ease of movement.

They said nothing but walked as close as they could to each other, not quite but almost shoulder to shoulder. They were so focused on experiencing the up swell of emotions, their new sense of each other, they moved as if blindly swamped by a sensory overload of colour and texture.

Which is why it came as such a shock when they walked full tilt into an invisible wall.

●●●

Interlude

BLAKE's colleague was back at his monitors. The boss was out. The darkened room was awash with a blue glow, making it seem like some underwater grotto.

The monitors opened windows to the sunlit worlds of Ruth, Pearce, Milla and Franklyn. It was a quiet time. Ruth and Pearce were eating fish in a beachside restaurant and the other two were preparing to go out to the swimming pool.

'I had a dream about her, you know.'

'Who?' asked Blake.

The other man was little more than a silhouette, his voice quiet and confidential in the blue-lit shadowy room...

'The blonde.'

'Do I want to hear this?'

'Nah not like that, it was fucking weird.'

'No surprises there.'

'D'yah want to hear this or what?'

Blake sighed, 'Go on.'

The man paused before launching into his narrative.

'We were at work, Blondie and me, and it was late. It was dark outside. We finished what we were doing, turned off all the lights and went out to the car park.

'That's when I found I'd left my keys on my desk so I borrowed hers to let myself back in and get them. She waited for me by her car looking kinda fed up about the whole thing...'

'I know how she feels.'

'Shaddup. Anyway I let myself in and go over to my desk without putting the lights back on. I'm in the dark, see. I pick up my keys and turn round to go back out the door. And there, right in front of the door, is this small dark girl all

*dressed in black with straight black hair. She's just standin'
there.*

*'Then from behind her back she draws this big fuckin'
knife with a white blade. Her face don't show nothin', man.
She's looking at me and holding the knife and I can't think
what the fuck is going on.'*

The man leaned forward in his seat.

*'Then, she started walking towards me. So I shoved the
keys in my pocket and looked for something I could use to
defend myself. I grabbed a chair, an old type, y'know made
of wood with legs. An' I held it out and I pushed her back. It
pinned her and her knife to the wall with its legs.*

'Man, I was thinking got you bitch *but then she just
started walking through the chair like it wasn't there. I got
out of there man. I ran for it. I got out into the car park and
there was Blondie. She was still waiting and there must have
been something about me because she says* What? *Then,
before I say anything, I turn round and there's that fuckin'
girl and her knife comin' at me again.'*

'Did you eat cheese before going to bed or something?'

*'Be serious, man, this was awesome. I looked at Blondie.
And she looked at the girl and said* Oh I know about her.
Then she says Hi *to the girl. She goes over and kisses her on
the mouth. The girl just kisses her back, then walks away
without looking round. I just knew, if I tried that I'd have
been split like a kipper.*

*'Then Blondie just holds her hand out to me and asks for
her keys, like nothin' fuckin' happened. I woke up, goin'
what the fu...?'* *He fell silent.*

*On Blake's monitor Milla had dropped her robe and
dived into the water. The cameras followed her graceful path
lovingly recording what the water was doing to her body.*

Blake's colleague groaned like a rusty hinge. 'Oh man.'

124

'Quiet,' barked Blake and his hands flew across his keyboard.

When Franklyn thrust into Milla, he had the penetration right there, centred on his screens, as seen from above, below and behind. Not a movement was lost, not an inch. He followed the couple back to the surface while wondering if any of this was going to be cut, all of it being too good to be thrown away.

On other monitors, against a tropical paradise background Ruth was weeping on Pearce's shoulder. But right here, right now, both men were rapt by events in a swimming pool in London. Blake saw Franklyn pull out with a sense of shocked loss. He couldn't breathe. The tension in the room was palpable; he felt a vein pounding in his head. Then Milla cupped Franklyn's testicles and when she said 'let me help you', the air exploded from Blake's lungs.

He sat tensely poised in front of his screens, an artist ready to perform.

'It's show time,' he breathed.

●●●

Chapter five: Don't Stop

MILLA felt the cloak of unreality settle more firmly on her shoulders, as she led Franklyn dripping from the pool to the sun lounger. *Am I really going to do this,* she wondered, *can I?* A slight breeze brought goose flesh to her wet arms and legs. She lay Franklyn down and sat lightly on his legs, trying not to look too closely at the mottled flesh of his belly. She raised the weighty cock in both hands and began stroking life into it. Franklyn looked like he was gasping for breath, so she paused. 'No, no – don't stop,' he said, 'please don't.'

She re-applied herself to the task of beating life into the beast. Under her hands it thickened, stiffened and began to bob. She put it between her breasts and pushed them together, trapping it in her cleavage, something she would never have been able to do in her own body.

And what about you, Paris woman? Do you do this for your husband, or is this the first time? Franklyn groaned and she watched the tip of his penis darken as it rose and fell against her blonde flesh. *Is this the time?*

She continued pumping the cock with her hand, as she rose to her feet and turned her back to the old man's face. She knew this would be easier if she couldn't see his writhing lips and bulging eyes, though she couldn't block out the wheezing sound of his panting breath.

Standing astride the cock she lowered herself, gently but firmly, onto its thick length. She rode it with an easy up and down stroke, lubricating the thing with a surprising amount of vaginal fluids. *Oh, this is unexpected*, she thought as her body began to take its own mounting pleasure from her actions.

Under her, Franklyn began a thrusting motion with hands firm on her hips and buttocks. She took a look around. His eyes were shut and his mouth shaped like a stretched 'O'. His head strained back and the tendons of his neck stood out like cords.

Without a pause to her movements, Milla flushed with her first climax and put her hand to her engorged clitoris to caress it and prolong the pleasure. It was a deep warm sensation that arched her back and had her squeezing joy from her breasts, her head tilted upwards to the sun.

Under her Franklyn stopped what he was doing and raised her from his lap. When he stood, the cock was barely above horizontal but rigid as a steel bar. 'I have to do this,' he said.

He bent her over the sun lounger and with instant understanding she raised her ass to him, spreading her legs. She felt his momentary appreciative gaze on her body, before he slid into her like he was sheathing himself in hot silk. Hands like iron welded to her hips, he rocked her in a counter rhythm to his own crouching and urgent motions.

They were lost in a maelstrom of slapping flesh and stimulated nerve endings, with gasping lungs and slurping, slippery friction. The man was making regular noises, something like a steady and increasingly forceful *haaaa, haaaa, haaaa, hnnn, haaaa*. Milla became aware that she too was making an involuntary noise, a sort of *mmmwah, mmmwah, mmmwah* sound.

There was no longer anything contained or civilised about what they were doing. It was primitive and touched down to something she had never felt before, something out of control and animal. The sheer force of physical desire, for this coupling, took her out of her body for a moment. She seemed to be above herself, watching her mindlessly rocking welcoming form – legs spread, head forward, getting ploughed by the pumping goat man with a cock as big as her forearm.

Her flesh dragged her back down into her hiccoughing pummelled self, and she almost drowned in the jolting, exquisitely pleasurable violence. She braced herself as his thrusting became faster and deeper, rocking her whole body backwards and forwards with an unstoppable momentum. The rhythm began to rock the sun lounger and she feared the whole thing would collapse under the hammering. Who knew the old man had so much life in him?

Then her second climax forced a grinding scream from between her clenched teeth, just as she felt a burning eruption in her belly and Franklyn groaned his release. His final spastic motions, slapping hard against her thighs and buttocks, made her breasts jounce and roll between her braced arms.

He pulled out just in time for his last jet of seed to spurt across the reddened globes of Milla's backside. Then he pumped the very last drops from his cock, with long lingering strokes of his hand trickling them onto her back.

She turned and greedily kissed the end of it, licked it and watched him wince with enhanced sensitivity.

They lay close together on the sun lounger, trembling and spent, while gathering their wits from wherever they'd fled during their brutal mating.

Franklyn coughed and groaned. 'You okay?' he said.

'I don't know.'

'What the fuck was that?'

'I seriously don't know,' she gasped, 'but we really have to do it again.'

'Okay, but next time easy does it or we'll kill the poor old sod.'

'Promise,' said Milla, as her hand stroked the flaccid tube between his legs with proprietary affection.

Chapter six: It can't last

PEARCE bounced off the unexpected surface and sprawled on his back next to Ruth. They were both more shocked than hurt by the impact, which combined a sense of walking into an elastic sheet with a gentle yet firm push away, like a benign 'keep out' order. Not a threat or a warning but a simple instruction. *Sorry about this but you go no further than here,* it said. *Have a nice day anywhere else you choose to be.*

'That was a natural 20,' said Pearce, getting to his feet and helping Ruth up. He was referring to the scoring system used in the popular game *20/20 Ricochet Jacks,* which was becoming something of a plague in the more densely populated urban sprawls.

A player would fire his Jack, a sort of small very bouncy ball programmed to eventually return back to where it started its journey, from an Ejector (the term 'gun' was considered too aggressive). On its high-speed return it was, hopefully, caught by the player in a specially designed Mitt. Some less capable players sported bruises caused by their Jacks, which they preferred to hide rather than display as trophies. Weaker players earned the sobriquet 'Long Sleeves' as a result of this cover up.

En route from Ejector to Mitt, the aim of the game was to bounce the Jack from as many surfaces as possible, the highest score of 10 being recorded for a ricochet from a window on which the ball would leave a minute 20/20 logo. Smart material in the ball, which computed its return trajectory, recorded the journey. It also impressed the score into the Mitt when it was caught, which could then be shared with other players.

The highest score for a single Jack free-flight recorded to date was notched up in Osaka during rush hour by Reginald Tanaka Ng. His Jack disappeared from view for over 11 minutes and he almost missed collecting it when it flew back to him from behind. His Mitt recorded a tally of 489, almost as high as scores attained under controlled conditions by the game's designers. It is believed that Ng's Jack got into a stream of cars on Osaka's principal autoway and bounced down the vehicles to-and-fro until it found a gap and escaped.

Some areas had become so pockmarked by 20/20 logos that the architecture seemed pixellated. Naturally non-players were far from pleased with the effect it was having on their environment, but so much money was tied up in the game's manufacture and distribution that it couldn't be stopped. It had, however, been banned from malls and car parks, though cars in transit were fair game for those trying to match Ng's score. Many a commuter forked out for the special cleaning fluid required to convert the removal of the logo from their vehicle's windows from an onerous chore to a simple wipe away.

Ruth nodded her agreement. 'Good call,' she said. The years had developed mental shorthand between the couple, a simpatico of shared thoughts and emotions. In one short statement Pearce had summed up exactly what this Body Holiday meant. Here in these perfect young forms they were little more than Jacks fired on a random trajectory. For the next month they would bounce around and leave their marks on all sorts of surfaces but ultimately they would end up back where they started, with just their memories to help keep score.

She remembered a director she'd worked with once, who compared one's effect on life to dipping your hands into a bucket filled with water. He said, 'You can reach down and

130

stir up the water with your hands as much as you like but once you take your hands out of the bucket the water settles back down again as if you'd never been there at all.'

In response she'd fetched a bucket of water, set it on the floor in front of him, then kicked it all over his shoes. She told him to give her a call when he learned something about positive reinforcement but the last he ever saw of her, in the flesh, was the sway of her perfect figure walking out the door.

The way Ruth saw it, yes, some people are, as Leonardo da Vinci had long ago remarked, little more than passages for food. But others leave a permanent trace on the consciousness of the world and what they do creates echoes in history. Great scientists, artists, musicians, writers, thinkers and soldiers shine with life from the annals of their time.

In her own way Ruth touched something in a lot of people during her career. She was sure that when it was time to finally take her hands from the bucket of water, the ripples she caused would continue flowing for quite some time.

Pearce raised his hand to the invisible wall and pressed in. It shrugged him off. He tried again but, no matter how carefully he did it, he couldn't find any purchase. 'You know what this is?' he asked.

'Some sort of barrier?'

'Yes, but you know where we are?'

'No.'

'This is the Town end of our beach. This incredible thing is here to keep people away from us, when we want to be alone. What kind of research went into creating this? I've never even heard of it. And it's very effective.'

He rolled up the legs of his shorts and waded a distance out into the sea, pressing against the barrier as he went. He came back and stripped off his clothes, causing Ruth to look around in alarmed caution. They were alone.

Pearce swam far out until she could barely see his head above the water. Then he dived and was gone.

After a while during which Pearce didn't reappear and Ruth began counting the seconds, she felt anxiety rising along with a little vomit in her throat. When she reached five minutes, panic began to set in. She started making short steps in different directions. She didn't know whether to follow him into the sea or run to Town and get help.

'Pearce!' she shouted his name, louder and shriller each time. 'Pearce! Pearce! Pearce!' She doubled over with the effort of trying to project her voice further out and down under the waves where she just knew something had gone wrong.

Had he met a predator, some great thing with teeth or tentacles that was even now peeling his flesh away from his bones? Was there a riptide dragging his weakening body out into the cold, deep sea and away from her forever?

'Pearce,' she said quietly this time, a cross between a prayer and a sob.

'What?' he shouted back. He was swimming strongly towards her and emerged striding through the rollers back onto dry land. Ruth didn't know whether to hit him or hug him, so she did both.

'Where...where did you go?'

'The barrier creates an enclosure. Now hang on. I'd better get my shorts back on if you're going to keep hugging me like this. We'll create a public indecency.'

Ruth looked down and saw what he meant. She stepped back while he quickly dressed.

'I dived down to see if I could get under the barrier but it goes down to the seabed. Then when I followed it, it suddenly wasn't there anymore. And I realised it had turned left, making a corner.

'I surfaced and followed it for a while. Funnily enough, though I could see you very clearly there was nothing of our beach. I waved but you didn't wave back and when I saw that you were getting into a bit of a state...'

'Bit of a state?'

'A bit upset...anyway I thought it best to come back.' He looked at the barrier with frank admiration. 'It lets air, fish and water in but keeps us out. We can't see through it or swim under it, and I bet we couldn't climb over it or spy on our beach from above.

'These Body Holiday people must either be wizards or they have access to technology I haven't heard about. Whoever or whatever they are, they're making totally sure we are safe in this place. Come on, girl, let's go home.'

Pearce took Ruth's hand and led her along the barrier to the path where they turned right, back towards their gate and the chalet.

A long way behind them in the Town, Reverend Pearly got the call from her implant and walked to her church where she received her orders.

As the evening became night and threw blue shades into the sky, she gathered her team and headed up the path towards the chalet, her expression grim, determined and resigned.

●●●

Chapter seven: Cooling to room temperature

MILLA swam in the crystal blue pool trying vainly to gather her thoughts. On his sun lounger, the old man was on his back snoring gently, dead to the world. *Let him sleep*, she thought. *After what we did this morning he deserves his time in the sun, even if it is with his mouth open and his eyes shut.* From the water she couldn't see his cock but it was there in her mind's eye and she examined it from every angle.

What happened here today? What happened to me today? What kind of woman am I? Thoughts and questions circled her mind while she circled the pool, allowing the cool water to soothe her bruised flesh.

Never before in her life had Milla been so out of control or so subject to the needs of her body. That much was true. But it was also true she had never been so completely in the moment as during the pounding, brutal act she'd been subjected to by the old man. She cast another surreptitious glance across to the slender, sleeping form on the sun lounger.

I have tasted new fruit and I want more of it, she realised. *I'm already like an addict after my very first experience of a new drug. I want more even though it hurt me.* She trod water and put a gentle hand down between her legs and felt the hot soreness there, a soreness that went deep into her belly. Her breasts ached from the way they'd bucked, jolted and rolled under the remorseless, battering fuck she and Franklyn had just shared. She felt physically abused, mentally confused and hungry for more.

That wasn't making love, what they did this morning. That wasn't some form of sexual dance done for pleasure between caring, sharing adults. It was bestial, raw and pure.

134

What they did was fornication at its most basic. It was hardcore and dirty. And it didn't need to pretend it was anything other than a fuck for fucking's sake. It didn't even insist on dinner and flowers. It was copulation as an extreme sport and it reached new heights of rampant pleasure in places she didn't know existed.

Milla knew she'd initiated proceedings out of a surreal sense of pity, while also under the influence of these glorious surroundings. What had she done? Above her the thick column of the sky tower soared up and away, something that couldn't even be seen close to it, from ground level, thanks to the anchors and buttresses surrounding its base.

The robust detail of the building became jewel-like as it got higher, until the microscopically thin needle of it pierced the dome of the sky. Some shift in perspective changed her viewpoint for a moment and suddenly she was looking along a bridge she could cross to a more blessed place, away from her confusion. Then it was a tower again and that expanse of arching blue was the sky.

She remembered from somewhere the word *welkin,* which described the arching dome of heaven. And under that dome, she thought, under such peerless beauty and flawless perfection they should walk as angels.

Her client's body might look like an angel but she had used it, and allowed it to be used, for baser things of meat on meat, squirting release and physical need. Almost distractedly she became aware of how she was still caressing and touching her inflamed mound. She thought of it as the open mouth of a starving beast, an animal with a thirst yet to be slaked and biting hunger still unabated. She was filled with heat and deep resolve.

She swam poolside and swayed to where Franklyn lay on his back, and there it was curving across his thigh. The serpent of temptation. She wanted to touch it, rouse it, put it in her mouth and taste it, ride it to catastrophe or be ridden by it to perdition. She put her hand out and almost circled its thickness, but instead she reached up to Franklyn's shoulder and shook him gently. He murmured awake, eyes coming to unfocused life while travelling the length of her body before resting on her face.

'Mgmnyah?' he asked.

'You were asleep.'

'Grrrmwhah, hah?'

'You might get burned in the sun. We should go inside.'

'Hnnnh.'

She got him to his feet and dressed him in his robe. She was very aware that he took every opportunity to touch her, caress her and make contact with her flesh. She encouraged it, even running the back of her hand down his cock; an action that brought sudden keen interest to his eyes.

She reached into his robe and stroked his weighted cock gently, making him close his eyes and suck wet air into his mouth with pleasure. 'Come on,' she said.

They met no one after they left the pool and entered the passage, which felt cool and seemed darker after their time outside. She led him to the apartment where, as soon as they were inside, she dropped her robe and turned to face him.

'A drink first, I think,' he said.

It felt strange, this violence of need, this wanting to get back to the mindless place they found by the pool. They drank quickly yet even before the glasses were emptied they began a fresh exploration of each other's bodies. Milla knelt and pumped at the cock, placing the end in her mouth and tonguing it until it stiffened with some sort of resolve. She put it between her legs and felt the longed-for sweet pressure once more begin to build. Franklyn put his hands both sides of her head and looked down at where he was penetrating this dream woman, watching the length of his cock slide in

136

and out, its thick curve of blood-darkened flesh stark against her pale belly. He felt something building to fruition.

'Ow, ow, ow youch,' said Milla, yanking at his arm. 'Something's pulling my hair out.'

Franklyn's Mediband was catching in her hair. Without even pulling out of her, he took the thing off his wrist and threw it on the table before resuming his thrusting progress.

'Not on the floor,' said Milla, pulling away. She led him to the bedroom, where she climbed on the bed putting her head down on the pillow and her arse in the air. The invitation unmistakeable, Franklyn quickly knelt between her legs and, enjoying the view before stuffing his cock deeply into her, he again began his pounding crescendo.

It seemed as if time became redundant, as they each worked towards their conclusions. He was roaring towards something that seemed hopelessly beyond his reach. She was pinioned on his thick length of hot meat like a witless puppet or a scientific specimen involved in a field study into sexual addiction.

There were moments when Milla wanted to scream at him to stop. These were followed by moments when she wanted to scream at him that he should never stop and instead just keep that piston driving and driving. She pushed back against him, wanting him deeper, and pulled away from the pain with equal vigour, until her first climax stopped both her breathing and any sensible thoughts.

Franklyn was making nonsense noises again but couldn't curb his pounding, panting momentum building towards orgasm. Milla whimpered, her breath ragged. Drool ran from the corner of her mouth and her second climax hit just as Franklyn began roaring behind her. He fell away from her, spurting a thin spray of seed across the bed. Then he lay spent on his back, his breath shallow, his body sapped of energy.

She climbed shakily to her feet and went to use the toilet, before having a quick shower and donning her robe. She fetched two fresh drinks and took them into the bedroom. On seeing Franklyn was spark out, she took them both onto the balcony and sipped gratefully while looking out across the view and feeling numb and shaky with guilty pleasure.

She opened her robe to the cooling breeze, washing some of the heat from her reddened loins. Behind her in the darkened bedroom Pearce's body began to lose body heat, as his death washed away warmth. He began cooling to room temperature.

Milla was just starting her second glass of wine when the medical team burst into the apartment and began the futile job of trying to breathe life back into the old man's corpse. She watched in mute shock.

● ● ●

Chapter eight: Sorry for the Inconvenience

PEARCE took time over preparing dinner. They weren't particularly hungry after their banquet of fish at lunchtime, but their hosts were evidently used to eating three square meals a day and must be catered for. Anyway, an afternoon of swimming and love play on the beach had soon whetted their appetites.

He made up little plates of tapas: chicken in a sesame sauce, meatballs in a tomato, parsley and basil sauce with pine nuts, and prawns butterflied and served in a hot and sour sauce. A bowl of young leaf salad in lemon and oil dressing, sprinkled with crunchy pan-browned pine nuts, and a platter heaped with strips of toasted pitta bread completed the table.

Evening drew late and the couple closed doors and windows against airborne ranks of nocturnal insects, which tapped regretful, yearning tympani against the glass. Under subdued light and with the room's air enriched by light classical music, they dipped mouthfuls from the board while talking with easy intimacy about the day. They sipped chilled white wine from tall glasses beaded with condensation sweat. They smiled a lot.

Their eyes never strayed far from each other's faces, drinking deep from youthful curves, full lips, dark tousled hair highlighted auburn by the tropical sun and a flush of freckles burgeoning across pink-tanned noses. They were like thirsty travellers in an arid land, knowing that drinking too much of the fresh cold spring water they found spurting from a rock would be bad for them but still wanting to drown in the icy deliciousness.

Pearce and Ruth were sharing the rarest gift – an opportunity to fall in love with each other all over again.

They were falling for new, fresh nuances in character, which each was demonstrating with youthful energy and verve.

Everything was brighter, richer and more profound. Their eyes sparkled with a healthy glow fuelled by both time-served wisdom and gleeful mischief. They were tired enough to sleep but also reluctant to give up one moment of their perfect day or lose one second of time with each other.

There were no clocks on the island to dictate how they spent their hours, their only entertainment consisting of books, music, food, drink, the island itself and each other. They knew they would find infinite variations in ways to spend the hours, all of them pleasurable, all of them to be stored in bright recesses of memory against the day the Jack returned to the Mitt and they were returned to their own flesh once more.

They discussed how they might make these host bodies exclusive for regular Body Holidays, how they might afford to do that and whether the hosts would agree. They agreed they couldn't bear the idea of other clients using this flesh, which had so quickly become beloved and as precious as their own familiar forms.

Their joy was limited only by a taint of sadness that it would all be over too soon, and they agreed that they would scrape this precious pot of youthful time together until the last scrap was gone. Then they would lick their spoons clean until they shone.

They were cuddled up, kissing, talking, and savouring their second bottle of wine when Ruth looked up and around in sudden alarm. 'Did you hear that?'

'What?' Pearce stood up and peered out into the darkness.

'Something...' Ruth couldn't explain. It was like an alarm going off in her head, heart and belly. 'Something's wrong,' she finished lamely.

'We're on an island surrounded by the sea, with an invisible barrier to protect us. We're as safe as it's possible to be in this chalet,' Pearce told her. 'Apart from insects and birds, nothing can get at us. What can go wrong?'

Ruth uttered a stifled groan and pointed at the window. Pearce turned and saw an expressionless male face gazing in at them. Flying things settled on the man's face but he made no move to wipe them away. He just watched the couple with a fiercely blank intensity, even as the bugs crawled across his eyes. Another man stood beyond the glass of the French windows, his form shadowy with arms crossed and looking massive like an antique wrestler.

Behind them the door to the chalet opened and closed quickly, yet not quickly enough. A small cloud of whining insects burst into the room and settled into a rapturous orbit round the light fittings. They were followed by the colourful bulk of Reverend Pearly. However, now there was no trace of the friendly, smiling face of daytime on her round features but something coldly *other*.

The couple said nothing about this unexpected intrusion. Ruth saw that Pearce had settled into a flat-footed stance, which she recognised from his martial arts training. He was ready to attack if anything gave him cause. For years Pearce insisted that Ruth practice various defensive fighting skills and she had become quite accomplished in the dojo. She'd simply never needed to use what she'd learned in anger. But now she got ready, knowing that if she needed to she would surely kill to protect her man.

Pearly spoke, her voice flat and empty. Ruth thought she was looking at something inhuman, some kind of automaton; an android. Pearce's sharp intake of breath told her he had reached the same conclusion.

'There has been an incident that needs to be addressed,' the large woman said. 'It requires that you return to London

141

by the quickest means possible, which means travelling by private ballistic from this island. The procedure is perfectly safe but very uncomfortable due to the high G forces you will experience.'

Ruth's eyes felt oddly heavy, her body weighted. Something told her she was just a puppet and any minute now someone would cut her strings.

'Therefore,' said the expressionless Pearly, 'it has been decided to render you unconscious until you arrive back in England.'

Someone cut the strings and Ruth fell with a boneless flop to the floor. Pearce staggered and did the same.

Like a bee buzzing in her ear, Ruth heard, 'This has been done for your own safety and protection. We are sorry for any inconvenience.'

Blackness, then nothing.

●●●

Interlude

WHEN the boss walked into the monitor room he could smell the sweat. 'Was it good?'

'In-fucking-credible,' said Blake. 'I have never seen anything like it before. I have a boner you could use to drive nails in with man. It was awesome.'

His colleague was silent, his mouth too dry to say anything, too overwhelmed to find words.

'We've made history,' continued Blake. 'Ruth Hudson so down and dirty she's like a bitch on heat without losing any of her appeal. She wanked the man with her tits and still looks like an angel. She takes it from behind twice and she's dribbling and I still want to lick the spit from her chin.'

'Shame we couldn't have a bit more action in the pool,' observed the boss, 'but the old man couldn't keep it up without drowning.'

'We've got the other two in the sea,' said Blake. 'That has beauty and grace, and a touch of comedy with the fish and all. But these two by the pool and in bed were so hot they set fire to the screen.'

'We edit the death?' asked the man in the corner.

'What?'

'We edit the death?'

'Of course we don't edit the death,' said the boss. 'We keep the fucking death in because it fuels the story arc. Ruth fucking Hudson fucks a man to death. She's so hot he keeps pumping even though it kills him. Who can blame him? What a way to go man. Why the fuck should we edit that? Get some music commissioned for it man. And put some rain on a hillside, whatever it takes to make it work. Get creative on its arse.

'We're right now in possession of the most sought-after scenes in porn TV history and we are soon going to be very wealthy men indeed.

'Now,' he continued, drawing his circled thumb and forefinger across his lips like he was closing a zip, 'keep 'em sealed until broadcast night. No need to spoil the surprise. And Potter,' he looked into the darkness in the corner where Blake's colleague sat mutely listening. 'Potter, you don't take these home to show your friends. You understand? Complete. Security. Blanket! Now send this stuff to the edit suite pronto. I've got work to do.'

When he left the room the boss's absence created a vacuum that Blake tried to fill with chatter. 'Man, the boss knows you, Potter,' he laughed. 'You're always taking work home that should stay here by rights.'

'You told him.'

'What?'

'You fucking told him, you brown noser.'

'No way, man, I don't need to tell the man what he can work out for himself. He sees you, man. He knows what you do and when you do it. He knows you're a jerk off but, hey, you're good at what you do. You love your work, perhaps a little too much, and you take it home for your personal pleasure. I know that. But I also know you aren't showing the goods to your friends. He's wrong there, man.'

'Thanks, dude, I 'preciate you saying that.'

'Sure, man, 'cause I know you ain't got any friends to show it to. You watch all this good stuff on your own with your remote in one hand, your cock in the other and a box of tissues by your side. And I'm guessing about the tissues.'

Potter didn't respond. He was watching Ruth and Pearce collapse to the floor in the chalet like boneless dummies.

He kept watching while the two men came in through the French windows and lifted the bodies to their shoulders with

144

easy movements, as if they were hefting nothing more than weightless dolls.

Pearly led her group out through the door and onto the path leading to the gate. She didn't bother to shut the chalet up after their departure and the light fittings were soon darkened by a swarming mass of roiling brown insect bodies. The noise filled Potter's headphones, deafening him to Blake's banter. The sound of classical music was drowned out.

He watched as the group of three took their captives to the Town. Nobody was abroad in the darkened streets. There were no lights in any of the buildings. None of the fishing boats had moved since Pearce admired them earlier. The Town was a sham, almost a film set, designed for the exclusive use of Body Holidaymakers. Now the clients were doped and unable to appreciate any of its charms, the Town reverted to passive mode. What was welcoming and beautiful under the sun had become dark and dead in the night.

Pearly opened the big church doors and led her men to the east end of the nave, walking through the building past shadowed, empty pews until she reached the last few rows. These were peopled with the silent, still, motley inhabitants of the Town. All sat slightly curved forwards, heads down, inactive until needed once more.

The Reverend walked behind the altar and opened a sliding portal in the floor. A pale light washed her from below. Potter sat engrossed. What had been hardcore romance was becoming something altogether more sinister, and he loved it.

He made some adjustments, and on monitor two the point of view altered. Now he was looking up at the trio, as they stepped down into the blue-lit crypt. The light came through thick windows that reached from floor to ceiling. They gave out to a view of the seabed and were filled with shifting blue phosphorescence.

Gravid shapes moved in the crystal shadows of the sea, sometimes coming into focus as recognisable marine creatures but mostly staying far enough away to tease and perhaps terrify the imagination. If Pearce had visited this place earlier he might not have been so keen to swim round the barrier, and Ruth would have had even more reason to fear for him when he failed to reappear.

Pearly opened the top of a fat tube that extended from the centre of the crypt, on through the wall and far out into the shifting stygian blue beyond the windows. Inside the tube was a capsule the width of a double bed, which she also unlatched. Her men brought the supine forms of Ruth and Pearce and lay them in the capsule, where they sank into gel foam. Pearly fitted breathers to both unconscious faces and stretched gel-based security rigging tightly across them.

She closed the capsule, sealing it firmly and swiftly, then dogged down the tube's hatch.

The entire crypt began to move as the electro-magnetic catapult, a ballistic launcher, was targeted precisely towards its destination while making exact alterations to allow for weather conditions en route. On the other side of the island was the mouth of a ballistic receiver, which was how Holidaymakers arrived on the island. In London, at the base of the Body Holiday Foundation's headquarters, a similar receiver was being prepared to capture and slow the island's capsule on arrival. The technology was proven and safe. Since the first commercial ballistic was fired from New York to Shanghai over 50 years previously, there had been no reported accidents.

None of this mattered to the occupants of the capsule as it was launched, in an instant reaching several times the speed of sound, in an arc that reached the very edges of space

146

before it fell like a bullet back towards Earth. Without gel foam buffering the forces, Ruth and Pearce would have been rendered to pulp.

Back in the church the crypt was resealed. Pearly and her henchmen took their seats in the pews, rocked forwards, and were still.

Potter took off his headphones. 'Guess we've got time for coffee. Want some?'

He missed the man who stepped out of the deepest shadows at the back of the church and then vanished.

●●●

Chapter nine: Die in his own skin

MILLA sat alone in what seemed to be a windowless hotel room. She was supplied with food and drink and the room had an en-suite bathroom. It was all very comfortable and quiet but that didn't stop her being chilled to her very marrow.

One minute she was luxuriating on the balcony sipping her second glass of wine while Franklyn caught up with his beauty sleep, and the next she was being bundled away by some sort of medical SWAT team and dumped here.

The Virtuo unit was fixed on a view of a forest clearing, which was nice enough. Long shadows were beginning to stretch across the mossy grass, which told her it was late afternoon. She had been back in the luxury apartment just a few hours earlier but now everything in her life, everything about this holiday, was changed.

She was still confused by her hungry, addicted reaction to sex with Franklyn in his client's body. And what was wrong with Franklyn? Nobody had spoken to her as they ushered her away from his still form on the bed. After delivering her here, she'd been left to her own devices. She was still wearing the robe she'd pulled on, after her shower just hours before.

She stood listlessly with a full yet untouched glass of wine in her hand. She'd poured it a few minutes earlier for something to do but some voice of caution in her subconscious mind warned her that alcohol might be a very bad idea under the present circumstances.

Framed by the Virtuo window a small deer with short, needle-sharp antlers entered the forest clearing, followed by a second then a third. Soon a small herd was nipping delicately at the grass, dappled by the sun. She walked up to the Virtuo unit and looked away to the left and right. The clearing was in the heart of an ancient forest: giant trees stretched up to a canopy of overlapping branches and fallen tree trunks woven to the forest floor with ropes of parasitic ivy. She wanted to step into the glade and escape, run away from all her confusion and doubt.

She hoped Franklyn was alright but somehow doubted it. Whatever the medical team was doing looked pretty desperate. Why did he take his Mediband off? Oh yes, of course. Her hair.

She began to weep, softly at first, and then in uncontrollable, stomach searing, wracking sobs. Fat tears rolled down her face and her mouth contorted into an open wrenching snarl of emotional agony. She shook with the force of her outburst, coughing and whooping air into her lungs, before jagging it out with a vomit of regret, sadness and fear.

It took several minutes to bring herself back under control, blow her nose and dry her face. Milla knew the weeping woman was still there, behind her eyes, when she looked in the room's only mirror. But otherwise, the face gazing back at her was untouched by grief apart from a slight redness round her nostrils. *Lady, you are some kind of special,* she thought.

The deer fled the glade as if spooked by her weeping, the sun dipping below the tree line.

This morning I woke in a luxury apartment, she thought, *and my only worry was what to do about Franklyn's advances. I have swum naked in a private pool under the shadow of a sky tower and probably killed a man with the force of my physical demands. Not bad for a diary entry when I come to write my memoirs.*

She tried the room's door again. Still locked. She drank some wine. As it was getting dark in the glade, she reasoned it was late enough for a drink and, anyway, after what she'd been through she deserved it. The same quiet voice that earlier advised caution with regard to alcohol now asked how it was that, in the midst of all her uncontrolled ecstasy of weeping, she'd somehow managed to keep hold of her wine without spilling a drop. She decided to treat the voice as a hostile witness and drained the glass.

She poured another and, this time, sipped it while it was still cold enough to chill as it slid down her throat and into her belly. She took a good swallow, another, and a third. She poured another glass and sat in a chair facing the glade, watching without seeing as night creatures climbed out of setts and burrows or swooped down from trees seeking small, warm life to feed from.

Death came to the night time glade under raking claw and razored beak, and that was good because animals need to feed – while she'd brought death to a bedroom with nothing more than lust. That was a hunger she could live with, without slaking.

She thought back to the killer at the NEC and how close she'd been to kicking his filthy brains out. His lust was all about taking power over women. Was she really so much better? Franklyn was dead, she was sure of it. And he was dead because she couldn't control her lust for the old man's cock. There it was, out in the open. So, was she really any better than the NEC killer; what was his name, Trapper?

She gave herself a mental slap. *Pull yourself together you little fool*, she spat. That murderer took girls against their will and did things no human should do to another. I killed a man with pleasure, and he was as much a part of the act as I was. If he'd said no, I would have waited until he was ready (*would I?* she wondered).

Now, what happened? Nothing can go wrong with a Body Holiday, they said. What was his name? Blake, yes, and Freedman too. Funny little man, Freedman.

She poured another drink and, when she found the bottle was empty, fetched a second from the fridge. This stuff must be low alcohol; it's not having any effect. She gazed at the label: 13.5%. She drank some more.

Franklyn was dead, dead in another man's body. Was that fair? He didn't even get to die in his own skin but in some skinny old guy's pelt with a cock like a hot hosepipe she would never get to feel again. And she ached for it.

You, my girl, need something to eat. She poured more wine. *So now what happens? Franklyn is dead in a client's body. So the client must be alive in Franklyn's. Makes sense, doesn't it? And the Paris woman is alive in me. So now what happens? And I'm alive in her. They can't allow that, can they? They can't let us live, can they? Not now we know it can all go so horribly wrong.*

The glass fell from her hand to the carpet, barely dampening the pile. Milla's head went back and down onto the arm of her chair, where she remained unmoving in the darkening room.

When the door opened and two figures entered the room, she greeted them with nothing more than a gentle snore. The door snapped quietly shut behind them as they approached her cautiously in the gloom.

'She sucks at the ambrosia'd tit of Morpheus.'

'She drained a coupl'a pints of Sauvignon Blanc is what she did, poet boy.'

'Stand clear.' There was a barely audible hiss and Milla's breathing altered to a deeper, more regular rhythm. 'I should take that stuff on dates, man. That's where I'm fallin' down with the ladies. I mean this lady has no idea what we're

151

doin'.' He reached out and caressed the recumbent woman, reaching inside her robe.

His colleague slapped him away. 'No playing with the merchandise, little bro. That ain't why we're here. We just got to take her where she needs to be.'

The man reached out again and hefted a breast. 'Oh, man, you have got to feel these. They look so wrong and feel so right.'

'Hands off, bro. We're paid good money to do this right and we're not going to queer the pitch. I was going to say you want the shoulders or the feet, but the way you acting you taking the feet man. Control yourself. In this we are guardians of the angel, till she flies again in heaven.'

'If this here is an angel, poet boy, I'm gonna be the best man on the block till I get me some in the afterlife.' Even in the darkened room the grin was obvious. 'Hey, man, I can see straight up her kilt from here, and the view is classic. Boy.'

●●●

Chapter ten: We're in Danger

RUTH was the first to surface from sleep. Her first care was for the discomfort caused by sunburned skin in a very tender spot. Her depilated groin was a mass of first degree stings. Then she looked around.

It was, at best, a bland room with no kind of windows or anything to break up the pastel green décor. She felt like she had gone to sleep and woken up in a therapist's office, centre core.

She thought of a man's face in a tropical night window, his features crawling with multi-legged, winged insect life, and he was apparently uncaring. How? Who?

Next to her was Pearce, still dead to the world, on his side and deeply sleeping. Beyond him, she was astonished to see some woman, some blonde tart, also asleep. She lay, curled around her centre, face down. Ruth raised herself on an elbow. *Looks like a Vegas showgirl*, she thought. *When did she get hitched to the party?*

She was so busy looking for things to knock about the snoring stranger that it took a while for realisation to come crashing in. Ruth couldn't summon a word for what happened when the mirror image of the woman she was studying flipped over. Something between 'fuck' and 'oh, of course' would have to do.

She had thought before that people only ever saw themselves, on a regular basis, in mirror image. They had to make real efforts with multiple mirrors, or be vain enough to get contemporary portraits made, to keep them up to date with their true likeness. But now she realised people also never expect to see themselves sleeping just a hand's breadth away from a recently young husband who has demonstrated enormously stimulated sexual energy.

153

Keep that bitch away from him, thought Ruth. *But, oh, my God, she's beautiful. I'm beautiful. I'm beautiful? What the fuck am I thinking?*

Ruth looked for those marks of time that had underpinned her personal examinations in the mirror over the past few decades. Sagging eyes, no; crow's feet, no; jowls, no. The girl she was looking at could easily be in her early 30s. She looked like an angel. *I never gave myself the credit I deserved*, she thought. Then the blonde farted, and the whiff was noxious.

We've all been there, thought Ruth, *me all too often these days*.

Something crashed into her consciousness; it was like a heavy blow. *It is me! This girl is me! Shit! Shit! Shit!*

Then, she thought, *why are we here?*

She reached across Pearce to touch the girl's hand (*my hand*) and the result was electric. The girl screamed.

Pearce woke and broke the contact by sitting up. The girl slumped back down.

'Is that you in there or you in there?' asked Pearce after a bit of eye rubbing, yawning and a visit to the pisser. He walked out of the bathroom with damp hands and an enquiring glance around.

'Me in here,' answered Ruth, 'but there's seriously something going on with our host there. I only touched her and she shrieked.'

'Where are we?'

'No idea, Hun.'

'Touch her again.'

Pearce leaned away, wincing in anticipation. Ruth reached out and touched her own body's sleeping hand and the girl screamed again, seemingly with terror. With an effort, the girl was roused from slumber but even so it seemed she wanted to flinch as far from Ruth's fingers as possible.

The two women looked at each other. Then the blonde shuddered, grimaced working her jaw, and asked, 'Can I hold your hand again?'

Ruth reached out and felt cool fingers enclose hers. *My hand*, she thought. *She looks good too*. The result was like an electric shock. They both gasped and pulled away, taking a moment's pause.

Milla studied her client. *Obviously didn't read the memo about not getting a suntan, but looks the way I always hoped I'd look after a bit of time in the sun. When do I get me back?*

Then a whole wave of anxiety swept over her and she held her hand out again, 'May I?'

Ruth clasped Milla's palm and the result was so electric she threw it away. 'Hngh, sorry, ouch,' she said. 'I didn't expect that.'

'Me neither,' said Milla. 'But, please, we have to try again.'

They reached out, clasped and held. Both looked at the door of the room.

Milla said, 'We're in danger. But you have a way out of this that I can't reach alone. Call someone called Ben, get him here in the car, the Lexus, and get him here quick.'

'He'll need somewhere to park.'

'Give him code...hang on...' Her eyes went blank. She was silent for some time, her eyes drifting under lids shut tight. Then they opened wide. '...AX20 West Side Outer LONtower. That should do the trick.'

All eyes were on Milla. 'It's what I do,' she explained. 'It's how I earn my living when I'm not in a mess like this. I'm a Shutterbox TP.' She continued, briefly telling the couple about the telepath sisterhood, with how she just sent out a TP 'shout' for help and how her friends had come to her aid. 'I know where we are and how to get out, once your friend Ben comes. Can you call him?'

Pearce walked across the room and activated his implant. He spoke briefly near the palm of his right hand and then nodded satisfaction. 'Ben will be here in about 10 minutes.'

'Great,' said Milla, 'but I think these are going to be 10 very busy minutes. Get ready either side of the door and, if you have any special moves, use them. These guys really seriously mean business.'

The girls released hands. Ruth and Pearce did as they were told, poised and balanced on flat feet with their centre of gravity low. Milla stood facing the door. With a suddenness that shook the other two, she shrugged out of her robe.

'Who wouldn't use a weapon like this?' she asked.

'Now,' said Ruth. The door opened.

The two armed men came in fast, low and deadly. But in the face of Milla's naked body, both stumbled and stood up, wide-eyed and slack-jawed. Pearce took out the second one, sending him through the door with a crunching blow to the throat. The first fell prey to Milla's precise and vicious palm-punch, rammed expertly up into his nose, which snapped bone and punctured the brain. Both dropped like sacks of heavy grain to the floor.

Ruth held the door open, while Milla regained her robe and picked up the gun dropped from her victim's hand. Pearce recovered the other. 'Come on.'

The three ran out into the corridor, the women holding hands as they made their escape. They were free, but free in the midst of an alert and armed enemy.

• • •

Part Four: Under Fire

Chapter One: Out of the Frying Pan

MILLA led the way as if she knew the route from long-earned experience.

'You been here before?' panted Ruth, breathless from exertion.

'No.'

'Then how do you know where to go?'

'Sent schematics by the TP team. You'll have to learn this stuff, Ruth.' Even as they were running for their lives it struck Ruth as incredibly strange to hear her name spoken from her own mouth.

'This is so weird, talking to myself,' said Milla.

'Are you reading my mind?'

'No. But shit, Ruth, it is just fucking weird. Isn't it?'

'Sure is.'

'He's here,' butted in Pearce, 'how do we get to him?'

Milla looked around briefly. 'Down here. Then out onto an open terrace. He should be there.'

Just at that moment Freedman emerged from a doorway, coming directly in their path. When he saw them running straight at him, he reared back and urgently thrust his hand into the shoulder bag he was carrying. Milla's lightning-fast spiralling kick to his head sent him crunching face first into the wall of the corridor. He left a flower of blood spatter where he'd hit, before he bounced and flopped inertly to the carpet. Ruth grabbed his bag, rummaged for a moment, and brought out the third gun of the day.

'I liked him,' said Milla. 'Who would have guessed?'

'Come on,' urged Pearce, 'Where now?'

'Wait.' Ruth turned and trained her gun back the way they'd come. The others followed suit. Seconds later four shots shattered the silence of the corridor and the four men

159

who sped into their gun sights, their own weapons raised, fell motionless to the floor.

'Touch, now,' said Milla. Ruth held out her hand.

'It's okay, let's go,' they said in unison.

'This is getting odd,' said Pearce as the three resumed their escape.

Milla opened a door and a cold blast of air struck her, which made her very aware that she was wearing nothing but a flimsy bathrobe. She was just as aware that her companions were better dressed for the tropics than London this early on a cold, grey spring morning.

'Shit, it's cold,' said Ruth.

'Keep moving.'

A shadowy figure rose up before them and Milla raised her weapon. Pearce knocked it down. 'It's Ben.'

The three ran forward but Ben only addressed Milla. He held out his hand, flat palm up, to the other two. *Stay back.*

'Where's Pearce and what's going on?'

'I'm here,' said Pearce.

'And you are?'

'Ben, it's me.'

'Who?'

Milla chimed in. 'Ben, we need to get out of here. People are dead and others want to kill us. We can explain everything better elsewhere. Let's get in the car.'

Ben looked over her shoulder for a moment, then across the three faces before him. 'I don't leave here till the boss arrives.'

Pearce stepped forward. 'Ben, can we have a word?'

Ben looked at the younger man with caution but followed him across the terrace to the car. Pearce spoke for about a minute. The whole time the girls held hands and looked around wildly.

'Let's go.' said Ben, gesturing the girls forward. Ben sat in the driving seat, Pearce beside him. The girls sat in the back. 'Belt up,' said Ben, just as the far door opened and dark figures spilled onto the terrace, guns raised and firing.

The Lexus dropped from the building like a brick, rapidly gaining speed, and quickly flew beyond the reach of its assailants. After settling the car into automatic, optimum flight, Ben sat back and looked around. 'Okay, what the heck is going on?' He was deliberately polite with his language.

Pearce did most of the talking. Ruth and Milla held hands and tasted what was happening to Ben's mind. Ruth was quietly astonished. It was plain how much Ben loved her; through Milla's talent she could see the emotion. She never knew. Faithful Ben.

Milla had another agenda. *Get this sorted out*, she thought, *or we are simply and royally fucked.*

Pearce was still talking. Milla gripped Ruth's hand tightly. 'Enough!' she shouted. 'Ben, my name is Milla, not Ruth. This tanned lovely is Ruth.' She indicated the woman sitting next to her. 'That is Pearce there,' she nodded.

'I have to tell you why all this is happening, because right now we are like very small people in a very small boat. And the biggest, most dangerous, fish in the world is swimming straight at us with its jaws open.

'I'm sorry, Ruth, Pearce...I think I caused this somehow. My boyfriend Franklyn died in Pearce's body. Now, I reckon, a whole barrel of worms has been kicked open because the Body Holiday Foundation just can't allow that to happen. So now they're after us with extreme prejudice.

'We have to die to keep things quiet; or else we close up a very lucrative revenue stream. Who would be stupid enough to take a chance on death just to earn money by being host to some old fart whose body may kick the bucket while you're in residence there?'

161

The temperature in the car dropped by several degrees. Pearce was looking out of his passenger window with an expression of deep concentration. Ruth was in shock, speechless and pale under her tan.

'Sorry. Present company excepted,' said Milla. 'Shit, it's been a tough day.'

'My horse died underneath me, Ben. Remember? So I said I wanted to try a younger, fresher body.' Ruth leaned forward, her young freckled face seemingly calling the lie to every word, no matter how true. 'This is all my fault.'

Pearce muttered a few words under his breath. The women in the back couldn't hear but they brought Ben up ramrod straight. He looked at the young face sitting next to him. Pearce nodded.

'We have to get back to your apartment. We can be there in minutes,' Ben said. 'We have to sort things out, so you can access bank accounts and keep tabs on business.'

'Remind me, whose idea was all this?' asked Pearce.

'Mine,' said Ben.

'Thank you my friend. It was a great idea, however this turns out.' Pearce turned to look at Ruth. 'Do you agree?'

'Oh yes.' She looked at the girl seated next to her. 'You are lovely.'

'Really? You're just beautiful.'

'Thank you.'

'Are we done now?' asked Ben. 'Because I think somebody just fired missiles at us and I need to deal with it.'

● ● ●

Chapter two: Curved Earth

RUTH was the first to speak. 'Down twenty degrees, right sharp, then over in a loop.'

'Drop and see what happens, dude,' said Pearce.

Ben ignored both of them, flying back towards the tower and aiming at the exact point they had just left. He slowed, acting as if his ass was the most tantalising thing in the sky. Well perhaps today it was.

Missiles smoked in and came close. At the last minute Ben kicked the car away in a curve. The projectiles sped past and erupted against the terrace he'd recently vacated.

Flame bloomed and billowed out as the shell of the sky tower opened and peeled back. A strange, rare bell tone stung their ears, like a guitar string plucked by God. The car bucked in the shock wave. The shape of the tower altered. It buckled and curved out and away from vertical.

Milla was looking out of the rear window of the Lexus when she saw pieces of the sky tower begin to fall. 'We seriously need to get off this planet, or find a place to hide,' she said.

'Can I wait until I have you good people back where it's safe,' asked Ben, 'or shall I just wait till we're all killed?'

Everyone in the car looked back. The strong central cable of the sky tower held true. But the circular building modules, at the epicentre of the explosions, were getting whiplashed around like bangles on a Spanish dancer's arm. Some huge pieces broke away and fell slowly in massive clouds of streaming dust.

Small dark shapes struggled and flickered as they dropped. 'My God, those are people,' muttered Ben.

'Let's go, now,' urged Pearce.

163

The car sped away from the carnage. 'Where to?' asked Ben. 'The apartment is back there under all that mess.'

'We have our implants for communication. Have you got a tablet in the car?' asked Pearce.

'Of course.'

'Then we don't need the apartment.' He looked at the car's dashboard. 'Beach house,' he said in a clipped tone. Nothing happened. 'Beach house,' he repeated.

'Doesn't know your voice, Pearce,' said Ben, then barked, 'Beach house, optimum.'

The car turned and at first seemed to be heading straight back at the dust-plumed wreckage of the stricken sky tower. The cable at its heart was so slender it created an illusion, as if the architecture above the breach was hanging lightly by magic in the air. Only the curvature of the Earth gave a sense of perspective and shocked the viewers' eyes into a realisation of just how immense the building was and how profound the damage.

'Nothing chasing us or firing at us now,' observed Ben, the strain tightening his voice. It was less than half an hour since he'd got the call from Pearce, and now his life was altered irrevocably. He finally got a few moments to realise just how much and to face the possible repercussions.

'Perhaps we should go to the police?' said Ruth, over his shoulder.

'It's an idea,' he agreed.

'Hands,' said Milla. The women sat in silence for several minutes, hands clasped. The two men also stayed quiet, waiting.

'Not the police,' said Milla. 'Something's going on there. My people tell me the Body Holiday Foundation has been in touch and asked to be informed if we contact any of the authorities. It doesn't explain why it wants us but it seems to have strong influence at some of the very highest levels. At the moment nobody's making waves or asking questions.'

The car flew on autopilot for the next several minutes. The seemingly endless grey towers and transport streams of London peeled away above, around and below them. Nobody knew what to say – they just wanted to escape.

After half an hour or so the first traces of greenery began to appear in the landscape and tension in the car began to abate. Ruth and Milla kept their hands locked together and Milla's head nodded as sleep threatened to overwhelm her. Suddenly her eyes flew open and she seemed to be listening to voices only she could hear.

'My people say good luck with whatever we're doing, and do we need any help? They also ask if we were able to steer clear of the terrorist action on London tower today. Body Holiday headquarters was completely destroyed, as were a number of residential floors. Luckily most people were out at work or shopping and fatalities were lower than expected. Oh,' She went quiet for a moment, then continued in a strange sing-song voice.

'Only! How can they say only?' She paused for breath. 'Only some 400 people are known to have been killed. But it's estimated there are about 700 more missing, believed dead. That number may rise. There was some collateral damage at ground level caused by falling debris. Casualty figures there will have to wait until the rubble has been cleared but it's hoped, and believed, the fatalities will be light.

'Another 20,000 people have been evacuated from the levels immediately under the blast. And desperate efforts are being made to stabilise the levels above it and seal the affected floors. Expert help has been called in and the original designers are now involved, one of whom is in his early nineties.

165

'News coverage states that sky towers are designed to withstand airstrikes. Reports about this event would seem to indicate the cause as a simultaneous explosion, of two large bombs or missiles, creating damage unprecedented since New York in 2001.'

She paused, listening to an intimate voice. 'Witnesses are being sought but it's believed that everyone who could say anything with certainty about the cause of the event was within the strike zone of the explosions and killed instantly.' She went quiet and put her head down. Her blonde hair, falling over her features, shadowed them.

'What have we done?' whispered Ruth.

'Survived,' answered Pearce, 'and that is just what we'll keep on doing. Ben, when we get to the house, sort out the programming for this car so it will respond to my voice. Then we'll create access to our accounts and personal Cloudware, so Ruth and I are back in business.'

He looked over his shoulder. 'Sorry, what's your name again?'

'Milla.'

'Okay, Milla, looks like you are on the team. We'll sort you out with passcodes and access. That should be simple, because voice and retina recognition is already in place.'

'How? Oh, of course, stupid of me.'

Ben said, 'We need a plan. We can't stay at the beach house for long.'

'We won't,' said Pearce, his words coming fast and clear. 'We do what we need to do, including grabbing some clothes. We can Quickprint some for us Ruth. Our own clothes probably won't fit and we don't have time for shopping. Milla – you can take a selection from the wardrobes. It doesn't look like Ruth will be wearing any of her outfits any time soon.'

166

'We should be there in about half an hour, allowing for black hat activity,' said Ben.

'We should be okay,' answered Pearce. 'Those missiles did us a favour by taking out the headquarters. You heard what Milla said. Remember, we are not to blame for what happened. It was them who fired at us but they reaped the bonus prize, thanks to your quick reactions, Ben. One of these days we must have a drink and talk about just what it was you used to do in the forces. Anyway, I think we are probably safe now.'

Milla laid her hand over Ruth's. 'No,' she said, 'no we're not.'

•••

Chapter three: Beach House

MILLA wondered why anyone would want to live in a sky tower, if they could be somewhere like this. Even an outer apartment with real windows and a balcony couldn't match the beach house's location.

The building was comprised of four floors, with just about nothing but tinted glass facing directly out to sea. The rooms were built back into a cliff face, mostly with an open plan design, though even areas sealed for privacy enjoyed natural light funnelled through cleverly designed conduits.

Space was broken into comfortable zones thanks to the clever use of living plants, carefully tended by discreet droids. All around her she had a sense of quiet activity, continuous but always just out of sight.

Pearce and Ruth had been scanned by the Quickprint machine, which quietly got on with churning out a good selection of bespoke clothes and underwear. Ruth helped Milla pack. The two bonded even further while they giggled through the wardrobes like old friends, discussing fabrics and the need for comfort during the journey.

Ben took up five minutes of her time, updating her implants with everything she needed to access specially created bank accounts and Cloudware. With something like an echo of her talent, she found herself responding to his gentleness and evident concern. She was also very aware of how he felt about Ruth, thanks to everything she'd inadvertently read in his emotions during that car ride away from London. Ruth knew it too.

Ruth was aching to ask what had happened to Pearce's body, what actually killed him. Milla's greater experience in the use of TP communication meant she was able to quickly find out. While she and Ruth held hands they joined in a comind link, across the talents of a number of colleagues and TP types.

At first the destruction of the Body Holiday Foundation headquarters made information gathering that much more difficult. Many of the minds who could have supplied information to an enquiring receiver had been lost in the blast. But facts could still be winnowed out from peripheral personnel.

He died of an aneurism caused by an already weakened blood vessel in his brain. It may have been caused by excessive exertion; it may just have been his time. Help was available and could have made a difference if it arrived on time. But Franklyn had removed his Mediband and the result was inevitable.

'Why did he take off the band?' asked Ruth.

'It was catching in my hair,' answered Milla.

Old eyes in a young face searched Milla's expression for honesty. Then the young face smiled and Ruth nodded, patting Milla's hands.

When Ruth was called over for a quiet word with Pearce, Milla realised she was in the way. While the other three continued with essential chores, and plans were hatched, she poured herself a drink and walked out onto the sun terrace on the seaward side of the beach house.

There was little sun to be had despite the time of year. Spring had arrived with a face of cold steel. Despite that, the panoramic vista of wide grey rolling sea, under a depthless pale pearl sky, allowed her to breathe freely; in that moment she could dispel deep tensions and assuage fears she hadn't till then been properly aware of.

She sat in a sun-bleached, slatted wooden chair, wrapped up against the chill; while a damp salt breeze coiled around her, hungry to leech away all trace of body heat. She sipped her vodka cocktail slowly, careful not to undermine her reflexes with alcohol but grateful for its bite and warm afterglow. She scanned the empty horizon and enjoyed the rhythmic flow and suck of the sea, its criss-crossing patterns meshing in perfect balance against a gusty soundtrack of wind-muted roar.

She watched gulls get picked up by the strong wind and bent back, to slide reluctantly through the air until thrown away like careless scraps of kite made from muscle, bone and feather. She felt unexpected kinship with them. *Is that us?* she wondered. *We make our plans and scheme our escapes but will blind chance just scatter us to our fate like these birds are scattered by the wind?*

Are we facing forces too strong for us?

She wondered at the way she had been so quickly accepted by these three people she had only met that very morning. They trusted her and she trusted them. They were willing to kill on her say-so, had done so without question. Their resultant actions had killed hundreds, perhaps thousands of people, even blown up a building. Then they'd come here, where she could breathe the salt air, this breath of freedom, with vodka in her hand and wearing clothes that cost more than a month's salary.

Where is my guilt? she wondered. *Why do I feel more alive now than I have ever felt? What about all those people in the London tower?* In her mind's eye she once again saw the desperate, hopeless scrabble of tiny figures tumbling to their death.

'It was self-defence,' came a light voice from behind her. 'Our only other choice was to be killed and we'd done nothing to deserve that.' Ruth came to stand beside her chair and perched her buttocks on its edge. The action was close and personal. It invaded Milla's space but she welcomed the company.

'I've always loved it here, especially out on this terrace,' continued Ruth. 'Pearce let me choose the house and its furnishings but these chairs are his choice. He wanted something that would survive the kind of weather we get here.' She stroked the pale slats, white as bone with a creamy under-colour, a man-made structure and organic at the same time.

'I'm becoming more aware of your talent, Milla,' she said. 'I'm picking things up from Ben and you, something stronger than just feelings, more like certainties. But I'm getting nothing from Pearce.'

'No, you won't,' explained Milla. 'He's in Franklyn's body and it's opaque to TP. That's why I settled with Franklyn in the first place, because we were just like any other couple. I always knew what other men were after, within a few hours of meeting them. And it was usually the same thing!'

Ruth snorted a laugh of understanding.

'But with Franklyn, I didn't know. He was always surprising me with the things he would say and do. It was his idea to be hosts for this Body Holiday thing, you know? No way he could have seen how that turned out. Who could?'

'I'm sorry you lost him because of us.'

'You, why?'

'If we hadn't chosen you as hosts, none of this would have happened.'

'If Franklyn and I hadn't tried to treat Pearce's body as if he were a 20-year-old, none of this would have happened. If he hadn't taken off his Mediband, none of this would have happened. If the Body Holiday Foundation wasn't run by greedy murderous thugs, none of this would have happened.

'Ruth, we can't blame ourselves. All the dominoes had to fall in the right way for any of this to happen. It's just our bad luck that they fell in our direction. If this had happened

171

to some other couples the chances are they would be safely dead by now and over a thousand people wouldn't be crushed by sky tower rubble. But it happened to us, the action dream team, and we took what they threw at us and threw it straight back at them with interest.'

Ruth took both Milla's hands with a smile. Both women froze. Simultaneously they looked out to sea. There was nothing to see, not even a tiny speck on the horizon. But something dangerous was on its way and it was coming fast.

'Pearce, Ben, we have to go now!' shouted Ruth as the women ran back into the house.

'How long do we have?' asked Ben, leaping to his feet.

'Don't know,' answered Milla, 'but alarm bells are ringing loud and clear.'

The threat was airborne. Both women were certain of that much. They shared the information with the men as once again they were running to the car, which, thankfully, was already loaded with all their gear.

Milla hoped she could hold on to her full bladder, which seemed suddenly in need of emptying, long enough for them to reach safety.

'Belt up,' bellowed Ben, as they threw themselves into their seats and he started the engine. The door to the car bay was slowly opening when the earth around them shook and the car was enveloped in flame.

●●●

Chapter four: the Ballistic

BEN responded by flooring the accelerator. To some degree their survival was aided by the force of the blast throwing the car forwards, in a gout of fire. They bulleted out of the car bay, as if shot from a cannon, and landed, tires screeching, several metres from the entrance.

Ben kept his foot down and put the car into a long skid to avoid getting thrown into an uncontrolled spin, or worse a roll. He forgot to breathe while he wrestled the car back under control, the action throwing his passengers around in their seats and bouncing the car off the path and into clinging sand. He eventually fought them to a stop behind a thickly skeletal, wind-sculpted hedge.

'Stay here,' he ordered, running from the car. The other three sat mute and breathless for the few minutes it took before he returned. He kicked the engine back into life and nosed the car away from the scene of the attack. 'I think we upset them,' he said.

'What was it?' asked Pearce.

'Wasp attack vehicle, still pouring cannon shells and scatter munitions into the beach house. Just sitting there, under its rotors, and blowing everything to bits. It might just wake up the neighbours.'

The Lexus climbed, gently following a rough, barely metalled path. Once he gained the proper road on the cliff top, Ben was able to ease the speed up to a respectable 60 klicks before he set auto and let go of the wheel.

'On the road, Ben?' asked Pearce, who was examining the sky with concern.

'I figure they followed us on radar or something like,' responded Ben. 'We leave a less obvious return on the ground if they don't know where to look. I'll take her up when we're out of their immediate air space. We need a town or somewhere with more air-enabled vehicles. We'd be a bit obvious out here, as one of the few airborne signals.'

'Guided by you, Ben.'

'Thanks, boss.'

Milla asked, 'Where are we going?'

Ben turned his seat to look at her, with a long look that said a great deal. Ruth smiled and looked out of her window. 'We need to get as far from here as we can, and as quickly as possible,' he explained. 'The car can take us a long way and needs no fuel to get there. But these people know about it, and it's an obvious target.

'Sorry, we haven't discussed anything with you, Milla. There just hasn't been time, until now. We are heading for St Pancras. From there we will board the Sydney ballistic, the fastest and one of the safest ways to get to Australia.'

He studied her face.

'We have booked you onto the flight with us. We are all in this together. However, if you have somewhere else you'd rather be, we can take you there and do everything we can to make sure you're safe before we leave. I am very much against that idea and so is Pearce. I believe we are all much safer together.'

'The dream action team,' said Ruth.

'Hm?' Ben paused. 'A nice way of putting it,' he responded, nodding.

'Without your help, we would never have got away from the Foundation,' said Pearce. 'Between you and Ruth we have an active alarm system that the Body Holiday people obviously don't understand. And you are good in a fight, obviously trained. I can do my bit, if need be. But I saw what you did back in the sky tower and you are good, very skilled. We need you, Milla, please?'

174

Milla took a deep breath. 'I'm in,' she said, 'but I seriously need a piss. That is, if I can take one somewhere without getting us all killed.'

She had to wait a matter of minutes before Ben could pick up speed on the A38 and then, with sighs of relief all round, stop at services just outside Saltash. All four took advantage of the facilities and enjoyed a quick comfort break before taking the opportunity to gather their wits over coffee. Back on the road it was a full stop-start hour through Plymouth and beyond before Ben finally took the Lexus onto the M5.

Very quickly after that, they left the motorway at the Exeter slipway and followed the ring road to the busy metroramp and then up into the air. When the car soared away from the urban sprawl of the West Country, it was already doing over 400 klicks. London was something less than an hour away.

While they travelled, Ben quickly ran through some details with the other three, making sure they remembered their new identities and had their new passcodes as primaries in their implants. The journey was uneventful, with little more than thermal turbulence at the edges of each giant urban development to break up an otherwise smooth flight. Soon they were gazing out across the seemingly endless panorama of the metropolis, which until very recently had been home.

Milla thought about how mindless this sea of buildings looked, compared with the careful crosshatching of the seaview she enjoyed recently, even though the jumble of buildings sprawled away to mist under the same pearlescent sky.

Ruth indicated the newly unfamiliar silhouette of the London sky tower, which was strangely truncated and still veiled in a pall of dust. Just a matter of hours had passed since the missile strike and here they were again, passing a scant few miles away from the scene.

Automated warning craft hovered all round, their flashing lights indicating detours. Any vehicles approaching the security perimeters too closely were met by uniformed guards on airbikes who calmly but firmly questioned the drivers. Some got sent on their way while others were escorted to a holding area on the ground for further questioning. Ben gave the area a wide berth. The women held hands but could feel no immediate threat.

Once it skirted the wounded tower, the car manoeuvred carefully towards the great bulk of the St Pancras TransCon. Falling into its immense shadow was like driving into night, and a sudden chill swept over the small group.

'The mechanism of the TransCon ballistic is much smaller than it would appear on the surface,' observed Pearce. 'Flights are precisely targeted to five receivers throughout the globe: Sydney, New York, Shanghai, Rio and Johannesburg. Each destination has its own electromagnetic ejector or launcher. They call them that because the word *cannon* has unfortunate connotations.'

He chuckled, 'I've got some money invested in TransCon, one of the best things I ever did. Safe and reliable, never an accident, precision engineering...'

Ruth butted in, 'Why are you telling us all this?'

'Because I've never been on the thing before, and I'm bloody nervous!' He paused before continuing, his voice barely controlled.

'I'll tell you how a TransCon ballistic works. Using electromagnetic fields, the ballistic is fired onto a precise path like a giant bullet. All the passengers and crew are wrapped in gel foam, against the G forces on launch. They're released during the *flight*, before being wrapped up again on *landing*.

'Only it doesn't fly. The crew has no control whatever over the thing. They're just there to check the manifest and make sure everyone is safe in the gel foam. Oh, they also bring round drinks and quick snacks, before carefully clearing up the scraps and litter before landing...' He paused for effect. 'You don't want anything flying around loose when the ballistic hits those reverse electromagnetic fields. It almost comes to an immediate stop.' On hearing him smacking his right fist into the palm of his left hand, his audience flinched.

'Imagine 800 people and their vehicles tucked inside a baseball when it's hit by a bat and then caught by a glove while going at full speed. That should give you an idea of what we're about to do. Except what we're going to be travelling in is much bigger and also much, much faster than any baseball.'

He looked up, bleakly, to take in the towering carbon fibre architecture, with ceramic-metal reinforcements, lowering darkly over his head.

'A lot of all this structure is false,' he concluded. 'The designers figured that nobody wanted to see the truth. Put simply, passengers on a ballistic are fired out of the barrel of one gun and caught in the barrel of another thousands of klicks away. There is no margin for error and no procedure to deal with it if anything does go wrong. Frankly people, knowing all of this doesn't make me feel any better about boarding the bloody thing.'

'And now you've told us,' said Ruth, her voice flat and icy. 'Thanks.'

'Yeah, well,' answered Pearce, 'we might have no choice. But at least we should know what we're letting ourselves in for.'

Milla spoke, her voice tight in her throat: 'But it's never gone wrong, right?'

177

'Never, in over 50 years, backwards and forwards, every few hours like an upturned pendulum on the world's biggest fucking clock.'

'Nice image,' said Ben.

The car dropped, gently, then settled into its place in the docking bay. They were aboard the ballistic.

●●●

Interlude

'We are way out of our comfort zone, boys. Can we cope?' The boss gazed at the smoking ruin of the sky tower on Potter's screen, before allowing his eyes to sweep the darkened room and take in the shadowed forms of his two men.

'Ah-maze-ing!' he said. 'A classic in the making. Do you two realise what we are creating here?' There were shrugs and mumbled responses.

'Our technology is cutting edge but we've had it easy up till now,' he continued. 'Now we find out just what all this shit can do. It's why I pay you the big bucks, boys.'

He reached down and put his hand on Potter's shrinking shoulder. Potter looked at the hand like it was a venomous giant spider or a live grenade.

'Are they going to lose us?' he asked.

'No, no sir,' replied Potter.

'Blake?'

'No way, boss.'

'Correct answer.'

The grin cut like a white crescent moon in the blue-tinged darkness.

'No matter where they go we can match them. No matter how fast they run we will keep up. They can dodge missiles and bullets but we will find new ways to test their mettle.'

The boss's voice took on a triumphant pitch. 'We will chase them to the moons of Jupiter and the ice fields of Saturn's rings. If they crack into the seas of frigid Europa, they will find us waiting. If they hide in the belly of a flaring comet we will follow them, from the very edges of the Sun's corona to the frigid darkness of the distant Oort cloud.'

'Boss, they're only going to Australia.'

'Are they? Do you really think so? Now where would be the fun in that?'

'Well they might do a bit more shagging. That would be prime footage.'

There was silence for a brief moment, followed by a sarcastic laugh.

'Is that all you think of, Potter? Your precious five-knuckle waltz while you lap up the fair ladies in action. Haven't we already got enough of that for flashbacks and reminders? Let's have a bit more of the big picture, Potter. Look at what they've done already.'

With a sweep of his hand the Boss took in the monitors showing frantic sex play, the fraught sky tower, crumpled forms in hotel rooms and corridors, the smoking ruins of the Beach House and the towering bulk of the London TransCon ballistic.

His voice sounded soft, almost caressingly so. 'All that in just three days. Three days! They think they are writing this script. They think they have the whip hand and they're trusting to God while they play it. And they are clever, very clever. They are so very sly. Well so am I! So are we! They think they're the action dream team, do they? Ha! Right, well meet the dream action team.

'We trade in dream holidays. Well, let's not forget that some of the most memorable dreams are really nightmares. When your heart is pounding in your throat, and your mouth is parched dry while your palms are wringing wet, that's when you know you're truly alive.'

Potter said, 'I have nightmares, boss.'

'Do you?' The voice sounded less than interested.

'Yeah, and some of them are really weird.'

Blake groaned and the boss's voice was edged with acid. 'Really?'

'Yeah. Last night I dreamt I was somewhere foreign, with this bloke. I didn't really know him but he was sort of a mate, I guess. Anyway, he did something illegal and really pissed off the locals.

'They dragged him up onto a sort of wide mud-brick wall, where everyone could see what happened next. He was struggling but couldn't break loose. The sun was flat and white like it is in really hot places, with all the shadows black.

'This big fellow, with wild hair and a dark face, took a mallet and, like, a big flat-headed spike. He used the spike to nail the head of a poisonous snake to my mate's shoulder. I forgot, he'd been stripped to the waist. Or did I say that?'

'No, and snakes are venomous, not poisonous,' said his boss, engaged despite himself.

'Well he was. Of course, the snake bit him. And its body wrapped around him, well it flailed about really. It whipped him. I saw the stripes. Then they brought my mate down, off the wall. The poison – sorry, venom, thanks for the tip – must have been getting to him because he began to stagger about and was trembling all over. Convulsing, that's the word.

'They stretched him out on the ground, holding his arms and legs rigid, and pulled out, like, a cross. The dark fellow with the wild hair bent down and sliced my mate's guts right open and with his two hands he held the belly open to the sky. And there he was, in the dust, foam on his mouth, eyes staring and his belly an open wound.'

'And?'

'This old woman walks over, all stooped and muttering. She might have been praying, you know the sound, like a chant? With both hands she's carrying a small cauldron full of the hottest, most wicked chilli ever made. It makes your eyes water from feet away, really nasty stuff. You wouldn't eat it, not with all the soured cream in the world.

'Then, while the wild-haired man stretches that belly open as far as he can, the old woman pours that chilli straight into my mate's open guts. I could see it in there blackening and scorching the flesh. Then she takes a big needle and sews him all up, though the stitches are smoking and the skin peeling from her fingers while she works. They all step away from my mate and his belly's like a red bowl, blistering. The venom is dripping from the wounds in his shoulder and he's writhing in the dust, which is caking across his eyes and mouth.'

Potter looked at his colleagues. 'He was calling me. But, I thought, what if they decide to have a go at me just because I know him? Except, his voice was getting weaker so I went over and said, What is it mate? and you know what he said?'

'No, what?'

'He said I bet this isn't covered in the fucking travel insurance. Things like this never are!' Potter looked at his hands, trembling with the effects of his crystal-clear dream memory.

'Boss,' he said, 'you're a smart bloke. What do you think it means?'

'It means I now have a great idea of what to do with you if you don't get back to work straight away. Get on with it. I've got things to do.'

•••

Chapter Five: Wheels or Wings?

MILLA was relieved when the gel web automatically pulled away from her face and body. Though it had cushioned the worst effects of the launch, during those long, aching moments when the foam had filled her mouth and nostrils also while pressing down on her eyes and into her ears, it had been a torment.

It had seemed to last for long minutes. She wanted to gag but couldn't. She wanted to breathe but a giant hand pressed her back into her seat and compressed her ribs until her lungs were useless. She felt like clay in a press, squeezed until every drop of water was wrung from her crushed flesh. Nevertheless, all the time it was happening, one clear thought stayed uppermost in her mind.

Then it was over and she dragged in a ragged but beautiful gasp of air, whilst opening her eyes to the cool light of the ballistic's cabin.

'40 seconds.'

'What?'

'40 seconds,' repeated Ben, 'The entire launch procedure took 40 seconds. It felt longer but I was counting. I'm surprised they don't lose more passengers during that time but they say never a one in over 50 years.' His smile vanished in the face of her anxious expression.

'Ben, I've just thought of something.' Milla leaned forward to push her face between the head rests of the seats in front. She glanced meaningfully at Ruth and Pearce, then back at Ben. Ruth reached up with her hand, without saying anything, and Milla lightly grasped her fingers.

The sense of mounting danger was becoming palpable, without yet screaming an alarm. Milla indicated her wrist.

'The Medibands,' she whispered. 'We're still wearing them.' She ripped hers off.

Ruth and Pearce followed her example by tearing the monitors from their arms, then pulled at toggles to bring their seats round to face their friends.

Everyone looked at Ben.

'Can these things be used as tracking devices?' asked Pearce, pushing the white band away with his foot.

'Don't see why not.'

'Shit.'

'They know where we are,' breathed Ruth. 'They must do. That explains everything. How they keep finding us. What happens now?'

'Don't worry,' said Pearce. 'We're safer on a ballistic than we were at the beach house. They can't catch us and they can't affect the flight. We have a few hours to plan what we do once we land in Sydney.'

Ben frowned. 'We know they like missiles,' he offered. 'What's to stop them trying a missile attack?'

Pearce shook his head. 'We're going way too fast. Can't catch us unless they try something from space and this thing has great defences to knock space debris out of the way. That should include missiles. The flight to Sydney from London is something over 17,000 klicks and the ship is doing just over 5,000 klicks an hour, faster at the top of its arc because atmosphere is practically non-existent. We should arrive in about three hours or just over.' He shrugged.

Milla looked around. 'But what happens when we get there? We've seen how ruthless they are. Why should we be safer there than we were in the UK?'

Pearce tried to wipe away the numb look of exhaustion that settled across his features. He wasn't used to having his plans questioned and had to fight back his resentment, but he pursed his lips and sucked air through his teeth before continuing.

'Have they got influence in Australia? No idea. We'll find out when we get there. But I have people there I can trust to do as they're told. They've been warned to expect us. Ben has also set up a protective cordon round Sydney TransCon. If I'm betting on anyone, I'm betting on us.'

'Australia is one of the least densely populated first-world countries,' continued Ben, 'and it has TransCon, so we can get to it quickly. We can get away from everything and everybody. We also have secure accommodation where we can rest up and catch our breath. That's why we figured Sydney as the obvious choice for a getaway until we can sort this out for good and all.

'Personally, I can't believe that every police force in the world is under the sway of the Foundation. That's conspiracy-theory thinking of the worst kind. We do have to find someone we know, though, whom we can trust to help. I've got friends in the media I can talk to, and Milla has her police TP contacts. Pearce, you and Ruth have built up a network of business and media people who owe you favours. Some of whom you can count on as friends. Surely, with all that behind us, we can find a way out of this mess?'

'All I know is a time bomb is ticking, somewhere, and we're still in range of the blast,' muttered Ruth. Milla took her hand again. The threat was closer. She nodded her agreement and the solid walls around her seemed suddenly flimsy.

They discussed options for an hour or so, hungrily wolfing down the light meal they were offered and waiting while an attendant carefully tidied away their cutlery and food trays. Milla took time to gaze out of the window, where she saw the darkness of the upper atmosphere give way to a heart-breaking blue as the air thickened and the ballistic began its fall back to Earth. Not long now.

'Excuse me.' Startled, the four looked up at a tall, striking-looking youth in TransCon livery, who had walked up beside their seats unnoticed while they were so deeply engaged in their planning. 'Excuse me, Mr Flagg?' He was looking straight at Pearce, who said nothing for a moment until he remembered his new identity.

'Ah, yes?'

'Sorry to interrupt, Mr Flagg. I was checking the manifest just now and I noticed you drive a Lexus ST270, the latest model. Is that right sir?'

'Yes, it is. You a car buff or something, son? We're busy here.'

'Not a car buff, sir, no. But I do know my manifest, and I keep an eye on developments. Can I ask, sir, your Lexus, wheels or wings?'

'Both.'

'What's the range, sir, in the air I mean?'

'For someone who ain't a car buff, you yap a lot of questions!'

Ben butted in. 'How important is all this...? Sorry what's your name?'

'Goodenough, sir, B. J. Goodenough. Very important.'

'Unlimited range and a honey bucket if things get uncomfortable on long flights. Can batten down for space if needed. We can fly until we starve or arrive at our destination, whichever comes first.'

'Very good, sir.' The youth turned from Ben back to Pearce. 'Mr Flagg, can I ask that you and your party accompany me to your vehicle with some urgency and as little fuss as possible?'

Pearce bridled. 'Not unless you tell me what this is about.'

186

'I can't sir, not here. Please come with me.'

'It's safe,' said Ruth, 'he's safe.'

Goodenough led them out of first class and down by lift into the echoing vehicle docking bay. Their footsteps clattered unnaturally loud in the silence of the bay, uninterrupted as it was by the sound of any engines.

Ruth spoke to the young man. 'It's very quiet.'

'Yes ma'am, I'm told the only thing quieter is a hot air balloon, but I can't speak from experience.'

'I like your name, Goodenough. Must come from an old family, I suppose. Quaker was it?'

The youth kept walking through the serried ranks of passengers' vehicles, all sealed for flight, and quickly led them back to the Lexus while he answered. 'No, ma'am, my mother gave it to me. She was a Chinese sex worker and, as you may know, they were only given first names and numbers.' He said it matter of factly, not looking at her. 'My mother is called Mishi 57. When she became pregnant, she decided her child was going to have a real name. So she saved up enough money to have my name registered on the official lists. When I was born she looked at me and said he's good enough, call him B. J., and that's what was entered on the list.'

Ruth swallowed a smile. 'I suppose that's fair enough.'

The youth looked at her with a raised eyebrow. 'Fairenough? She's my sister!' He continued to the car. Ruth stopped and looked at Goodenough's back. Milla took her hand. When she did so, they at first looked at each other in shock then ran to catch up with their party.

'Whatever we're doing we'd better do it soon,' Milla breathed.

The gleaming Lexus was just a few metres away, when Goodenough finally turned to the group and said: 'Your only chance of survival is to get off this ship. It's dangerous. But if you don't go, you will die with the rest of us. I promise. There's no way out of it. This ship and everyone on it is finished.'

•••

Chapter Six: Tokyo Bound

RUTH was stunned into silence but not Pearce. 'What are you talking about boy?' he spat. 'This is a ballistic. Never an accident. Never a problem. And to my knowledge, never a car taking its leave half way through the trip. This crap stops here. Do you work for the Foundation?'

'What Foundation? What do you mean? I'm just trying to save you. Please believe me.' Goodenough was almost in tears. Ruth registered the way his mouth was working and how his eyes took on a wet gleam. So young, she thought, and every cell in her body told her he was speaking the truth. She touched his shoulder reassuringly but instantly recoiled in horror as his naked emotions washed over her. The youth, mortally terrified and barely controlling his fear, was purely trying to help them, strangers who had a chance of escape.

'Trust him,' she said firmly.

'But...' Pearce turned on her.

'Trust him, while there's still time,' she said flatly. Then she looked steadily at Goodenough. 'Tell them, please.'

'Get your car ready while you listen, please. There's so little time.'

While they worked to unseal their vehicle Goodenough explained how he, alone of the staff on the ballistic, always checked flight details once he was out of his gel web. His colleagues considered him more than a little anal as a result, but he got a thrill from seeing the ballistic's careful curve up and away from its launcher to the very brink of space. He revelled in predicting the brief touch of weightlessness at the apogee of the curve. 'Most passengers don't even notice,' he admitted, 'though some feel a bit queasy.' He would then follow the craft's journey down to its destination.

'On the way down I can enlarge arrival parameters on the screens. You know, watch how it pops into the pocket well in advance. I love the precision – never get bored seeing everything work just right. Only this time it doesn't pop in the pocket. It misses the receiver completely. I think this time it's targeting a retail centre and residential block on the outskirts of Sydney's TransCon complex. And it's going to arrive at full speed.'

'What will that mean?' asked Ben.

Goodenough's voice faltered. 'I've only seen the models, it's never happened for real. But the result of over 8,000 tonnes of ballistic, hitting the ground at a terminal velocity of over 5,000 klicks, will be very similar to the detonation of a small, clean, thermo-nuclear device. Most of its mass will be converted to heat and energy.

'It's estimated that the shockwave alone will bring down buildings to a radius of about two or three klicks. Most people up to a klick away will be instantly vaporised. The TransCon complex is hefty enough to create a brief shadow for those lucky enough to be on the lee-side of the detonation event. It should hopefully cushion some of the worst effects.'

He shook his head as if trying to scatter the vivid images playing in his brain. 'But the inevitable result will be the loss of thousands of lives, perhaps hundreds of thousands. And there's nothing we can do about it.'

'Surely we can warn Sydney?' said Milla.

'They already know. There are alarm systems in place. Even as we speak this ship is being targeted with missiles, in the hope it can be blown down over the sea or at least partly reduced to lessen the impact. But it won't work. We are too large and too fast for anything other than a nuke to be effective. And that would mean the payload would then arrive somewhere as a radioactive dirty bomb. Tough call, huh, so what do you do?'

'Can we take you with us?' asked Ruth.

He smiled. 'Thanks, but no. I'll have to override the bay doors' security protocols to let you out. And you'll need to be going at a good speed to exit safely, otherwise our slipstream slams you against the ship's outer skin and its game over. I can't promise you safety but I can promise it's the only chance you have.'

He paused briefly. 'Are you ready?'

The four nodded. Milla mouthed 'thank you' as her door closed and secured. Ben took the Lexus straight up and held it steady while they watched Goodenough hurry to a seat in front of a small control panel. The youth pointed across to the wall of the docking bay, where Ben could just discern the outline of a substantial portal set flush to the surface.

Goodenough pulled gel foam webbing down over his torso before attacking the controls with lightning-fast touches of his fingers. Ben saw the portal push out from its surrounding wall, then crack down the centre. Everything not strapped down began to eddy and stream towards the opening; some pieces ricocheted from the windows and body of the car. The car began to slide in the air, tugged fiercely towards the enlarged opening by the sucking stream of air. Ben waited, holding the vehicle steady.

'Fuck, no, boot it!' yelled Pearce and Ben floored the accelerator. The car leapt forwards and cleared the doors by scant metres. It was instantly whipped away and backwards, along the massive roaring length of the falling ballistic, before being swept bucking into its turbulent slipstream. Ben fought to leech away the insane speed they'd been lent by the falling ship and clear the Lexus from the clutching, dragging effects of its immense bulk. Then the ballistic was gone and they went from bucketing frenzy to relative calmness, in a matter of moments.

191

'Thank God the atmosphere is thinner up here,' Ben told them. 'If we'd come out further down, we'd probably have burned up. This car isn't designed for that kind of speed. Hey boss, what was all that shouting about back there?'

Pearce answered: 'I was watching the boy. He told us he had to override the protocols to let us out, which is why he couldn't come with us, yes? Well he passed out, I saw him, and I reckon without his fingers on the buttons the doors were about to slam back shut and lock us in. It was then or never Ben, and you did it.'

'Just,' agreed Ben. 'That was skinnier than any skin I know. Teeth are fat by comparison.' They smiled at each other.

Ruth began to cry, wiping the smiles from their faces. Milla took her in her arms and, as she did so, tears sprang into her own eyes. The women hugged and sobbed while the men maintained their silence. Ben looked in the direction of the falling ballistic but it was gone. Not even a diminishing dot remained.

'Bastards,' he said.

'Yes,' replied Pearce, 'bastards.'

For some minutes the car fell towards thicker air, Ben feeling increasing response from his controls. He broke the blanket of silence. 'I need some direction here, please. Where am I going? Just now we are falling. But we're still pretty high up and, from here we can take a good poke at going anywhere east of Europe, quite quickly.'

Pearce replied, 'Japan?'

'Yes.'

'Tokyo?'

'Doable. Take about an hour and a half. We're lucky the ballistic's curve took us within shouting distance of the islands.'

'Sky City then, Ben. We've got an apartment there that shouldn't be in any database. We need time to plan, time to think. We must surely be off the bastards' radar now we've ditched the Medibands. Let's buy some time, enjoy some peace and quiet out of the limelight.

'These bastards have no respect for life and we don't want to put anyone else in the crossfire. There's too much scope for collateral damage every time we stick our heads up. Let's keep them down for a while.'

Ben nosed the Lexus round and aimed for the land of the rising sun.

●●●

Chapter Seven: Effective Limits for Survival

MILLA sat with Ruth and watched the news stream from Australia. It was two days after their fraught escape from the ballistic and they were sitting side-by-side holding hands, a position they took whenever they could. The relationship between the two women was maturing apace and was unlike anything either had experienced before. If it was friendship, it was developing into something beyond mere physicality or intellectual equality. If it was love, it went so deep that neither felt the need to put it into words.

They were in the spacious lounge of Pearce's Tokyo Sky City apartment. Both were freshly showered and each was wearing a crisp linen kimono. They cradled long glasses of cool cocktails but neither had taken more than a sip of their drink. They were too absorbed by the words and images unfolding before them.

After a hectic time of confusion, the news broadcasters were beginning to make sense of the horrific events unfolding less than 48 hours before. The ballistic arrived, striking Sydney like a judgement from an 'Old Testament God' according to some, like a 'cruel stroke of fate' according to others. Pundits were theorising on the causes for the accident, stating that the 'peoples of Earth and beyond were in shock at the sheer scale of carnage visited on the Australian economic capital'.

Goodenough had been right. Desperate attempts were made to bring the hurtling mass of ceramic steel and carbon fibre down over the sea but they all failed. The nuclear option was considered and rejected as an even more dangerous ploy than just letting the ballistic strike its target. The people of Sydney were, reluctantly, surrendered to their fate.

Futile stabs were made at evacuation but with only a scant hour of warning those who tried to flee by road just got in each other's way. The resultant gridlock clogged arterial motorways beyond redemption. The roads came to a hopeless standstill.

Those few who could flew to safety. Most, though, had no choice but to become reconciled to their fate. Many chose to meet death on their knees while others turned to drink, drugs or final desperate orgies of physical pleasure. None of those in the targeted area had much time in which to make peace with their God, their loved ones or themselves. So many plans, so many schemes and so many futures came to an abrupt halt. Communication networks crashed due to the sheer volume of people trying to say their final goodbyes.

Death came with devastating effect. Missile strikes, those that got through the ballistic's automatic defences, succeeded in knocking pieces away from the body of the craft. It was a bad idea; those chunks continued on the same path and arrived at the same time as the main mass, effectively broadening the parameters of damage by creating their own storm of fire from the sky.

The noise of impact was reported hundreds of kilometres from the epicentre, while the dust it raised caused astonishing sunsets and sunrises around the globe. The only visual records of the impact, of any use, came from satellites and space stations. For most observers on the ground, events simply happened too quickly to make any sense.

Some compared the pattern of the disaster to that of a massive bomb blast. Wiser observers declared the impact to be more along the lines of a reasonably sized asteroid strike, although the damage caused by a similarly sized asteroid would undoubtedly be much worse. After all, the ballistic was hollow. Few could imagine just how much worse such a strike could be but the thought sent a shudder around the world.

The time frame to tragedy was short. Once the ballistic hit the ground, everything happened in the blink of an eye. In that brief cluster of seconds, the dreadful cascade of grim events scarred the heart of Australia to its very core.

No one saw the smoking mass of missile-pocked wreckage coming; it was just too fast. Low-level clouds were swept from its path like smoke, just milliseconds before it hit, and an almost perfect hemisphere of white-hot plasma rolled out across the flinching city.

Another of Goodenough's predictions held true, but not for long. The squat bastion of the TransCon complex protected some of the land that fell under its shadow, but only for the few moments before its massive fabric also boiled away. Elsewhere, the circle of destruction rolled out from the strike centre unimpeded by brick, steel or flesh.

Something resembling a mushroom cloud cast its stark shadow across kilometres of crowded humanity. Boiling billows of dust lifted high into the stratosphere then spread for miles on urgent wind currents. The dust brought rain, and whenever the rain fell onto people's property its resultant tan-coloured residue was almost always washed away with frantic haste. So many souls had been incinerated in the initial strike that their flesh and bone had surely to be part of that falling ochre slurry. The thought of that was too much to bear.

The ballistic's crater was gouged over 900 metres across and almost as many deep. It surgically cut through mains services, causing power outages and water shortages across over half the city. It also severed one of the busiest lines of the Sydney Metro, taking away nearly a kilometre of tunnel. Superheated gases spurted down the exposed Metro tunnels. As the gases became compressed in the tunnels they unbelievably became even hotter. Nothing as flimsy as a passenger could hope to survive even the briefest contact with such searing heat. People were wiped away in an instant, erased by a careless storm of blue-white light.

Nothing of the ballistic, its cargo, crew or passengers, remained. Observers said it would probably take state-of-the-art spectroscopic analysis of the glass-like floor of the crash site to recover even the most elemental traces of the huge craft. Carbon in the flesh and bones, of passengers and ground-based victims alike, just added fuel to the expanding globe of red-glazed desolation.

How many died in the initial blast? Nobody knew, perhaps nobody would ever know. Emergency services and rescue workers, coming in from beyond the blast zone, were forced to pick their way carefully through ever-increasing levels of destruction. As they worked their way to the centre of the blast, rescuers found injured and shocked survivors becoming rarer, as did the number of blinded and deafened victims found numbly stumbling their way through the wreckage. The violence of the event was just too immense for the human mind to encompass.

Then they began to find corpses, scraps of human detritus tumbled pell-mell around the shores of what seemed an unbelievable lake of ruin thrown up from hell.

'We penetrated further in, towards the blast centre, and started to find people washed up against buildings like broken spindrift against a sea wall,' an exhausted woman in a dusty and bulky uniform told a sombre-faced reporter. The woman's face and hair were coloured with the same nondescript tan as her clothes. Her shockingly clear green eyes flicked briefly, to camera, then returned to contemplate the blank horror of things no one should ever need to see but were now burned deeply into her memory.

When she opened her mouth to speak, the pink of her tongue and her white, carefully tended teeth looked wrong. It was as if the exhausted, shocked Earth had begun to talk.

'There was a mother and baby. The baby was in a papoose, a kind of sling, you know? She was holding the baby in front of her and it was protecting the mother's chest. That was the only part of her that wasn't flayed away, not burned to the bone. The baby and the mother's faces were fused together, as if she was caught kissing it goodbye. The last thing she did was kiss it goodbye.'

The woman took a long draw from a paper cup, of something steaming. Her tears left big dark splotches on her uniform. 'Excuse me,' she said, getting to her feet. 'Things to do.' She crushed the cup and threw it down onto the rubble-littered pavement.

'Litter lout,' she said to no one in particular. 'Someone will need to pick that up.' She drew a deep breath and walked steadily back to her work. For a few moments the camera followed her departing back then turned to frame the reporter, who looked somehow shockingly clean and neat. With a sweep of his hand he indicated the fractally shattered ruins of his immediate skyline.

'It's hard to imagine how much worse this can get,' he said. 'We are just over 300 metres from the beginning of what rescue workers have begun to call the iris of impact; the crater is the pupil.' In fact nobody involved in rescue work had time to come up with anything of the sort. They used practical terms like 'further out', 'further in', 'impact site', 'effective limits for survival', and 'how did this fucking thing happen – anyone know? *Someone* should know.'

The reporter's immaculate face was replaced by aerial views of devastation, while his clipped, trained voiceover continued: 'The pupil is the impact crater. It is scoured clean of life and the heat of impact has melted the soil and bedrock like glass. In the iris zone we estimate thousands of victims have lost their lives in this catastrophic accident, perhaps hundreds of thousands.'

The camera was back on the reporter's face. It zoomed in until his features filled the screen. 'But was this an accident? TransCon has been plying its ballistic trade for over 50 years, with never an accident in all that time. Are we meant to believe that its luck just ran out, and that this bloody carnage is the dreadful result?'

He shook his well-tended head before continuing. 'Or...is this horror really the result of deliberate sabotage?' The camera came even closer. 'A spokesperson for TransCon indicated today: the company is looking closely at the idea that its computers have been hacked by an extremely sophisticated program. If so, it is just possible that this tragedy will prove to be much more than a terrible accident.'

His eyes became glittering slits and his voice sharp as cut crystal. 'Have the bloody fingers of cyber-crime killers deliberately sent an innocent ballistic and all aboard her to their fiery deaths, and in doing so wreaked flaming murder across a peaceful city? What would be the motive? Is all this tragedy a sick political statement or the result of some hate-fuelled vengeance? Or is it something even more sinister? Is this unthinkable destruction actually some kind of business ploy? Who would benefit most from the demise of the lucrative ballistic trade?'

His voice now became barbed and weighty in tone. 'Whoever it is, their days are numbered. Of that they can be absolutely sure.'

He gave his name and signed off.

The women switched to other channels, hoping to hear more about the possibility of a hacker. Both of them were pretty sure they knew the truth, but what could they do?

Where could they go? What if what had happened to the ballistic was really nothing to do with their escape from London but rather some dreadful and unlikely coincidence?

The Japanese news channels made much of the aid being sent from its mainland to the stricken Australian megapolis, though recognising it would be slow getting there. The quickest routes had always been via TransCon ballistics from Shanghai but now that avenue was closed to them – nowhere to land. And it was becoming increasingly obvious that few passengers would be willing to risk a ballistic flight following the unfolding nightmare.

Milla and Ruth held hands closely, sweat mingled between their palms. *Safe*, the talent said. *Safe*. But were they? Were they really?

● ● ●

Chapter Eight: Making Firm Plans

RUTH watched the bloom of yet another unparalleled sunrise spread across the Eastern horizon, with the dust from Australia high in the atmosphere lending its poignant touch to the dawn of a new day. These breathtaking sunrises would continue to mark the catastrophic events in Sydney, until time washed the last of the dust from the sky. Until then, the sun would be born each day into a lake of blood.

Its rays warmed her face, minutes before illuminating even the tallest buildings in the cityscape stretched out below her. Since the advent of fusion power had ended the reign of fossil fuels, the vistas open to any viewer became clear and sharp and their colours bright. There was no trace of the oily sepia blight that once smeared even the most remote horizon. Though the population of Earth was greater than would have previously been thought possible, the air was cleaner than it had been for millennia. Ruth was a blissfully ignorant child, born under a clean sky, and she had never known anything different.

Even from her position on its rim she couldn't see down into the shadow cast across Tokyo Under, by the great white disk of Tokyo Sky City. However, she was aware of how reflectors, carefully designed and directed, were even now washing clear daylight down into its crammed streets and avenues.

Some years before, she allowed Pearce to take her for a trip into Tokyo Under and was astonished at the cleanliness and order she found in what must be one of the most densely populated places on Earth. The people of Tokyo Under were drawn to the place by one of the most magnetic forces known to mankind – wealth. Wealth brings work and Tokyo Sky City was inhabited by great wealth.

201

It had been created over two hundred years before and featured many architectural details picked out using natural materials, something become increasingly rare and expensive for most recent buildings. Ruth ran her hands along the smooth natural wood that topped the railing around the apartment's balcony. The rail had been polished and smoothed by many hands before hers and, though its pale blonde character seemed as fresh as the morning awakening around her, she still felt their touch down through the years.

This was the only balcony in the apartment and for very good reason. Some sacrifices had had to be made to balance the living space to weight equations during the original design.

Sky City hovered hundreds of metres above Tokyo Under, the only such permanent airborne structure ever built. It was one of the seven wonders of the modern world, matched with sky towers (all of them), the 'even greater' wall of China (which now really could be seen from space), the Hilton hotel at the base of the thick Antarctic ice at the South Pole and The Falls Restaurant built under the thundering curtain of the central Niagara cascade.

The Pyramids of Giza and Stonehenge added gravitas to the list; and though some still believed these ancient stones had been left as messages, by an alien race more advanced than current-day humankind. Others smiled at the idea and waited for some kind of proof.

There were as yet few signs of life beyond Earth's atmosphere – other than fossil bacteria on Mars and a curious, yet scientifically fascinating, genera of aggressive mobile plants swarming across the sea bed of distant Europa (an actively volcanic ice-bound moon orbiting the great gas giant Jupiter).

There was now quite a lot of human activity around Saturn's rings. These iconic planetary features proved to contain some of the purest water ice to be found anywhere. Mining it for human consumption was big business. But despite all the activity beyond the asteroid belt few spacecraft approached Europa, and the exploratory drones sent there were programmed to land, report and remain. Who knew what would result from the introduction of truly alien species of bacteria to the Earth? By common consent caution was deemed the best option, at least for the time being.

Many thousands of people were plying their trade off-planet, much of which activity reinforced Pearce's fortunes, and advances in technology brought the furthest reaches of the solar system within touching distance.

Ruth wondered how people out in space could live, without ever seeing the achingly beautiful blue of the sky. She wondered how they could accept their permanent exile from Earth, once time combined with low gravity wrought its inevitable physiological changes. Some moon or planet-based outer-worlders might be able to return, with difficulty and careful support, but most off-worlders became outcasts from the home planet.

This far-reaching train of thought, which had little to do with the dissipating wisps of shell-pink dawn melting in the vast sky before her, had been set in motion during a conversation over dinner the evening before. Pearce talked about making firm plans, in the event that the Body Holiday Foundation had survived the missile strike on the London tower and, perhaps, had even been behind the Sydney disaster.

'We have to act as if we are still firmly in their sights,' he said. 'We need to make exit plans, to go where they can't touch us. We seem to be okay here, so far. You girls aren't sensing any threat but neither of you felt anything before we boarded the ballistic, and look what happened there.'

'It has to be an imminent threat, Pearce,' explained Milla. 'There would be no point in knowing we are vaguely in danger sometime in the near-ish future. The psychic alarm is triggered by a kind of standing wave of mortal danger. We pick it up just before it spikes, kind of on the lower slopes. That warning should give us a clear opportunity to get out of the way. Unless, of course, we're trapped in a ballistic screaming towards certain destruction, that might well cause unforeseen complications.'

'Sorry, Milla,' replied Pearce. 'It would be useful if your talent was a bit more predictable, I admit, and handy if it gave us a bit more warning. But we probably wouldn't be here at all without you and that makes you aces with me. Both of you.' He looked from Milla to Ruth and back again.

He continued, 'Ben and I have been looking at our realistic options. If Tokyo gets compromised, which it just might, where can we go next without getting royally screwed by the bad guys? Ben, over to you.'

'Boss.' Ben collected his thoughts. 'We have a few options open to us. We stay here until we know whether we're safe or not. That's number one and I quite like it. It gives us a chance to finish protecting our new identities, something I've already started on. What I've done already, while we were at the beach house and since then, was pretty tight but I left a few loose ends and they needed tidying up. Most of that is done now. So staying here is good.'

He took a sip of his wine, nodded his appreciation then counted off on his fingers: 'Option number two: we stay on the move, keep one step ahead of them. Perhaps even get another car, something more robust. We don't know how much of a signature they have for the ST270. I think they've been tracking the Medibands, because they completely ignored me at the London tower until I had you three on board. Then they started throwing missiles. It's possible they haven't a clear picture of the Lexus but, if they're still out there, do we want to take that chance?

'Option three: we have a facility off-planet that is totally secret and completely mechanised. Even the people who built it don't know where we put it. We can go straight there, from our launch pad in Namibia. Frankly, I can't think of anywhere safer than space. People say it's getting more and more crowded, but that's just bull. Everyone living out beyond the atmosphere even now would easily fit onto the Isle of Man, and they could still safely run the TT races around them without risk to life or limb. Space is a big place. We could vanish completely, like ghosts in the morning.'

He paused for another sip then said, 'The Foundation would just have to wonder if we died on the ballistic or crashed trying to escape. Either way they'd be out of our hair. We'd be able to research them and plan ways to get back at them, if we want to.'

Ruth broke in, her head spinning. 'But hang on. If they think we're dead already, and remember we left the Medibands under our seats on the ballistic so there's no reason they should think otherwise, why are we worrying? And, if it was some sort of business coup that crashed the ballistic into Sydney, how do we know a fully operational Foundation even survived the missile strikes in London? We could be making plans to fight an enemy who's already beaten. What if it's us running away from ghosts and not them chasing us?

'Ben, Pearce...what if we're already home safe and just jumping at shadows?' She spread her hands. 'I really don't know if I can take much more of this. I want to wake up in the morning knowing that I will be sleeping soundly and safely in my own bed come nightfall. I am not a fugitive, damn it. I've done nothing to deserve this.'

She took a breath, fighting incipient tears. 'And what about Milla? The more I've got to know her, the more I see a brilliantly complex and wonderful woman. She's lost her home, her job, her identity and even her body. She's lost her youth and, let's not forget it, she lost her boyfriend just a few days ago. She sits there wearing a brave face but I've felt her pain. I *share* her pain. So do we really want to take away her sunrises, her summer days and winter snows? Do we want to take away her rain? Because that's what running to space will mean. No more fresh breezes, no more walks on the beach. Do we really want that, do we?'

Milla stood and walked round to where Ruth was sitting. She crouched down and hugged her hard. Ruth felt tears begin to come, even while part of her was checking for danger in the talent.

'I can live without sunrise if I have to, Ruth.' Milla's voice was catching in her throat. 'But I'm not sure I can live without you. If space means life I embrace it.'

Standing in the glow of the day's strengthening light, the following morning, Ruth felt her vision blur as her eyes were once more made brilliant with tears, and she smiled. She quickly walked from the balcony to Milla's room and knocked firmly on her door. She opened it and put her head round, expecting to see her friend's head on her pillow.

The room was empty.

●●●

206

Chapter Nine: Are you Awake?

MILLA was feeling guilty. A cascade of events had left Franklyn dead in Pearce's body and hundreds of people killed in London. Who knew how many had lost their lives in the ballistic strike on Sydney? The past few days had seen her lethally defending herself against Body Holiday Foundation operatives and somehow surviving attack after attack by the very skin of her teeth. She should by rights be feeling physically and emotionally wrung-out, morally exhausted, a borderline nervous wreck.

A Shutterbox TP develops a defensive skin against her more invasive kin. She also learns to see into her 'self' with utter clarity, examining motivations and reactions with razor sharp integrity. Milla had to admit to herself that she was feeling guilty because she was enjoying herself, very much so.

Her senses seemed heightened by danger. She revelled in the freedom allowed by the concept of 'kill or be killed'. A lot of dark matter lay behind her crunching strike at the gunman's nasal bone as he came through the door back at the Foundation's headquarters. And she bathed once more in remembered pleasure, when she felt that crunching bone driven back into the man's brain. He was dead before he hit the floor. *Good.*

With Ruth and Pearce she found a family she could relate to even more than her TP sisterhood. Also more than her parents, whom she knew were embarrassed by her unexpected differences and what had happened with her grandfather. No, strike that thought, they were embarrassed by what her creepy grandfather had tried to do to her but still they blamed her for it. As if being young, attractive and female was some sort of crime.

She wondered what mum and dad would have made of how she looked now and the things she'd done with the old man by the swimming pool and in the apartment's bedroom. She'd never been like that before with anyone – *never, never.* She shut her eyes and replayed the urgent, out of control physicality of sex acts she'd performed just days before; acts that set this whole train of events in motion.

She was still confused by her actions with the old man. Milla had never been overly inhibited. But in every other sexual encounter she was always aware of the quiet observer at the back of her mind, watching and judging her partner, all the way from the very first curious touch to the final sweaty conclusion.

Something else had happened at the swimming pool and afterwards. Something broke open inside her and released a torrent that swept her out of her comfort zone into a dark, exciting and mindless place. An animal place.

Yet still, right now, she felt like a gleeful child on an impossible adventure and she didn't want it to end. She was living the glamorous lifestyle Ruth and Pearce took for granted, except it was like a dream for Milla. And there was no reason it should end. After all, Ben and Pearce thought they were safe.

The Medibands were still on the ballistic when it struck Earth, so the men reasoned the Foundation had to believe they had all perished in the super-heated explosion. Yet would they? There wouldn't have been any signals from the bands, for the last hour of the journey, so the Foundation could well be suspicious and still be on the lookout for the escapees.

She'd raised her concerns with Pearce. He dismissed her ideas, asking if anyone would really believe it possible to escape a ballistic in mid-flight. The speed alone would render it all but impossible. If he hadn't been part of it he wouldn't believe it himself. True, without Goodenough's sacrifice they would all be no more than a molecule-thick smear across part of the glass-like surface of the Sydney blast crater.

Pearce still wanted to explore options raised by Ben and he still wanted to maintain caution until safety was proven and they could relax. Yet, in his heart, he thought they were home clear. He would start to lay plans against the Foundation, as soon as he put some practical ideas together. For now, they should all relax and enjoy Tokyo.

He'd grinned at her in a way Franklyn never had, then said, 'Milla, I'm going to introduce you to baby octopus, so fresh it will wrap itself round your tongue.'

So what happens now? The four of them had newly created identities. Mr Flagg and his group perished in Sydney, so Ben activated other names and histories. Pearce was still fully in control of his business empire and fortune, thanks to Ben's help. Ruth had already changed Milla's original hairstyle to something a little less Bohemian, while Milla loosened up Ruth's patrician formality. Only Ben remained as he was, all apart from a name change, and even here he kept his first name. He was still Ben, and Milla was pleased about that.

And Ruth had finally assuaged Milla's curiosity, when she admitted that, yes, she had once shared an apartment in old Paris with Pearce. And, yes, she would sometimes perform her exercises naked. Funnily enough, she also pointed out that quite often if the exercise became more rigorous she would have to wear a support bra.

When Milla told her about the scene in the Virtuo window and the effect it had on Franklyn, Ruth didn't know whether to be flattered or offended. She had no idea the film had been made.

When she and Ruth held hands to make an alarm sweep, there was no apparent threat. Yet, opening the Shutterbox eye laid more than impending danger before its gaze. Though the women still failed to sense anything from Pearce's mind in Franklyn's TP-opaque body, they were both warmed by the concern and care that shone from Ben. That, and so much more.

Ben. More and more her thoughts turned towards Ben. Suddenly decided, Milla took a deep breath, slipped a robe over her shoulders and slid her feet into her slippers. Under the robe she wore nothing more than a tee shirt that barely preserved her modesty.

She gazed at her reflection in a tall mirror by the door. She supposed she would have to get used to seeing the tall curves of this beautiful blonde creature looking back at her. However, she also recognised something of her own impish features in the mischievous smile tugging at those perfect lips.

She slipped across the lobby to Ben's room and knocked gently at the door, letting herself in without waiting for an answer.

'Hello, Ben. Are you awake?'

The bed was untouched and empty, while the wall lights were lit. She looked around. Though the room had a warm feeling about it, the décor was a little Spartan and decidedly male. Her heart was in her throat; he wasn't here. She had just began to turn, in order to leave, when the bathroom door opened, issuing a cloud of steam. Ben stood silhouetted by the brighter light behind him.

The towel he was wearing enhanced the narrowness of his hips and the breadth of his shoulders. He was towelling his hair into a mop of short, tight curls. She couldn't read the expression on his shadowed face.

Opening her lips to speak, she couldn't think of anything to say. She let her robe drop to the floor and stepped out of her slippers. She moved towards him.

He said, 'Milla, this is so unexpected.'

Then she kissed him, hard.

●●●

Interlude

'THEY can't really think we've finished with them, surely?' Blake's voice stuttered with barely suppressed laughter. 'We don't let them off the hook that easy.'

'They might,' mused Potter. 'I tell you, they're putting us through one hell of a chase. I thought they were going to lose me after London, let alone what happened in Sydney.'

'That was genius, dude. You kept right up with all of it.'

'We have the technology. You hear what the boss says – we have the technology so we might as well use it.'

'Hey look, the Ruth girl is getting jiggy with the home help.'

'Man, I would change places with him in a heartbeat.'

'She's going hardcore on his ass.'

'What's her name?'

'Milla. Where's your head been?'

'Just keeping up with the action, man. What do names matter when a woman has an ass as sweet as that? Just look at her. I wouldn't know where to put my hands. I'd want to touch everything at once and taste it too.'

'Looks like he's taking your advice, Potter.'

'A moment on the lips then plug it deep in her hips.'

'Shush now, I don't know where you get it from.'

'Are the others doing anything?'

'Not now, sleeping like babes.'

'Then bring some extra viewpoints to bear on these two.'

'Will do.'

There were a few moments of silence while the two technicians swiftly changed viewing angles to better record the couple on their screens. Milla was increasing her pace astride Ben, whose dark hands were splayed firmly around her buttocks. His mouth was ranging from her nipples to her *mouth and back again. The pair began panting and emitting small groaning noises.*

Milla was gazing at Ben's face, an almost quizzical expression in her eyes. His eyes were shut, his mouth a stretched rictus. Corded tendon stood proud of his throat. Then, almost as if surprised by her climax, Milla shut her eyes and shuddered, while arching her back. Ben slipped out of her and an arc of seed splashed up her belly and breasts. She took him in her hands and pumped him until he quieted. Then she stretched full length against him and tasted his lips with her tongue before resting her head on his shoulder, her hand still gently working.

The two men in the darkened room finally remembered to breathe. Potter's main monitor featured the long-fingered pale blonde, her hand absent-mindedly stroking a length of darkly engorged penis. Blake framed pale pink-nippled breasts against a broad dark chest, and a tangle of sweat-drenched blonde hair curled in loops, to frame a perfect child-like woman's face.

This was when the technicians earned their crust. Anyone can aim a sensor or point a lens at a man and a woman coupling and hope for the best. But that would merely capture the act of sex. These two were obsessed with framing beauty.

Their subscribers belonged to a very expensive, invitation-only channel of exclusive erotica and more. They wanted much more than they would find by downloading amateur footage, of which there is plenty, or even watching recordings from Skinfests.

Potter's and Blake's creativity was fuelled by dream and vision. Their light didn't reveal performers and expose them to stark, unedifying view. No, they caressed and delineated them, presented them as visual poetry for the watcher's hungry gaze.

213

Potter was almost certainly sociopathic. But his psychotic mind threw horror into his dreams, rather than let him run amok with an axe amongst his fellow men.

It was his eager pleasure to share his dreams with any colleagues who would listen, often in stupefied admiration while his baroque fantasies took shape. Potter's dreams could probably earn a lucrative following all of their own. But his banal phrasing precluded his entry to the canon of imaginative fiction and instead his dreams fully informed his expert camerawork.

Despite his fantasies of bloody violence, Blake slept the sleep of the just, uninterrupted by even a hint of Potter's personal horror show. He was a pedantic perfectionist and his creative psychosis demonstrated itself by a genius for detail. His screens glowed with high-definition 3D and his speakers with sound designed to fill the Grand Canyon, let alone a cathedral.

Separately, these men were masters at their craft. Together, they were a unique talent. Ever since Ruth, Milla, Pearce and Ben got in front of their sensors, they had been able to craft exquisite scenes of such erotic purity that they would have tried even St Anthony at his most pious.

Even so, neither of them would be welcome as an entertainer at a child's birthday party.

Blake crowed, 'Ding ding, here we go. Seconds away, round two.'

At his post, mouth drooping open, Potter began to dribble onto his new waterproof keyboard.

●●●

Chapter Ten: Tokyo Under

RUTH was relieved when her friend came out of the bathroom and gave her an easy, relaxed smile despite being naked.

'Nothing you haven't seen before,' said Milla while spreading her arms.

'True enough.'

'Give me five, and I'll join you for coffee and a bite. I'm famished.'

Ruth watched Milla as she climbed into her underwear, pulled on a pair of blue jeans and buttoned up a crisp white blouse. She slid her feet into expensive, vat-grown leather sandals then ran her hands through her hair. She was wearing neither make-up nor lipstick. She looked fantastic.

'Ready when you are.' Something in her friend had changed since last night. She seemed perkier, almost jaunty. A smile played around her mouth and her eyes sparkled. Even her step was lighter than before.

Milla looked at her as they walked. 'Do you miss it?'

'What?'

'This.' Milla indicated her body. 'Being you.'

'I haven't had time to really think about it. Do you miss this?'

She looked down at the pert, coltish body she took such joy in.

'Not really, but then I'm not as striking as you.'

They reached the kitchen and ordered coffee and scrambled eggs with toasted ciabatta, continuing their conversation while their food was prepared. Milla said, 'I went for a walk to the mall on my first day in this body. It was my first taste of what it's like to be truly strikingly beautiful. People couldn't take their eyes off me. Men even followed me. It really got to me, you know? I couldn't wait to get back to privacy and away from all those eyes.'

'I think you're lovely,' answered Ruth. 'Don't put yourself down. I bet if we went out now for a walk, you'd attract just as much attention as me. You're younger and just so incredibly pretty.'

Milla pointed at Ruth's face. 'Pretty enough, though you look back to front because I'm used to seeing me in reflection.' She pointed at herself. 'Beautiful, so much so I almost fancy myself.'

The women laughed and ate their breakfast. There was no sign of the men. Ruth thought they had gone off to sort out some business matter. 'Why don't we do it?' she asked conspiratorially.

'What?'

'Go for a walk. Go down to Tokyo Under.'

'Are you kidding?'

'Why not? There aren't any monsters down there anymore.'

'Monsters?'

'You know, like in the old movies. Men in rubber suits tearing down toy buildings.'

'Sounds dull.'

'Pearce loves them. He's a bit of a movie buff when he isn't doing business or planning menus.'

'You two are good together.'

'Yes, yes we are.'

Half an hour later the women were sitting in a crowded floater and drifting down towards the heart of Tokyo Under. Ruth found herself explaining how they were still in daylight thanks to what were commonly described as light sails, despite being slung beneath such a massive construction as Sky City. Then she explained how Sky City hovered precisely over Tokyo Under.

216

'The designers wanted something even more reliable than nuclear fusion,' she said, 'so they used something that can be depended on no matter what happens to fuel cells or the world economy. Solar power.'

Milla looked up at the massive floating bulk of Sky City which, due to the effect of the light sails, was beginning to melt and merge into the blue background of the sky. 'You're joking, right?'

'No. Did you notice on our original approach Ben had to go round Sky City rather than over the top, which would have been more direct?'

Milla nodded and shrugged. 'I didn't think anything of it.'

'Well there's a good reason for the detour.' Ruth leaned closer, her voice dropping even as her eyebrows rose. 'Above us, in space, a cluster of huge dedicated solar panels collect the Sun's energy. Reflectors bounce sunlight to the panels when they move into Earth's shadow They are geostationary, miles up, and can't be affected by earthquake or weather. Tokyo has been subject to earth tremors in the past, some of them quite severe. Anyway the energy the solar panels collect is processed into a microwave beam and targeted to a massive collector at the heart of Sky City. It keeps the City in the air and also supplies power to Tokyo Under.'

'A microwave beam?'

'Ah, yes. A microwave beam. The technology works and has done for decades. The science was proven before the framework for the city was built in space then lowered into place on the same impellers that keep it in place even now. It isn't anti-gravity, that doesn't exist yet, nor does it affect anything under the City.

'The microwave beam is every bit as intense as you might think. Nothing must fly through it. If you did you

217

wouldn't break the connection to Sky City or anything that drastic. But the beam instantly vaporises anything it touches. Have you noticed how few birds there are around here?'

The floater landed and its passengers walked down steps to Tokyo Under's meticulously clean walkways. Ruth and Milla were too deeply engrossed in their conversation to be aware of the intense scrutiny that followed them down the street.

Milla looked up at an apparently flawless sky. Sky City was there, she knew it was. But it was rendered invisible by its clever array of prisms and reflectors. 'It sounds really dangerous, Ruth,' she said.

'Not at all, Milla. It's tried and tested. It works.'

'Isn't that what everyone said about the ballistic?'

In silence the two women headed for a mall where they hoped to enjoy a little retail therapy and grab a coffee and perhaps a pastry. Milla's pithy observation dampened both their spirits briefly but they soon rallied and began to enjoy the day.

Perhaps an hour later they found a patisserie they both liked, ordered coffee and lemon tart then took a seat towards the back of the room. They began to feel increasingly exposed to the gaze of people around them and Milla was once more reminded of her experience in London. Ruth took her hand, planning to reassure her and instead they both instantly sat up, fully alert. There was danger coming their way and, whatever it was, it was going to happen right here, right now.

● ● ●

218

Part Five: An Unfortunate Slip

Chapter One: Always Fear Sharp Suited Men in Tokyo

MILLA looked around the café using Ruth's borrowed talent. Both women were tense, their nerves stretched like violin strings. 'Down!' gasped Milla and the two ducked just as a 20/20 jack whirred at high speed over their table and ricocheted off the mirror behind them, missing them by centimetres before rocketing around the room and back out the open door.

A flying jack, while not dangerous to life, could cause bruising to skin and worse if it hit an eye. Most players tried to avoid what they called 'bystander strike' in order to keep play legitimate, but even so the game was banned in enclosed spaces.

Whoever fired that jack into the café was either stupid or deliberately dangerous.

The two women sat up and found themselves suddenly confronted by the broad smile of a slender young Japanese man, seated uninvited at their table. He had taken his place while their attention was diverted. He was dressed in the height of modern fashion, his glittering jacket was zipped from knee to throat and its fabric streamed moving images and lines of Japanese text, which seemed to coil and play around his torso.

His mop of jet black hair curled up from his scalp and down onto his brow. He was good-looking in a pampered, cat-like way and the fact that he knew it was stamped plainly across his every gesture.

'That was a narrow escape,' he said in almost accentless English. 'It would be a shame to see such lovely faces damaged by a flying jack. You were lucky to duck just in time.' He spoke through white smiling teeth but his eyes were appraising them coolly, judging.

'Your reactions must be extraordinary,' he continued. 'Most people cannot see a jack coming in time to avoid it.' The smile widened a touch. 'But then just looking at you both would tell anyone how extraordinary you are.' He gestured: 'The light angel and the dark, how brightly you shine in this darkness.'

He looked around and as his face fell briefly into shadow, Milla stiffened.

Ruth was looking away, already bored with the glib boy. In her time she had heard just about every variation of chat-up lines known to man (and most of those known to women). Nothing new here.

Then she heard the nervous acid in Milla's voice. 'Who asked you to sit here? Who are you?'

'I'm sorry,' the boy purred. 'I am Richard Tagaki. My friends call me Rich. Rich by name and generous by nature. I would love to find out more about you both. May I treat you to lunch? I know the finest places. Better than here.'

He rapped on the table top and looked around again. His face once more fell into shadow. Milla flinched by Ruth's side and took her hand. There seemed no sense of threat but Ruth became very aware that Milla was clearly disturbed. 'No,' Milla said quickly, rising to her feet and gesturing for Ruth to do the same. 'We have to be going.'

Tagaki also stood. He took Ruth's arm but she pulled away. He looked crestfallen. 'But dear ladies, I would love to show you around my proud city, and perhaps I could introduce you to some friends up in Sky City, who would also love to meet you. Nothing seedy,' he said to their retreating backs, 'just some celebrated fashion editors and photographers.'

As they left the café he raised his voice in a last-ditch effort: 'I could put you on the opening pages of the best magazines, and you would be very sought after. I could make you famous.'

'If only you knew, buster,' breathed Ruth, 'if only you knew.' She looked back at the café to make sure he wasn't in pursuit, then shook her head. 'What a creep.'

She looked at Milla who was frowning and seemed distant. 'Don't do that dear,' she said. 'You'll give me worry lines.' She smiled but the look on Milla's face dashed the smile from her lips. 'What is it, Milla?'

'Let's get out of here, please – let's get back up to the apartment.'

'Of course. We can be in a floater in just a few minutes. What's the problem?'

Milla stumbled as she hurried along the path. 'Didn't you see?'

'See what?'

'That man, that Rich creature...' She paused, searching for words. Then, as if spurred by a dreadful memory, hastened on her way.

Ruth quickened her pace to keep up. She said, 'You should always fear and avoid sharp suited men in Tokyo, they say. But he was just an egotistical boy. He was a slimeball, sure, but nothing to be scared of. I've been approached by men like that all my life. Just shrug him off and forget him, I say. Don't let him ruin the day.'

'I don't think you've ever been approached by a man like him before, I really don't,' said Milla. She was determinedly silent for the remainder of their walk to the floater terminal, and looked anxiously out of the window of their craft until its doors closed and it took gently to the air. She released a breath.

222

'What is it, Milla?' Ruth's youthful, lightly freckled features didn't suit the grave expression she wore. Milla looked around the floater to see if anyone was listening in on their conversation. Once again the two striking women were drawing sly glances from other passengers and they were receiving more attention than she felt comfortable with. Somehow Ruth's habitation transformed Milla's face and figure into something even more attractive. And Milla simply couldn't shake the ingrained radiant glamour that clothed the body she now wore.

It was stupid to think they could go anywhere or do anything without being noticed, but that was just the lot of beautiful women. She was learning to live with it. Most of the time. But who was that dark creature who approached them in the café? Who and what was Richard Tagaki? What she saw in the shadows of his face filled her with dread.

Milla shivered and cold sweat prickled her armpits and trickled down her spine. She locked eyes with Ruth, took her hand and stretched the talent as far as she could. Something was coming; clouds were gathering on a distant horizon. Yet here, on this floater rising up to dock back into the slowly emerging structure of Tokyo Sky City, they were safe.

So what had she seen in the café? What did it mean?

Perhaps it was true about sharp dressed men in Tokyo: you *should* always fear them. Even if he wasn't necessarily a man.

• • •

Chapter Two: Need to be More Careful

PEARCE raised his voice in disbelief. 'How could you do that? How could you both go swanning around in Tokyo Under, as if we didn't have a care in the world? We didn't know where you were or what you were doing. It's just thoughtless risk taking.'

Ben joined in, his deep steady voice more measured. 'You need to be more careful, ladies. We can't afford to let anything happen to you. Either of you.' He remembered at the last minute to look from Milla's face to Ruth.

Ruth was very aware that Ben's attitude to Milla had changed over the last 24 hours, and she had a pretty good idea why. She wasn't sure how she felt about it. There was no precedent for what they were living through. If Milla and Ben were taking comfort in each other's arms, it was none of her business. Though, what was going to happen if they ever reclaimed their own bodies?

She thought: *write me a protocol or design me an etiquette for this social behaviour. Why don't you?* Through lidded eyes she watched the lovers' interplay of covert glances. She felt a growing closeness and depth of play between one of her oldest and her newest friends. She decided to worry about it later, if she was ever back in her own body, but wondered at the psychological complexity of just what Ben was feeling and doing.

Who is he really making love to when he lays down with Milla embodied as me? What is he feeling? And why is Milla so careful to be back in her own room in the morning? Is she feeling guilty? Does she worry about hurting me? Or is she just protecting her privacy?

Ruth loved both of them too much to want anything other than happiness for them, but this relationship of theirs was going to mature into a tangled cat's cradle of hurt. Of that she was sure.

Her attention was tugged away from her thoughts and back to what was being said.

'What was wrong with his face?' Ben paced in front of Milla while Pearce stood arms akimbo.

'It was wrong,' answered Milla. 'It was just wrong. He looked okay in the light but when he turned his face into the shadow he was, like, his face looked...hollow...it freaked me a bit, well a lot actually. I mean what was he?'

'There was no sense of threat,' said Ruth.

'No, no. None,' agreed Milla, 'and the talents working because we saw the jack coming, or we knew something was coming, and we got out of the way. But I've never seen anything like Tagaki. In the shadow his face became hollow and had kind of greenish lines, where the eyes and mouth should have been, like a drawing done with a laser. Then he came back into the light and he looked solid as you do. I can't explain it.'

'Hologram perhaps?' thought Pearce aloud.

'Did you touch him?' asked Ben.

'He banged on the table firmly enough and he touched my arm,' answered Ruth. 'I had to pull away. He felt like flesh to me.'

'He was creepy. No, look, it really spooked me when I saw how his face changed,' said Milla. 'I clearly saw it twice. I just can't explain it.'

Pearce was looking at her with doubt, Ben with concern. Neither seemed convinced but Ben seemed prepared to give Milla the benefit of the doubt. Ruth butted in: 'I saw how Milla reacted. She was genuinely scared by what she saw, and we know she doesn't scare easily.'

'That's true,' agreed Ben.

Milla looked from one to the other, gratefully.

Pearce raised his hands in the air then let them fall by his side.

'Okay, okay. Milla saw something weird,' he breathed. 'Let's agree on that. But this is Japan, they do weird shit here all the time, and they are amongst the cleverest people on the planet.

'I bet Tagaki was just wearing some kind of new face cream that only shows up in the shadows and makes glowing lines out of his features. I've never heard of it but I wouldn't put it past someone here to come up with it. Kids would love it.'

The effect of Pearce's words was palpable in the room. Milla started nodding as he spoke and looked as if a dark curtain had been pulled from her eyes. 'Yes, that would do it,' she smiled for the first time since leaving the café. 'I am so stupid. I bet people are wearing the glowing cream all over Tokyo but we just didn't notice.'

'Pearce, you are just too smart sometimes,' said Ruth, laughter in her voice. She fetched drinks from the cooler and handed them round. She raised her glass. 'To face cream,' she said.

'To face cream,' the others agreed, touching glasses together with a slight clink.

'I am just so gullible,' sighed Milla with a rueful smile. 'Why didn't I just ask him why his face was doing that?'

'Too familiar,' answered Ruth. 'He was a creep – why ask him anything at all?'

'That's true,' agreed Milla.

Pearce's theory cleared the air and relaxed the women, setting the scene for what was to develop into a thoroughly enjoyable, if somewhat alcohol-fuelled evening. And, for each of the two couples, an equally enjoyable night.

Milla was grateful to Pearce for his fast wit and pragmatic attitude to even the strangest events, and to Ben for what was rapidly becoming a very deep relationship.

Of course Pearce's highly plausible theory was completely wrong.

•••

Chapter Three: The Birthing Stone

RUTH stumbled nakedly through the concealing bushes and held her protruding belly in as tight as she could, while she pushed her way through the narrow opening into the cave entrance. She followed a dark passage until it opened out into a round cavern, at the centre of which was a carefully tended pile of sweet burning logs.

The smoke from the fire was drawn away and lost in an up-draft towards the blackened ceiling. The air in the cavern was sweet but scented with smoke.

She became painfully aware of the baby moving, straining inside her. Her distended belly thrust out before her, looking even larger in the cave's flickering firelight. Her black shadow, thrown onto the lichen spotted stone wall, looked almost akin to a fertility talisman from race memory: great belly, swollen breasts, prominent buttocks and a small, almost negligible, head.

The movement of dancing flames made her pregnant, bloated shadow float and quiver across the walls, even as she hunched over her increasingly urgent spasms, which were building to a muscle-wrenching climax. Her baby began to fight its way out towards the smoke-scented air.

Ruth panted and, battling to slow her panicked breath, rallied her strength to meet these final moments. She stopped, momentarily transfixed, as a long thick-bodied cave snake rippled across the beaten earth floor towards her. Blind and pinkly translucent the snake tasted its way through life, tongue flicking in and out.

It swept past her, barely touching her bare feet with its sleek muscular length, then rose up and thrust itself into a tight cleft in the rock wall close by her hip. Even as the last inches of its tail slid away, out of sight, another powerful contraction brought Ruth to her knees. *They* came to her then, the old ones, and they laved her belly and vulva with warm oils. They shaved her vulva smooth and kissed her face and breasts. That is where things began.

In the red firelight her heavily pregnant body glowed with fertile grace, in stark contrast to these stringy old ones with flat exhausted dugs, sagging creased bellies and bushes of cobwebbed shadow topping their bowed, mottled thighs.

These are the old mothers, she thought. *These are the knowing ones, ancient in knowledge, their sinewy desiccated bodies depending from clay masks, first fashioned in the early times and patched countlessly over many hundreds of years.* The daubed patches of clay smearing their masks further dehumanised the withered creatures who gathered around her. Yet their confident movements helped calm her mounting fears.

The old mothers muttered, hummed and twittered, voices rustling like the rasping scales of serpents. They brought with them a fetid air of faeces, stale spices and old leather, which overlay the gentle perfumes in the soothing oil. Their touch was papery, light and dry, somehow, despite the amount of warm oil they worked into Ruth's tautly bloated belly.

The waters came gushing then, hotly flooding down her thighs and over her feet, and the old mothers hissed, prodding and pushing her towards a long curving stone smoothed with centuries of use. The Birthing Stone.

Apart from newborns, and they always forget, only mothers and incipient mothers have ever seen this place. It was forbidden to men, boys and virgin girls. It was sacred to the act of birth, to the emergence of new life. These stringy old mothers were handmaidens to Eostre the spirit of life and birth, Goddess of the sacred cave, wife of the everlasting fire.

229

The dark shadowy spaces around Ruth took on a sparkling life of their own. Blue lines made them seem somehow hollowed out, or like unfinished sketches. The same was happening to the old mothers' masks. Like a clever illusion, it entranced her for a moment. Then a powerful contraction brought her straight back to the matters at hand.

Ruth tried to lie back on the Stone but the whiskery old voices castigated her. Light practiced touches manoeuvred her round into a kneeling position, knees apart, and pushed her forward until her forearms were slotted into polished grooves and her hands gripped the time-rounded edge of the Stone.

The pain of the birth lessened somewhat, though the urgent peristaltic contractions redoubled. She pushed harder and felt a sudden release. But it was just her bowels emptying. The mothers cleaned her then prepared the floor between her knees, for the child's delivery, by laying down soft mosses and fine dry grasses.

As she moved back and forth, pushing and pushing, her highly sensitised nipples grazed the Stone beneath her, making her thrust up away from its abrasive touch. That was enough to finally bring a rush of redness and weight, falling away from her and down into the carefully laid nest.

The mothers whispered with a happy sound like dry leaves in a breeze, like the voices of leathery wings. They gathered the child and hustled away, leaving just two masked attendants to deal with the placenta and once more clean Ruth's body.

One of the two carried the placenta away reverently, while the other took Ruth's hand. She dipped the hand into the blood between Ruth's thighs and then made her press it against the flat wall beside the Birthing Stone. As she did so Ruth realised with shock that the whole wall was dappled with hand prints, streaked and overlapping palms impressed with maternal gore layered so deep its surface was cracking and so old it was faded in areas. Ruth was a mother touching the hands of mothers over millennia, perhaps even longer. The act stopped her breath and touched her heart.

The old mother brought a clay bowl of warm water and helped Ruth clean herself with fresh soapwort to wash away the sweat, fluids and blood. She then presented Ruth with a gown of fine white material, woven with red threads and detailed with silver runes. As she pulled it over her head, Ruth smelled all the other mothers who had worn the gown before her.

She was surprised when she pulled the gown all the way down and her breasts fell out of a specially designed panel cut in its front. The old mother nodded and twittered reassuringly, handing her a short cape to drape around her shoulders and preserve her modesty. After what she just experienced, Ruth was confused by her shyness but perhaps as a new mother she now needed a sense of decorum.

The old mother led her, trembling with exhaustion, to a low-seated, tall-backed wooden chair carved with animals, fruit and vegetation. She sat, and within moments her baby was brought to her and placed in her arms. With its head laid against her under the demure cape Ruth felt the baby begin to suckle, heard its greedy sighs and gasped as it did so. Not until that moment did she truly realise what had just happened. She was a mother, this was her child, and its toothless gums were clamped to her in need. Under the cape her fingers found the soft down of the baby's cheek. Its need to feed overrode her desire to see her child. She wanted to give now, not take.

The emotion flooding through her at that point was unlike anything she had ever known before. It went beyond love to a place in her heart she had never found before, deep and fiercely protective. She almost crushed the baby to her beating heart, wrapping it tight in her enfolding arms, wanting it to feel her love and know she was its mother.

There was sadness too. Ruth knew she could never again be her own person, never be truly care-free. This little creature feeding from her would, from now on, require constant attention and care.

The old mother who took away the placenta returned with a plate piled with scraps of pale cooked meat. She offered it first to Ruth and then the other old mothers. They lifted their masks and ate solemnly. Ruth chewed the metallic-flavoured protein and swallowed it before realising what it was. There was no place for a meat store in this cave. She had just eaten a piece of placenta. She fought the sudden rising gorge in her throat and forced a smile. *It must be alright*, she thought, *at least I know it's fresh*. She smiled and the old mothers whispered and clucked around her.

The baby released her teat and sighed, sated. It breathed a tiny belch. It was now time to see what this brand-new intimate little stranger, who had ridden into her life on a scarlet flood, actually looked like.

She lifted her child out from under the cape and gazed for the first time at its tiny pale face.

Her scream woke her and Pearce beside her; it even brought a concerned Ben and Milla bursting through the bedroom door.

●●●

Chapter four: Baby Talk

RUTH took a moment to come back to herself, warm and safe in her comfortable bedroom, and shook off the last clinging strands of her dream. The others were throwing concerned looks and questions at her but they might just as well have been using the incoherent rustling clicks and whispers of the old mothers. She needed time to recover her wits and stop her body's involuntary juddering. The dream had been so detailed, so logical, so real, it was hard to shake it off and climb back up to reality. Even so, a part of her mind was working just fine and that part was focused on Ben and Milla.

Despite her trembling confusion she noted how dishevelled, hastily dressed and bedewed with sweat they both were. Also, they arrived at exactly the same time. Her previous vague presumptions about their deepening relationship anchored down into firm certainty, though she decided she would worry about it another time.

'Sorry,' she said. 'It was a dream, just a very strange dream. It rattled me, that's all. Please, go back to sleep all of you.' Ben and Milla made cursory protests. Milla wanted to make sure it wasn't the talent's alarm sounding and warning of imminent danger but she quickly surrendered to Ruth's protestations. She left after receiving a kiss on the cheek, a brief hug and the promise of a good girlie chat in the morning. Ben, trailing mutely behind her, closed the door with a firm click.

'Girl's got Ben's cock in a noose, I'd say.' Pearce was looking at the closed door with pursed lips and a glint in his eye. 'He's following her around like a new pet puppy.'

'You saw it too?'

233

'Saw it, smelt it, almost tasted it. I like both of them a lot and I wish them well, though this sure complicates things.'

'Hmm?'

'Ben's had the hots for you forever, Ruth. I've known it for some time. He's rubbish at hiding it but it's you in that body he wants. And now he's getting plenty of your body by the look of things. But there's nothing in there of you. Problem is that fine body has a new tenant just now, and that complicates things. So just how are things going to pan out, if those two develop a real relationship and you girls manage to switch back?'

'Ben will just have to wake up from the dream, same as I just did.'

'Of course – your dream. Noticing what was going on with those two drove it clean out of my mind. I'm sorry, Hon. You gave me quite a start there when you woke up screaming. I tell you, I was nearly halfway to the car and ready to run for it! Do you want to talk about it?'

Ruth did. Pearce fetched them both a drink from the room's cooler and they sat at the table in the window bay. Her gaze flickered from the endlessly moving streams of red-lit traffic criss-crossing the Tokyo sky to the intense handsome young face that disguised her husband.

She told him of the cave, the fire and the snake. She detailed the old mothers' preparations, the Birthing Stone and the bloody network of hands across the cavern wall, an ancient maternal mosaic of blood and tenderness. He shook his head in awe when she described the mother's gown with built-in boob access. 'I'd like to see that,' he chuckled. 'What an imagination.' He winced when she told him about eating a piece of placenta, while allowing that he had heard of it happening even in civilised society.

As he rose to refresh their drinks, he offered, 'It's meant to be quite nourishing and helps rebuild the mother's strength after the sheer exhaustion of the birth. I think I heard that animals do it. But what was it that made you scream?'

She told him of the suckling child, how she felt about it all. 'I was there, Pearce, it was my child. I knew I had to care for it. I loved it. I got my head wrapped round it and the sweet little sounds it was making. When it took my nipple in its mouth it created a short-cut straight to my heart in a way that nothing else has ever done. It touched the deepest most secret part of me and I felt complete like never before.'

Her hands were trembling as she took a deep draught from her glass. She gazed out of the window at the orange streams of vehicles across the darkened sky. So many firelights in heaven, she thought, so many children loved by mothers and so many secret hearts touched.

There was a catch in her throat, something stinging in her eyes. Pearce said nothing; he just sat waiting, giving her time to put her story into words.

She took another healthy sip and another. 'We've never talked about children, Pearce. I've never thought about it before now. Well, maybe in passing but never with the raw ache I felt in the dream.'

She rolled the glass in her hand, emptied it and fetched two more. Any more alcohol and sleep might claim her again, right where she sat, but she felt she needed the booze to fuel her tongue. 'Then the baby finished suckling and I thought it was time to say hello. I brought it out from under the cape and looked straight at its little face.' She paused,

'It was me, Pearce.'

She pointed at the door. 'That me, the one Ben is probably playing hide the cave snake with right now even as we speak. She was a tiny yet perfect me, complete with tits and hips and everything, like a living Barbie doll. Tiny little fingers with perfect nails perfectly polished. Perfect tiny

235

eyelashes beautifully mascaraed, perfect white teeth. I hadn't felt teeth while she was suckling but there they were.'

She gulped her drink, her movements a little wild. She was fighting for control. 'Then I realised, the only thing I had ever given birth to was me. It was me, in my secret heart. I'd made that short-cut years ago when my parents did what they did to me. I realised then, I had to love myself because nobody else would.'

She indicated her body, looked down, hiccoughed and giggled. 'I mean when my parents did that to her, to me, to her now, the poor bitch. Why does it have to be so fucking complicated?' She indicated the door again. 'Her out there, probably fucking Ben's eyes out, God bless them both. But my bastard parents, they took something essential away from their young daughter all those years ago.'

Pearce sipped his drink. Something was coming, he knew, and it would be worth waiting for. The Freudian aspects of Ruth's dream hadn't escaped him, though considering what they'd been through over the days since their abduction from the island, he wasn't at all shocked by Ruth's epiphany.

'That's what woke me up. When my eyes opened and I realised the truth I screamed. That scream was a scream of utter rage you all heard. I suddenly realised they'd not only taken my body and my childhood. They took my chance of motherhood as well.'

She tapped herself on the chest and nodded, looking at Pearce with sly complicity, her dark mass of curls flopping over her forehead. 'But that's okay, because you see I'm this me now. I'm her and she's me. I've got my youth back and so have you.' She chuckled with drunken glee. 'We've pressed the biological reset button, Pearce. So I'm asking you, what's to stop us making a baby, Pearce? We've read the manual and we've done the training.' She chuckled again. 'As of tonight, I've even had some virtual experience of giving birth.'

Her eyes were big as fluorescent pearly light washed over the couple from the full moon that had been inching across the sky as she spoke and now flooded through the window. It cast a translucent radiance into her eyes, an ethereal otherness into her face. Pearce was sure she never looked more beautiful than she did just now.

'What about it, Pearce? Why don't you and I make us a baby?'

•••

Interlude

'DREAM sequence? She had a fucking bizzaro, your fingerprints all over it like a rash. Dream sequence? Give me a break.'

With the boss out of the room Blake once again adopted the mantle of authority; a position never formalised but tacitly understood between the two of them. It's true, Potter was some kind of technical genius and his set-ups were things of beauty. The only thing you could be sure about, when Potter was at work, was total surprise. But, and it was a big but, he needed guidance or he'd swing way out of control.

On the quiet, Blake was a little in awe of Potter. But Potter needed a firm hand, a guiding hand, and when the boss was away Blake bellied up to the plate.

'Care to explain what you were up to, Mr Dream-meister Potter?'

'That cave thing was just so cool man, I loved it! Giving birth like a dog, with her tits rubbing on the ground. And she shit herself first! I didn't see that one coming! So awesome. I nearly shit myself in sympathy.'

'You didn't send it?'

'No way, how could I man? I was so busy watching what she was doing, the camera had to practically take care of itself. That vision was complete man, it was layered, iconographic. She should dream professionally, I tell you. We just have to stay tuned to her frequency.'

'You have to have been involved. The mothers' bloody handprints; that snake thing. Even the blue tracery in the shadows. All of that is just so your signature, Potter.'

'I don't copyright dreams, dude. Everyone has them, even you. But no, you don't do you. Anyway, not my play this

238

time. Ruth Hudson is more than just a fine figure and a walk you should set to music. She's a woman, all woman, and she's hurting way down deep.

'Now, if the snake was venomous and bit her. Or the old ladies had knives and slashed her up. Even if the snake raped her or did something really nasty, you could look my way and I'd put my hands up. In her dream all it did was disappear down a hole like Alice, not even subtle symbolism. Are you calling me for that?'

Blake said nothing, just turned back to his monitors. Still nothing happening. Ben and Milla were asleep in his room. Their earlier exertions, though interrupted by Ruth's scream, had slaked their passions for the night. Each took a shower, kissed deeply and thoroughly, then retired to a dreamless sleep.

Ruth and Pearce sat like sculptures cast in silver-blue alloy, gazing at each other. The air crackled between them. Then, as though obeying a silent command, they stripped in the moonlight and coupled with an almost animal fury. Despite all the energy they were putting into the act, it was strangely un-erotic. It had intensity beyond the usual sexual bonding; it was more akin to a frenzied ballet. Blake couldn't resolve what was happening into usable material. He sat and watched for a few minutes in frustration then turned round.

Behind him Potter was creating angles that highlighted the otherworldliness of the scene. In his monitors the conjoined lovers glistened and flowed, hard bodies splashing against each other like ice cold yet still fluid lava.

'Beautiful,' Blake heard him say. 'Mother's bloody handprints on the wall. Just beautiful.' Blake wondered what it was like to be in Potter's mind, what it was like to have his eye, his imagination.

239

Then he shuddered – no, not worth it. *He turned back to his screens. He couldn't make the art like Potter but he could edit some sense into it. He downloaded the scenes from Potter's monitors and started work. The pain he always felt between his shoulders, when he worked these long hours, intensified.*

●●●

Chapter Five: Morning Glory

MILLA was still fast asleep when he woke with an erection. He didn't know at first if it was a reaction to the firm peach-scented flesh of his sleeping woman or the urgent signals coming from his bladder. Morning glory jutting stiffly out, as if sniffing the air, and he knew exactly where he wanted to plant it again and again.

But first an urgent call to be answered. He got quietly out of bed and crept to the bathroom, where he held his stiff cock and brokered it down until he was finally able to have a welcome piss. The water was strong and yellow. He took some time to have a freshening shower, warm water washing the sweat of the night's exertions from his skin and hair. His body was hard trained and lean with wide shoulders. He felt he was a better partner for Ruth's honeyed beauty than the old man had ever been, even if he was now coupling with Milla in Ruth's flesh.

His cock may not have had the majestic length and thickness of the old man's but it was enough to pleasure a woman. For the right woman it could offer repeat performances, and that was more than the old man used to manage. Mind you, he chuckled, these days the old man was younger than him.

Or so he thought.

He heard a sound, turned, and through the misted glass of the shower cubicle saw Milla perched on the toilet, urinating while watching him as he showered. She patted herself dry with a small wad of paper, flushed the toilet then joined him under the shower. The cubicle was just big enough for two grown people to be intimate, if they didn't mind pressing happy flesh against flesh.

They didn't mind.

241

Later they were cleaner, fresher, and enveloped in gentle post-coital languor, sitting in thick white robes and hunched over big mugs of hot strong coffee. Milla swept the hair from her eyes and looked quizzically at Ben. 'When we do that, who are you fucking?'

He was taken by surprise, 'Hm?'

'Me or Ruth?'

'You, of course.'

'Are you so very sure, Ben? I mean, this is Ruth's body and you've known her for quite a long time. I can't blame you for fancying her, after all she's quite a babe. I just need to know. Be honest, is it me or her? I won't mind.'

'You, it's you all the way. Ruth is lovely but she has never been impish like you. She is some kind of woman, yes indeed, but she has a seriousness about her that plants her aloof from the rest of the world. Pearce has a similar quality. Those two fit together like pieces of a puzzle.

'But you, Milla, you have mischief in your eyes and dimples in your cheek. You even put dimples in Ruth's cheek. How do you do that? You bring freshness to that flesh you're clothed in, like I've never seen before. And I have to say, it's a welcome change.'

Milla grinned, displaying those dimples, and came round to sit on his lap. 'Thank you. And you know what you were saying, about how Ruth and Pearce fit together? Well it's funny but there's something familiar about how we make love, like I've known you before somehow. Do you know what I mean?'

Ben's eyes looked momentarily veiled as if he was searching for the right answer to her question and thinking furiously about it, then he nodded. 'I know what you mean. You know I thought it was just me. When we're together it feels like I'm home, it just feels so right. It's a cliché but it really is like we're made for each other. Is that stupid?'

242

'No.' Milla snuggled her head against his shoulder, wafting faint coffee breath against his cheek. Then she asked in a quieter voice, 'What happens when Ruth gets her body back?'

'Will she, do you think?'

'Isn't that the aim, in the long run?'

'I don't know – is it possible?'

The couple remained quiet for a few moments then Ben stood up, lowering Milla back onto her feet. He said, 'Just now I really don't know if we're safe enough, here in Sky City, to even be thinking about transferring you and Ruth back into your own bodies. Can we even do that, without the Body Holiday facilities? We are apparently off the Body Holiday radar, just now. But how long will that last?

'My priority is to keep you three safe and keep myself alive, while I'm doing it, no matter what gets thrown at us. And our attackers have proved very resourceful. God only knows what they'll do next. But, Milla, I can't explain it except what's happening here between us is unexpected and beautiful and very welcome. I'll think of the right word in a minute but survival is our principal goal. And believe me, I want you alive and with me more than anything else in this world.'

The kiss they shared was completely different from anything they'd done before. It was deep and warm and intimate, and seemed to last for long ages. Then at last it ended with a quick swipe of Milla's tongue against Ben's lips, and their touching lips stretched into broad smiles. 'I think that says more than any word you could think of,' Milla breathed.

'I think you're right,' agreed Ben. 'Come on.' He continued stroking her flank with a proprietary touch she quite liked. 'We need to get dressed. I don't know what the time is but Pearce was talking about us going to Kyoto today, to see the temples and try shabu shabu in a restaurant he knows or heard about from somewhere.'

When the couple walked into the living room, some minutes later, it was unoccupied. The kitchen was also vacant. So they just made more coffee and sat by the apartment's balcony sipping their brews in companiable silence.

'Glorious,' said Ben.

'The view?'

'Us.'

Milla shook her head, with a chuckle. 'Pre-ordained.'

'Don't be daft.'

Despite everything, it was still only 9am when Pearce and Ruth joined them for breakfast and the four made plans for the day. Each couple sensed a change in the other and secret smiles were exchanged. Whatever Ruth had been up to, last night, her dimples were very much in evidence this morning, thought Milla. *Why, she's positively glowing*, thought Ruth.

All too soon the smiles would be swept from their faces. But not just yet.

● ● ●

Chapter Six: Kyoto in spring

RUTH was the first to see Mount Fuji, its snow-capped peak barely shrouded with thin clouds. The lower flanks of the oddly symmetrical volcano were crowded with buildings but it still stood high and proud against the clean blue of a perfect spring sky.

'I can see why a primitive people would worship such a thing,' observed Pearce, as the scene flashed away and out of sight.

After breakfast the four had taken a floater down to Tokyo Under and then boarded the famous Kyoto Express, the latest incarnation of the iconic Bullet Train. Smooth and quiet, as only the most superbly engineered vehicles can be, the express flew the 364 klicks non-stop, from geographical capital city to cultural capital, in just 45 minutes. A brief slow stretch gave passengers their passing glimpse of the sacred mountain.

One of the world's great tourist destinations, Kyoto boasted ancient temples, excellent restaurants, lush parklands and geisha girls in traditional costume. In late spring cherry orchards were heavy with blossom and beggars, dressed like mediaeval peasants, bowed to tourists and handed out blessings in exchange for money.

Pearce observed how the geishas' stark white faces and precise, red painted lips made their teeth and eyes look oddly dark and unhealthy. 'Not a natural look at all,' he said.

They took a horse-drawn open landau to the city's old quarter where they walked the crooked narrow streets to the Kiyomizudera temple, a pile of great gabled roofs sweeping out from its massively braced wooden legs. It loomed above them like a spread of great dark wings, over sacred orchards of milky blossom.

245

Pearce read from the guide: 'Kiyomizudera, which means literally Pure Water Temple is one of the most celebrated temples of Japan. It was founded in 780AD on the site of the Otowa waterfall, in the wooded hills east of Kyoto, and derives its name from the fall's pure waters. The temple was originally associated with the Hosso sect, one of the oldest schools in Japanese Buddhism, but formed its own Kita Hosso sect in 1965.'

He allowed his voice to become sing-song: 'Kiyomizudera is best known for its wooden stage that juts out from its main hall, 13 metres above the hillside below. That's where we're standing guys. The stage affords visitors a nice view of the numerous cherry and maple trees, below, that – and I quote – erupt in a sea of colour in spring and fall as well as of the city of Kyoto in the distance. And so it does.' They all agreed. Pearce continued.

'The main hall, which together with the stage was built without the use of nails, houses the temple's primary object of worship: a small statue of the eleven faced, thousand armed, Kannon – the Goddess of mercy.'

Around them the Japanese took photographs of each other and themselves, planted directly in front of their lenses like grinning pointing children and almost completely blocking the view. *Why do they bother going anywhere?* wondered Milla. *They could take pictures of each other at home.*

Ben and Milla swung the great wooden beam to sound the prayer bell and each made a wish before moving on. It was Ben who pointed out how many of the younger Japanese had strangely hollowed-out faces in the shadows, much to Milla's relief. A little later Pearce spotted an ad for 'Ghost Face' cream. 'Well I never,' said Milla. 'You were spot-on.'

They next visited Sanjusangendo, a temple in eastern Kyoto famous for its 1,001 golden statues of Kannon.

Reading from the download to his implant, Pearce explained how the temple was founded in 1164 and rebuilt a century later after the original structure was destroyed by fire.

He continued: 'At 120 metres, the temple hall is still Japan's longest wooden structure. The name Sanjusangendo, literally *33 intervals*, derives from the number of intervals between the building's support columns, a traditional method of measuring the size of a building. In the centre of the main hall sits a large wooden statue of a 1,000-armed Kannon, flanked on each side by 500 statues of human sized 1,000-armed Kannon standing in ten rows. Together they make for an awesome sight.'

'Very much so, and they did all this without computers or printing. That truly is awesome,' said Ruth. 'The 1,000-armed Kannon are equipped with 11 heads to better witness the suffering of humans, and with 1,000 arms to better help them fight the suffering.'

'They haven't got 1,000 arms,' said Ben. 'I count...hang on...42!'

'Ha,' mused Pearce. 'You have to subtract the two regular arms and multiply the remaining 40 by the 25 planes of existence to get the full thousand.'

'Twenty-five planes of existence,' laughed Milla. 'We're having enough trouble with just this one. I couldn't cope with sorting out another 24.'

'Yes, well, at least we'd have more options, for places to hide, if we need them,' offered Ruth.

Later that day, after the sun dipped below the horizon the shabu shabu meal proved to be everything Pearce had promised. Tender thin slices of beautifully marbled raw beef were wrapped around a selection of vegetables then one by one, using long chopsticks, plunged into a seething cauldron of boiling water set into the centre of their table. They then dipped the stuffed meat into bowls of sesame sauce before placing it in their mouths.

Apart from Pearce, the group were a little tentative about their first mouthfuls. But once they realised just how delicious the meal was, they quickly became adept at the art of 'select, wrap, seethe, dip, chew and swallow'.

All too soon the meat and vegetables were gone and the little group looked quite crestfallen, until Pearce called over a young waitress. She was prettily dressed in traditional costume, though without full geisha make-up. All four friends appreciated the smiling, bowing girl's fragile, almost porcelain-like beauty, and her musical yet incomprehensible sing-song chatter.

She deftly skimmed away the scum from the surface of the liquid in the cauldron before adding more vegetables to the broth, stirred for a few moments then ladled it out into bowls and handed them around. The soup was flavourful without being too rich and, served as it was with small cups of blood-warm sake wine, it completed the meal perfectly.

Afterwards another short trip in an open landau, the night air chilly against their alcohol-flushed faces, brought them back to Kyoto station and the Bullet Train to Tokyo. Within 15 minutes they were relaxing in their seats and on their way while luminous ribbons of light flowed past their windows, the only sign of the murmurous and ubiquitous advertising which streamed across the night dark Japanese landscape.

On the crowded floater back up to Sky City, the day came close to being ruined. An anonymous commuter took advantage of the standing room only situation and slipped his erect penis between Milla's mini-skirted legs, then began rubbing it against her thighs. She pointed out to Ben what the man was doing and he had her duck quickly to one side. The punch he threw was fast, hard and accurate.

When passengers vacated the vehicle on arrival at Sky City, they left behind a bemused floater operator. Scratching her head she wondered what to do about the unconscious man she found crumpled on the floor of her vehicle with his flaccid cock drooping out of his gaping pants.

When she checked with her supervisor, a woman with many years' experience about what some men do on crowded transport, she was instructed to post a photograph of 'the filthy flasher who's got his come-uppance' online, just as he was. 'If anyone wants him they can come and get him,' she was told. The operator complied with a fierce grin.

•••

Chapter Seven: Die Happy

MILLA vigorously showered away any possible trace of her molester, with something of a shudder, before joining the others in the living room and gratefully accepting a large glass of red wine.

'Chateau Petrus,' advised Pearce. 'A nice Bordeaux merlot. I think a glass of this will nicely round off a rather excellent day.'

When Ben whispered how much the wine cost per bottle, Milla curbed her initial intention of throwing the wine down her throat and instead relished its intense nose and long, complex draw.

'Sorry about that prick on the floater,' continued Pearce, 'and I mean that in every sense of the word. There's a tremendous culture of face saving here in Japan, and part of that makes them amongst the most pleasant and polite people in the world. But there are some men who take advantage of respect and *face* on busy transports, such as trains and floaters, to touch-up and even, in extreme cases, attempt rape on young girls who are forced up against them by the crowd and can't move away.

'The girls blame themselves for looking too seductive, or something equally stupid. The men perform their sick activities below the line of sight of other passengers, so they get away with it in the crush. It isn't that common but neither is it rare, unfortunately.'

Pearce's loquacious monologue rambled on and Milla realised he was becoming quite tipsy. Ben looked askance at her and, with an almost imperceptible movement of his head, made it clear he was ready to retire for the night. She realised she had all but finished her wine while Ben barely touched his. She put her drained glass on the table, bade everyone goodnight, and went to wait for Ben in his room.

She heard a mumbled conversation at the bedroom door and fought down an impulse to hide in the bathroom. She and Ben had nothing to hide, for God's sake. When the door opened, Ben walked in alone and joined her in a seat by the table in the window bay. He placed his glass of wine on the table before her. 'Pearce topped it up for me, so it's just about full. You seemed to enjoy it so please feel free.' He fetched himself a glass of something clear, chilled and slightly greenish from the room's dispenser and rejoined her. 'You okay?'

She sipped the wine. 'I have never drunk *anything* this expensive,' she said.

'Not many people have.'

She leaned over the table top and kissed him, then sat back and grinned. 'Great punch Ben, worth it just to see that filthy fucker decked out on the floor with his cock out in plain sight.'

'You looked back then?'

'Of course.'

'Me too. But I saw his face when he was still conscious, the creepy little wanker. Ah, Milla, you would have really enjoyed the look of surprise he gave me, when he saw what was about to happen and realised there was nothing he could do to stop it. Then pop,' Ben threw a punch into the air, 'he was down and out for the count.'

'Nobody else on the floater did anything about what you did either. You realise, it could have been reported as a common assault? You could have been arrested.'

'I think they all realised what the old creep was up to and why I did it. Who knows? Some of the women passengers might have been victims of the little creep, in the past. Anyway, that's all done now. Bottoms-up.'

251

Milla took a long sip from her rich ruby-coloured wine, while Ben downed a good mouthful of his drink. She said, 'Ben, despite everything that happened leading up to today, I really can't imagine being happier than I am right now. How can you improve on a day like today? I've had a great day out with good friends in a land saturated with peach and maple blossom. I've seen some of the most beautiful sights the world has to offer, eaten a great meal, drunk great wine and had my big knight in shining armour punch-out a sleazy little creep who was trying to touch me up. It just doesn't get much better than this, does it?'

Milla wondered how much of the emotion washing through her was down to honest feelings and how much was due to the booze she'd sunk. 'You know something, Ben,' she said. 'You want to know something? I could die happy right now, I really honestly could.'

'Don't talk daft, girl. We've got years before us now, and there are sure to be other days just as good as this one.'

'Will there, Ben? Are you really sure?'

'Promise you, cross my heart.'

'And hope to die?'

'If you need me to, love, I will. Yes.'

They both carefully put their drinks down on the table. But the sudden violence of Milla's launch, into Ben's arms, nearly knocked the table flying and his chair teetered backwards. He recovered his balance then carefully manoeuvred her to the floor, where they fought their way out of their clothes while keeping their mouths locked together.

The first time he entered her their sex was fast and a little delirious. The second time a few minutes later was gentle, considered and completely gratifying. Their coupling ended with a mutual sigh of release.

What Ben said afterwards touched Milla to the core, and she clung to him as he carried her over to his bed. She wept freely and happily, with her face buried against his neck, and told Ben she loved him too.

She chattered drowsily about the future and what they would do together, until sleep finally calmed her voice, hushed it down to silence and soft open-mouthed breathing.

She descended swiftly into a deep, deep sleep, sated and slightly carpet-burned on her knees, elbows and buttocks. Had she been awake, Milla would probably have questioned the strange look on Ben's face as he gazed down on her sleeping form.

He was smiling – and his smile was not that of a lover.

● ● ●

Chapter Eight: They know we're here

RUTH gazed into her big bathroom mirror, brush in hand, while trying her hair in a more tousled style than she was used to. In fact, she suddenly realised, it was a style more like Milla's original look when she very first saw her face on the Body Holiday host list. Ruth customarily preferred a more controlled style when in her own body (*how strange is it to think like that?* she mused) but something gypsy-like in Milla's appearance called for a more relaxed approach.

She liked the way Milla's womanly, yet elfin, face was framed in a cloud of dark curls. And she admired the tilt of her eyes, dark yet aglow with warm light and mischief. She liked her pert nose above her angel's bow of a mouth. Yes – an angel's bow; no Cupid was ever lucky enough to possess such smilingly full Italianate lips.

Ruth loved how her rounded, dimpled cheeks fined down to a pointed, perfect chin, and how the whole was poised on the graceful column of her neck. *It would take a Leonardo to capture this face with all its nuances*, she thought. She stroked a possessive hand through her hair, down her cheek and neck and down again until she cupped her right breast, its pink nipple standing proud from her smooth, sun-blushed skin.

The love affair Ruth found she was having with Milla's body no longer worried her, nor did her hunger for Pearce in his current guise as a young lusty man. Their recent lovemaking had lost some of its original urgency but none of its pleasures. Her fingers constantly longed to explore his hard body while he gratefully took every joy to be found in her supple firmness.

She wondered how things would be if she fell pregnant as they'd discussed. How would Milla react to such an infringement of her sequestered body? Then she wondered whether something had been implanted in the host body to avoid such an event. Plentiful sex seemed as much a part of enjoying a Body Holiday as its promise of regained youth. *Let's be honest,* admitted Ruth, *finding themselves to be up to a month pregnant, after the Holiday was over, might just put some female hosts off the whole idea.*

Maybe host motherhood would be a viable proposition under a different sort of contract, with different payment arrangements, she thought. After all, the Body Holidaymakers would have all the fun of making the baby while the poor host would have to carry it to term.

I'm sure a number of people would happily pay to have someone else do all the morning sickness, big belly, baby kicking and contractions stuff, she reasoned with some amusement. The sly smile she now saw on her reflected face and the arch look in her eyes made her laugh out loud. She realised just how much she was coming to love this girl, and the way she wore her thoughts on her face with such undisguised honesty.

She understood how this elfin charm wasn't really anything to do with her. It was no more a reflection of her own lost youth and beauty than the virile cocksman's body she was sleeping with was really Pearce's. These were borrowed gifts and this fact gave her a brief pang of remorse.

Pearce's body was cold in a morgue somewhere or lost in the fall of London's sky tower, so he was now trapped in his host's flesh. Such was not the case for Ruth. Her host was still walking tall in her old body and looking damn good in it too, evidenced by Ben's dog-like attentions. But surely one day she'd want to swap back, if such a thing ever became possible again.

What then for Ben and Pearce? How would they feel about the change in partners? What then for herself, Ruth, after so happily tasting the joys of youth once more?

She was momentarily distracted and lost in thought. Then, when she re-focused her gaze on the mirror, she jolted backwards with shock.

The face looking back at her was silently screaming in stark terror.

Pearce began to smile when his wife ran naked into the bedroom, where he was sitting at the table reading from his crystal pad. But his expression altered to one of intense concern when he saw the agitation and fear on her face.

'Pearce, we have to leave, leave now, they know we're here. We have to go straight away. Come on!'

He rose to his feet, saying nothing, and just took her elbows to look keenly into her eyes.

'I mean it, Pearce, we have to bring the car round to the balcony now, right away. And we have to get Milla and Ben ready.'

Every member of the group had cases packed and stowed away in the car, ready for just such an event. They could be on their way in minutes but Pearce was wary. This was the first time Ruth demonstrated any predictive talent, without first channelling through Milla's more experienced mind, and he wondered if she could be relied on. Then again, he reasoned, it would be very useful to have a practice run at the escape plan, so why not?

'Get dressed Ruth, you're not going anywhere like that,' he said. 'I'll get the car and bring it round while you wake the others and get them ready. We should be out of here in about 20 minutes.'

He kissed her cheek, grabbed his jacket and ran from the room, his crystal pad tucked under his arm.

Ruth was in a hurry too, so of course she made a mess of getting dressed. However, she finally pulled on her shoes while hopping to the bedroom door. She walked through the now surreal calm and serenity of the apartment, fiddling with catches and buttons while alarms roared through her mind. She was still tucking her blouse into the waist of her denims when she began hammering on Ben's door.

An insistent klaxon call was flooding her body with adrenalin and she was quivering, almost whimpering, with her urgent need to get away, get free from threat. She was desperate to live a while longer, to enjoy this body for another day, to breathe for just another hour.

'Ben, Milla, come on!' she shouted. She knew they were together in there. She could almost smell their sex through the door. She hammered again then pushed the door open.

Ben was sitting up and cast a quizzical gaze at the interloper while Milla yawned hugely, rubbing her eyes. The bedclothes puddled around their waists.

'We have to go. We have to leave.' Ruth strode to stand beside Milla's befuddled recumbent figure before reaching down to take her hand.

Milla jolted fully awake, in sudden shock. 'Fuck it, Ruth, we have to leave right now.'

'Pearce is bringing the car to the balcony. We'll see you both in five minutes.' Ruth hurried out of the room while behind her the couple threw aside the bedclothes. Milla was panting with barely suppressed terror.

Without pausing for underwear, she and Ben tugged on the clothes they'd scattered on the floor the night before. Ben grabbed his small case and nodded at Milla, his face an exercise in focused control.

He pushed her through the door and followed her across the hall into the living room, where they could both see Pearce at the car's controls and Ruth beside him urgently gesturing them forward. The back door of the car was open and safety beckoned.

Then the floor of the apartment lurched sideways and Milla was thrown to her knees.

•••

Chapter Nine: A Seed to grow a Girl Child

PEARCE cautiously tracked the moving balcony with the Lexus, while Ruth screamed at Milla and Ben to get a move on. Ben reached down and dragged Milla to her feet then ran her across the drifting floor. Gravity felt wrong – down was relentlessly moving around towards the walls.

They had reached the balcony when Milla suddenly reared back, her head catching Ben on his upper lip and mashing against his teeth. His trickle of blood angled sideways; he tasted the raw iron of it on the right side of his tongue.

Milla was struck witless by paralysing fear. She had seen how there was increasingly clear space between the balcony edge and the safety of the Lexus. She also saw how the car was desperately bucking to stay close enough for her to jump. It was terrifyingly clear how a missed leap would mean a long, long fall to Tokyo Under, with no chance of rescue. Her knees buckled and bile came into her throat.

'There's no time for this,' roared Ben, close to her ear. She felt strong hands grip her waist and heave, propelling her forwards and out into the void. Reaching out to safety, the world seemed to pause for her. And she nearly made it, so very, very nearly.

Her arms were stretched out to reach through the car's doorway and her long legs stretched straight behind her like a diver's. The open door of the car loomed large and safe in her eyes. Behind her, Ben was taking a few steps backwards before taking his own running jump to safety.

Then Milla felt something touch her, press down on her. It was something light and warm, less than a breath, not even a caress of a breath, yet it stopped the breath in her throat stone dead.

The car was no longer in front of her – nothing was – and she was spinning down to Earth from a clear, uncluttered sky. The landscape swept past her eyes then the sky filled her view once more. Her last coherent thought was one of sadly curious surprise. *Oh no. After all that?*

Above Milla's spinning form, Ruth was trying to come to terms with what she'd just witnessed. One minute Milla was on the verge of safety and the next she was swiped clean away, as was Ben behind her and the balcony he was standing on. It was so shockingly sudden, like something had taken an eraser to them both. They were gone.

Pearce was all action. He hit the controls to close the doors and set the car into a rolling dive. Ben was good but Pearce knew he was better. They were going to survive this shit. Through the windscreen they both saw a spinning thing flickering below them. It looked like a sycamore seed drifting in the air. Pearce dived.

As they got closer they saw the streaming blonde hair and blank-eyed face. It was just the head, shoulders and arms of Milla dressed in Ruth's murdered flesh, spinning blindly yet gently to the ground. Ruth felt sick, gagged and retched, bringing up nothing but bile in a dry heave.

Pearce swore and turned his car away from Tokyo, conclusively away from the strangely beautiful yet horrific thing drifting propeller-like to the distant soil. And away from his suddenly vanished best friend.

His mind racing, he wrestled with his controls, long enough to first set the car on a trajectory away from harm, before keying the navigation system to head towards his Namibian facility.

In the rear-view mirror he watched the immense bulk of Tokyo Sky City continue its slow tilt down towards the crowded, neatly cluttered, streets of Tokyo Under. Streets doomed to die, crushed beneath its huge and increasingly darkening shadow.

'The microwave beam,' he spoke rapidly, 'it moved. It can't but it did. They were caught in the microwave beam. Every cell it touched would be instantly boiled and vaporised, Ruth. There could be no pain, nothing. They didn't feel a thing. They went easy. But look at that behind us. Sky City can't fly without the microwave beam and that means millions upon fucking millions will die when it falls.' He slammed the steering wheel with the heel of his hand, his mouth open and twisted in confusion, his eyes creased in concentrated horror.

'Are they really doing all this just to get at us? Are they that insane? That's a whole city down there: children, women, and centuries of art...'

As if in answer, the car was lifted up off course by battering turbulence. They heard a roar growing louder and louder, a roar that became tooth-splinteringly intense and pounded on them for what seemed ages. It was a roar filled with the screech of twisting metal, the grind of crunching stone, the tear of ripping plastics, the clatter of shattering ceramics and what ultimately sounded like the voices of millions of people screaming in fear before they became suddenly quieted.

And then there was a hush, heavy as granite, unapologetic and unexpected as a tooth on a pavement. It was all over and in their car they breathed – they still breathed.

Ruth shamefully thought: *This is my body now. She's gone and it's my body now. Mine. We can have children, if we want.*

Pearce accepted her sudden collapse into heaving, gulping tears as the result of her loss. Her new friend and old colleague were both gone, all at once in a God-like murderous swipe. Who could blame her? Now, he thought, is the time to escape, get away, reach safety, run.

His mind reeling, he angled his car south-west towards Africa. New plans began to burgeon in his mind. *Ah, he thought, yes.*

He took the wheel in his hands and started to plan his line of flight, looking at his wife as she began to recover from her crying jag. *She's calming down. Good, calm is good. We have to get way. We need to get away.*

There was a brief hiss before the car's speakers came alive around them. After a moment's pause, a slightly mechanical yet refined and strangely familiar English voice said, 'Sir, you are in physical control of your vehicle, yet I perceive you have been drinking to excess.'

Pearce looked around wildly. The skies were clear.

'Sir, I ask that you relinquish control of your vehicle to the onboard AI. Immediately. Your blood alcohol levels are unacceptable for you to be flying a vehicle in this airspace, under current legislation: airspace ruling 26, 2165, sub section 12a, note 57b. Your implant is advised.'

Something akin to an electric shock struck his hands away from the wheel of the car, and the dash display changed from orange to a mellow green. The onboard AI was now automatically in charge.

'Sky City just crashed into Tokyo Under,' Pearce screamed, 'and you worry because I've had some fucking wine, you arsehole? Millions of people are dead or injured, you fucking cretin. Why don't you go do something useful?'

There was a tap on his side window and he saw a ball no bigger than a clenched fist swinging back onto its parallel path, flying alongside the Lexus. A bright light at its heart flashed from red to blue and back again. Pearce got the feeling it was gazing straight at him and it wasn't impressed.

262

'Your AI is enabled,' said the traffic droid. 'Keep it that way until you sober up or sod off out of my airspace. And I'll thank you to not call me a cretin, on a day like today, you arsewipe.'

Pearce kept his hands away from the controls until the glowing fist-sized ball pulled away and headed back towards the growing dust cloud that had once been a unique twin city and was now a disaster almost beyond imagination.

'Who did that little pipsqueak think it was, calling you an arsewipe?' asked Ruth.

Pearce was silent for a few minutes before he suddenly began to laugh. It was such a free, full-bellied laugh that Ruth wondered if recent events had loosened his sanity to the point of collapse.

'What?' she asked.

'One of mine! It was one of mine,' he gasped, tears stinging his eyes.

'What? One of your what?' she asked again.

He heaved a sigh and caught his laughter up into a hiccoughing chuckle, then put his hand up and waved it for a moment. 'I designed it,' he said. 'I call them cunt cops, sorry. Sorry, Hun.'

He shook his head for a moment then continued: 'They're designed to be a solution to a problem that exists between some people and legitimate droid law enforcement. Most droids are so polite they can't be taken seriously. But my droids are algorithmically programmed to respond to abuse with equal abuse until they're talking like total bastards. I designed the algorithm and even scripted the words. I've just been shouting at myself!'

He glanced across at Ruth. She was looking steadfastly out of the windscreen.

'Pearce, what do we do now?'

'Hon, to be honest, I've got no idea. Give me a minute.'

263

Many minutes earlier in the streets of Tokyo Under, Reginald Tanaka Ng played his last jacks of the day under the fluorescent sky sails of Sky City. When the light suddenly tilted and the bright sky unexpectedly went dark, he stood with his mitt held up to catch the jack for just a few, brief, futile seconds before he mouthed, 'Awesome.' As the immense screeching bulk of Sky City impacted with unprecedented force onto Tokyo Under, he promptly dissolved and was gone.

Out beyond the great collapse, also beyond a wall of orange dust that palled the Tokyo sky to almost total darkness, stood aged mother Susan Wang. Susan was not too sure about things these days. She was a farmer's widow rendered down over the years to the status of just another benefits woman, living in a tiny house on the outer suburbs of Tokyo.

Old and frail, living with just fleeting glimpses of sanity, but only when it waved its rare hello through her mind's window. She was gently making her way towards final extinction with a drooling smile and the help of neighbours.

Then the girl spun out of the sky, spinning like a sycamore seed, and landed in her garden. It collided and tangled with her cherry tree. The sight was unmistakable to an experienced gardener like Susan. The seed was bruised and a bit crooked but when she saw the seed's face she wilted. This was a girl seed: blonde because she was ungrown, and bloody because she was full of juice.

Susan buried the blood-rich seed by the roots of her cherry tree. *Who knows*, she thought, *this girl seed might one day grow into a daughter. One day. God willing.* And then something ran through Susan like a tremble of doubt and horror. *This is a body*, she realised, *a dead girl's body thrown down out of the sky!* But she smothered the doubt, smiled her drooling smile and patted the earth over the girl seed, into a neat mound.

•••

Interlude

'Ha haa – it worked.'

'What did?'

'Killing Sky City.'

'What are we doing to these people?'

'Giving them a holiday they'll never forget.'

'Giving them a holiday they'll never recover from, more like.'

'A holiday you'll never forget is worth all the angst, surely.'

'I'll come back to you on that, if I may.'

'The sex has been good.'

'The lighting could have been better but there you are.'

'Fuck off.'

'All of it. All of this is down to you, dude.'

'Some of those effects are spectral.'

'Through the window doesn't count, moonlight doesn't count, fucking fish eating semen doesn't count. Oh, I don't know what to say.'

'Boss is with her.'

'Lucky fucker.'

'I liked her.'

'She's fucking dangerous. She needs to be dealt with.'

'Fuck off.'

'I mean it, man. She's a problem to be addressed, and I mean with extreme prejudice. Lose her.'

'Not down to me.'

'No, pussy boy. You like the ladies. I just want to survive this and keep my job. Lose the lady.'

Blake sat and once again watched the spinning remnants of Ruth's body (Milla incumbent) after the microwave beam dissolved every delicious inch of her below her armpits.

266

He watched Potter follow her flight from his work station: her flutter down as a spinning thing, head upwards and blank eyes staring.

When Susan Wang plucked the truncated body away from her cherry tree and buried it in order to grow a girl child, Blake looked across at his colleague Potter. Once again he imagined the improvement he could bring to the average sanity of mankind, as a whole, if he smashed that seething mess of a brain with a brick.

Potter grinned, showing his teeth. Blake grinned back, or was that a snarl?

●●●

Chapter Ten: Slow Arousal from Death

MILLA was already adjusted and making dispassionate plans around the idea of her death. Why fight it? How could she fight it? She'd been killed, okay, job done. And so far, it wasn't so bad after all.

She at first watched the blue sky spin above her in a breathless (literally breathless) whirl. There were some things she saw that were massive and loomed above her then slid away. But they didn't really register in any coherent way. And then, all too soon, there was darkness and quiet.

Death descended over her bringing calm stillness, peace and endless clinging blackness. *But hang on...* she thought some kind of music was missing from this scene. A big event like death surely needed a child choir singing in Latin or at least a plangent organ ringing across the welkin.

Never mind. This is it, she thought. *St Peter bring on your book.* And she smiled the smile of the innocent while hoping she looked convincing to the powers that be.

At first being dead felt like being rolled back and forth in warm chocolate. It was quite nice if you didn't mind ending up in hell afterwards, she supposed. Inwardly she laughed, very aware that you need lungs for outward laughter, and resigned to the fact that she was now very light in the department of lights.

She hoped Ben was okay and he'd managed to get in the car. He'd been a good point to finish on but that was all over now. At least her death was quick and painless, and a pretty solid escape from all the running and the dread about the Foundation. *Okay so far*, she thought, *but now where will I go – up, down, sideways or nowhere?*

'Laydees and Genamen, lay your bets.' She could almost hear the voice ring out like an actor in an old play and was all too prepared to answer it: *who fucking knows? Dead is dead*, she thought. *Dead is..? Hang on...*

Then some fucker changed all the rules. *Bugger!*

She took a shuddering breath and opened her eyes. Her eyes were crusted and she wiped them clean. Her mouth tasted foul and was very, very dry. Her tongue felt thick and cracked. She was experiencing slow arousal from death, and needed to fully pluck herself from its clutches before entering into any kind of mental debate about what was happening and where she was lying.

Dark was the clue, her mind told her. Death isn't dark, it's dead. Where are your optic nerves when you need to see darkness and you're dead?

'Hello Milla.'

Shocked, alert too quickly, she retched, drooled bitter bile then sat upright. She realised she was naked, on a gel bed, in a familiar Spartan bedroom lit from above by a shifting light source. She also became very aware that she was now being keenly observed by a fully clothed man standing at the end of her bed. 'Welcome back.'

'Fuck.' Her voice sounded old, rusty and raw in her ears. 'Whose body am I in now?'

'Take some time to relax. It's hard to come back, I know.'

'Franklyn? *Franklyn!* Fuck..? Is that you? Fuck. Fuck everything and fuck you too. You're dead!'

She realised with some surprise that, despite everything she'd been through, she was feeling very well. She felt light, healthy and pain-free, like a taut cable all set to whip. So she levered herself out of the gel bed and stood tall on her own two feet. Then she hauled back and smacked Franklyn so hard across his face that he stumbled sideways into the wall. Franklyn crouched down into a flat-footed defensive position, and her TP alarm roared.

She backed away. *I'm back*, she thought. *This is me and I'm in trouble here.*

'Clothes,' she said. 'I want clothes, right now, and some sort of explanation.' She pointed an accusing finger. 'I saw you die. You let me think I killed you. What the flaming fuck happened? What did you do?'

'Shower,' he said. 'Then I'll tell you everything.'

'But...'

'Hang on...you need to get clean before you put a scrap on. And, let me tell you, you need some solid food in you too, girl. You've lost a few kilos you didn't need to lose.'

After her shower, Milla spent a moment in front of the full-length mirror in the bathroom. Her belly was too hollow, yes. Flat, yes, too flat. *Okay.* But she was also surprised to see the pubic bush at the junction of her legs. She'd recently seen Ruth naked in her host body and her pubic area was completely depilated. She herself had always kept a neat, well-trimmed pubic patch, when she could be bothered.

But now she was completely *au-naturel*. Her armpits were patchily dark with hair too, as were her legs. She checked her upper lip. Nightmare!

She was quite a while in the bathroom, taking advantage of every facility. Franklyn finally resorted to tapping on the door and asking if she was alright. She ignored him. When she finally opened the door she was refreshed, depilated back into her physical comfort zone, clothed, finding it difficult to walk on her own two feet and starving.

Franklyn dealt with the latter before explaining the rest. The small bowl of warm metallic-tasting porridge he gave her to eat started off tasting awful. But she found she couldn't stop bolting it down. She ended up scraping, licking and lapping at the bowl like a hungry dog.

He then placed a polished and smoothly curved piece of wood before her, on which were presented three variously

270

coloured cubes of jelly sprinkled with chopped leaves. She quickly wolfed all three.

She had a salt thirst she thought would call for an entire ocean to quench. He gave her a bulb of orange liquid, open at the top like an accepting belly. She drank. He gave her another and she drank again.

'Body Holiday's a sham isn't it?' she said. 'No one goes anywhere.'

'They do where it counts.'

He tapped his temple and smiled the smile of a lizard, or worse the smile of a politician and diplomat. She wondered where her trust in him had gone. Evaporated under the heat of recent events, she supposed. She compared him with her calm and capable Ben, and found Franklyn seriously wanting.

Alarms mounted inside her like wads of physical material, building up until they seemed jammed in her throat. She almost choked in fear. He smiled again. 'I'm not surprised you're edgy after what you think you've been through. But don't worry, you're back and you're safe and everything's okay.'

'Franklyn, I've met a man called Ben and...'

'No, Milla, you haven't. You haven't met anyone at all.'

●●●

Chapter Eleven: Why we call it a Dream Holiday

FRANKLYN led her away from the bland bedroom and out into the corridors of the Body Holiday Foundation. All the time he was talking she recognised the places she and the others had left in such a hurry, and even where they shot and killed members of staff.

Shouldn't all this be gone, in a missile blast? She stopped mid-stride. 'London, the beach house, Sydney and Tokyo – all that was a dream. Wasn't it?'

'Not a dream, as such, no. A construct, a bit like virtual space.' Franklyn was still as opaque to her talents as he had ever been. But she was getting something from him now, something like a taste on the side of her tongue.

'How can that work? And what was all that killing and chasing about? Why would you do that to anybody, when they've paid to have the holiday of a lifetime? And what are you going to do about Pearce's body? The poor man died.'

'No, he didn't. But he would have.'

He led her up into a dark gallery, from which angled windows overlooked a room lit only by a number of large 3D monitors. The light was blue and gave the room an underwater feel, though crowded with gleaming stacks of black computer towers. Two men sat in the shadows: one fatly crouched over his keyboard like a toad, the other poised and playing his keyboard like a concert musician.

On the monitors Milla clearly recognised the images of herself and Franklyn, alone in the front seats of the Lexus. Ruth and Pearce were on the run again. Ben didn't make it then.

'Ben was killed, like me. Was he?'

'Ben was never there, any more than you were, or they are now.'

Milla took a seat in the gallery and felt Franklyn settle down beside her in the darkness. 'The technology needed to transfer minds from one body to another does not exist, yet,' he explained. 'However, the ability to put a human mind into a completely convincing body construct, and then place that construct into an equally convincing spatial environment, has been with us for quite some time.'

He sounded like a bored tour guide.

'It dates back to a time when pilots were first out mining the rings of Saturn, performing tasks using constructs. Some pilots created some really accomplished constructs, giant versions of themselves that could reach out and grab great chunks of water ice and precisely throw them back towards collecting stations around Mars. Of course, that was before Mars was completely roofed over.'

She heard the seat creak as he sat back, and continued, 'Not many people know it but there was a project established back then to harvest freshly dead human brains and use them to steer spaceships and calculate the correct trajectory for throwing the ice. It was a complex business and scientists then, as now, realised that the human brain is one of the most astonishing calculators for its size the universe has ever seen. Brains were used in the mining ships' computers, hell they *were* the mining ships' computers, though the pilots never knew.

'Then one year there was some kind of accident and one of the pilots took her ship over Saturn's event horizon. She was lost beyond any hope of rescue. The gravity well was too strong to escape and much too much for successful rescue by another ship, though it was tried.'

Milla was partly captured by the story. She was caught between watching her friends on the monitors in the room below and growing curiosity about why an accident to an ice miner, somewhere around Saturn, could have anything to do with the plight in which Pearce and Ruth were now trapped.

'The gravitational stresses the fabric of her ship suffered did something unique. Something that's never since been replicated, in any lab. The personality of the donor brain woke up. It scared the shit out of the pilot, Vesper her name was, but the end result was that there were now two people faced with certain death.

'That was until the mission manager for Saturn, based on Iapetus, worked out a way to tap into Vesper's construct and upload both personalities from the ship and store them in the system's accountancy computers, the only facility big enough for the job.

'They lived together in a virtual world for years after that. In fact they were very important in developing core technology at the heart of the Body Holiday Foundation.'

'What about the woman's body and the brain on the ship?'

'Crushed and never recovered. Vesper died that day, as did the brain. His name was Eddie, Eddie Plowright, I think. But their virtual personalities lived on, for decades after. They may even still be going, somewhere, in some research program. Who knows? But what they did then provides us with the technology we use today, to offer people the ultimate great escape.

'They get to take time out of their active bodies and away from their mundane lives. They step straight into a great big breathless adventure. That's why we call it a dream holiday. Except you're not asleep when you live it. In fact, you're one hundred per cent awake and one hundred per cent alive.'

'But surely, it's a con?'

'What con? Did you feel conned? Do they feel conned? Look at them – they've never felt more alive.' Franklyn was silent for a moment while they watched the scene unfolding on the monitors below them.

'When they wake up they'll feel refreshed and excited,' he continued. 'Their bodies will feel better than they ever did before the transition. They will look better too, shaved and washed the way they like it. What's more, Pearce can get treatment for the incipient aneurism that killed his avatar in the construct. The Foundation has given him years of extra life. Where's the con in that?'

He stood and reached out his hand. 'Come on.' Milla followed him, out of the darkness and suddenly into a blindingly bright corridor. She walked beside him down to another room, where food and drinks were laid out. They both ate and drank while Franklyn continued his monologue. He explained how he'd been kept comfortable while waiting for her return, and how the Foundation gave him all the information he was now sharing with her.

He also explained why she had to be killed in the construct, because Pearce and Ruth were demanding more and more memory for their Holiday. 'The Foundation tells me it's never had a sequence like this one,' he said. 'It's got those guys and their technology stretched to the limits, to keep up with the demand.'

Milla realised how Franklyn was now trying to convince her that he was nothing to do with what was happening here. Yet the sense of threat never diminished the whole time he was talking.

'They are worried about you being a telepath, though.'

When he said it, she looked straight at him, and in return found herself the subject of intense scrutiny. 'Why?'

'Well, you know. You signed a confidentiality agreement when you agreed to be a host, same as I did. But can't your TP chums just, you know, look in your head and see everything?'

275

Her crawling skin was ready to flinch away from the violent attack she was sure would come. She tensed, hoping to get ready for defence without alerting him. She took a better grip on her dinner knife. 'No they can't, it isn't that simple. They have to be invited or know what they are looking for. It isn't like opening a box or reading a diary, you know. Thoughts aren't linear or mechanical; they aren't there for anyone to read like the pages of a book.' She paused then reconsidered.

'No, hang on. In a way thoughts and memories are like a book. But it's a massive book, with hundreds of thousands of pages and links to lots of other books, and without any index. What I mean to say is that there is no way any TP can look in my mind and read anything I don't want them to see, no way.'

Like a switch turned off, the atmosphere at the table lightened. Imperceptibly tightened muscles relaxed. Franklyn smiled. 'I'm told our money is already in our accounts. We can afford a proper holiday ourselves, if we fancy getting away from it all, for a while. What do you say?'

You have got to be fucking joking, she thought. She smiled, clamping down on the surge of nausea holding her in its grip.

'Franklyn. Look, I need a break. I do. But I need to spend time on my own first. We've both just been through a pretty traumatic time and I need to get my nerves back into shape. I want to go back to my apartment and enjoy some peace and quiet, alone. You do understand, don't you?'

He reached out and took her wrist in a vice-like grip, his hand easily encircling the slim column of flesh and bone. She was suddenly aware of just how powerful he was. He squeezed. 'I don't want to lose you, Milla.' His voice was flat and steady, his eyes glittering, not menacing as such but the implied threat was real enough.

'Look, I had an affair with Ben over the last few days, when I thought you were dead. And it was really good. I need to know how I feel about that, now. I need some space. Please.' His grip on her wrist tightened. 'You're hurting.'

'That was me,' he said, releasing his grip. 'The only person ever to have sex with you, in the construct, was me. That's the deal, when you go in.'

He smiled a tight smile. 'Someone had to animate the Ben character, even though he wasn't a host or a client. He still needed to do more than some of the other people you met, so he needed a driver. The only choice was me but I couldn't tell you about it until now. I'm sorry, Milla, but the only affair you had recently was with me. Now, can we stop this and go home?'

Milla opened her mouth to answer but no words emerged. No wonder Ben's lovemaking seemed so familiar, and there was also his quick and easy acceptance of her into his life. Everything was explained now, of course. Or was it? 'Hang on. How could you be Ben?' Her voice was insistent. 'Ruth and Pearce know Ben and have done for years. How could you fool them? This is bullshit.'

'No, no, it's part of the algorithm of the construct,' Franklyn gestured at her. 'While working in the virtual space, the system has to read clients' and players' expectations in order to meet them. I suppose it is like reading minds but we can only read the current thought in a person's head. In the construct thought is linear and we see things in real time. You know something? The team can even see into dreams, and some dreams are awesome.

'Anyway, it's the only way to let people exist in construct space. Otherwise they would, say, turn left and the street would stay where it was. Or you could raise a glass to your lips,' he let his actions match his words, 'and the glass would stay on the table.'

He looked at her, willing her to believe. 'I knew just what Ruth and Pearce expected from Ben, because they were telling the team everything we needed to know. You didn't know him from Adam, so we didn't need to read you. But the other two were painting a clear picture of how I should act and even what I would say.'

He pulled a wry face. 'If anything, I guess, I became a little too predictable. But I wasn't with them long enough to rouse suspicion. I spent most of the last few days with you.'

Milla stood up, walked round the table and pressed her lips to his. She resisted her urge to shudder. She pulled away when Franklyn opened his lips and tried to embrace her. He was still so maddeningly opaque to her talent but she knew a creepy bastard of a liar when she heard one.

At least he was a bad liar, give him credit for that. He gave himself away over and over again. That he was a genuine cog in the Body Holiday machine was a given. Okay, it was him who got her involved in the Holiday. In fact, it was him who first flirted with her all those months ago. Had he been planning all this, for all that time? The thought took her breath away.

She finally convinced him that she just needed a few days' grace and, in the end, he reluctantly fetched her belongings and called a cab to take her home. He tried to kiss her again, before she left, but she held him at arm's length and asked him to wait until she called.

The last words she said to him were, 'See you soon, I promise.'

At least, she thought, *I'm a more convincing liar than you.*

One thing was true, as she found as soon as she reached home and checked her bank: the promised money was in her account. She quickly made her arrangements.

By the time Franklyn turned up and tried his key, the lock was changed. And she didn't respond to his increasingly violent pounding, because she was already long gone.

•••

Epilogue

WHEN he walked back into the fuggy darkened room, Potter and Blake looked up at him, evidently startled.

'Hello, boss,' said Blake. 'We thought you had something to be doing elsewhere with the lovely lady.'

'I'm going to miss her,' said Potter.

Franklyn ignored them both. 'What's happening?' he said, testily.

Blake answered, 'They are going to Africa. Pearce has a facility there, from which they can launch into space. Ruth wants a baby, so he wants to make sure they're safe from us first.'

'That's nice. They would make nice parents,' crooned Potter.

'Where in space?' barked Franklyn.

Blake fired back, 'Lagrange II, the big ESA cylinder.'

'Up there, they can fuck in zero G,' Potter offered. 'That always makes for good viewing.'

'Doubt it – they'd have to do it out in the open in mid-air at the centre of the cylinder,' said Blake. 'That's the only zero G up there. And they'll have to watch out for recreational fliers too.'

'If we let them live that long,' rasped Franklyn.

'Ah boss, these two are great value. Let's not snuff them yet, please,' pleaded Potter.

'Okay, let's see what they do,' answered Franklyn. 'Let's see if they can come up with something new every day, like Scheherazade. If they do they can have their 1,001 nights. But as soon as I get bored...'

And as for that bitch Milla, he thought, she's dead as soon as I find her. And I will, I promise you, I will.

All three men looked at the beautiful flushed faces on the monitors.

Potter sighed.

'Whatever you say, boss.'

Franklyn sat before his own bank of monitors and watched the young couple make their escape. The switches he needed to turn off the construct and snuff their virtual lives lay directly under his hands. He paid particular attention to the borrowed face of Milla Carter, a face he had come so close to loving but one he would now like to see pulped to a bloody ruin. Bitch to treat him like this, how could she? I'll show her, he thought. He squeezed his eyes tight shut then, when he opened them again, they were awash with pain and anger.

'Come on then, entertain me,' he snarled.

•••

Postscript

MILLA sipped her cappuccino then nibbled her lemon tart. She looked out over the immaculate and crowded streets of Tokyo Under and up at the sky illusion created by the practically invisible Sky City. She was glad all that destruction was a lie. London Sky Tower and Sydney were also intact and the world network of TransCon ballistics still had a 100 per cent safety record.

She turned off the pages of her guide book then looked up annoyed as someone stood before her and blocked her light.

Both men were young. One looked a bit familiar but the other had an extreme, almost beautifully alien, Asian face. It was the latter who spoke first.

'Miss Carter, may we join you?'

Surprised to be recognised she nodded, and the Japanese man bowed slightly before they both took their seats. No sense of threat from either, in fact an increased sense of safety. Who are these guys?

He continued, 'My name is Reginald Tanaka Ng. My friend is William Macready. You may call me Reg and him Bill.'

'Please, call me Milla.'

'Thank you, Milla. Bill has met you before, you know, but you did not look as you do now.'

Of course, the man who followed her from the café in the mall and called her Ruth. But wait, that was...

'Of course, that was when you were both in the construct created by the Body Holiday Foundation.'

Reg went quiet when the little waitress came over and took their order. Milla asked for another cappuccino, again without cinnamon. Both men chose Americanos, with cold milk on the side.

As soon as the waitress left, Reg leaned towards Milla and spoke quietly.

'Potentially, you have a very dangerous problem with the Foundation. Your friends are still caught in the construct. And I would like to suggest we work together, to get them out of there before it is too late.'

'Reg, surely they're perfectly safe in the construct! It's just a virtual world where they can't be hurt, isn't it?'

'No,' said Reg, and calmly began to outline some of the dark secrets behind the Body Holiday Foundation.

• • •

Milla Carter will return in Body Holiday: Shadow Players

Other 2013-14 GB Publications

Christopher Ritchie

isbn 9780957297050

ForeWord Reviews Book Of The Year 2013 Horror Finalist

Vitina Molgaard, Horror Novel Reviews: This story *"needs to be read to even begin to grasp Ritchie's vision"* His *"alternate worlds... may throw you for an entertaining loop."*

Rebbie Reviews: House of Pigs will *"horrify you with some really gritty and gory events... I love the imagery and the pace."*

DeepStorm OutTack

George S Boughton

isbn 9780957297081

From Earth's overcrowded megacities a new generation must rise...or die

By the 2060s – the march of megacities across the globe has finally stopped but the population must still grow.
Now mankind turns its eyes to space – building the Near Earth Territories and peopling them with youngsters DNA-primed to survive there.

When a planet-destroying cosmic disturbance bears down on the Earth, a team of Territories' researchers scrambles to respond with enhanced talents and hard science.

More than just science fiction *DeepStorm OutTack* is based on a decade of intensive research. Enjoy the story but heed the warning – mankind could go the way of the dinosaurs.

The Full Story
Cpt George P Boughton

isbn 9780957672826

Times Literary Supplement *"His book is genuine sea salt..."*

John O'London Weekly: *"An excellent book"*

Lloyds List & Shipping Gazette: *"one of the best books on life at sea..."*

The Spectator: *"recalls emotions* [on sea-life] *that have fleeted from the minds of most"*

Lightning Source UK Ltd.
Milton Keynes UK
UKOW02f0243040914

237989UK00002B/16/P